Between More Sisters

Book Two

Also by The Queen

Between Sisters (book one)
Tapioca Pudding Next Door

NOTE FROM PUBLISHER:
If you have not read Between Sisters (Book One), please stop here and read it first. Between More Sisters is book two of the Between Sisters' series.

Between More Sisters

Book Two

The Queen

Queendom Dreams Publishing
www.queendomdreams.com

Queendom Dreams Publishing
PO Box 93832,
Las Vegas, NV 89193

Copyright © 2009 by The Queen

All rights reserved. No part of this book may be used or reproduced by any means, graphic, electronic, or mechanical, including photocopying, recording, taping or by any information storage retrieval system without the written permission of the publisher except in the case of a brief quotations embodied in critical articles and reviews.

This book is a work of fiction. Names, characters, places, and incident are the product of the author's imagination or are used fictitiously. Any resemblance to actual events or locales or persons, living or dead, is entirely coincidental. So, if by chance you see yourself in any of the aspects of this novel...good for you.

If you have purchased this book with a "dull" or "missing" cover, you may have purchased an unauthorized or stolen book. Please immediately contact the publisher advising where, when, and how you purchased the book.

Printed in the United States of America

First Edition
Series Volume: Two

ISBN-13: 978-0-9827-2230-5
ISBN-10: 0-9827-2230-X

Cover Design: Candace Cottrell

For information regarding special ordering for bulk purchases, please visit www.queendomdreamspublishing.com.

Website: www.queendomdreams.com

Acknowledgements

First & foremost, all thanks be unto Jehovah God, my father, for without, I am nothing. Next, I must thank **YOU**... for without you, I am merely a person writing words and not the success you give to me through your love and support. Thank you!!!!

The Queen...

Between More Sisters

Book Two

The Queen

Queendom Dreams Publishing
www.queendomdreams.com

Prologue

1

"Damn, girl! You sure know how to love your man on Valentine's Day."

Lying on her side, Charise twisted her face and rolled her eyes up at the multicolored bamboo fan hanging from the mint green painted ceiling. "Arnold, please, let's not get this twisted. This is just sex."

Arnold's neck almost snapped off from turning his head so quickly to look back at Charise, still with her sweaty breasts pressed up against his back. "WHAT! And why exactly am I here with you in Cancun for your sister's wedding?" he asked, pushing away from Charise and swinging his legs off the side of the bed to sit up.

"I already told you that I don't want to have to deal with my sister Sandy's crap. You are here only for image, and I need you to remember that we have to appear as a happy couple. Damn! Stop trippin'!"

Arnold shook his head in disbelief as though he was hearing these words for the first time. "You know, Charise," he chuckled to mask his hurt, "I have been your fool for almost a year now. I dropped my whole life to be with you in Houston. I have been a damn good father to our son and have jumped through all kinds of hoops just to get a

smidgen of respect from you. After this trip, you and I . . . we're done. I don't need you calling me to satisfy your sexual needs. I don't want you calling me to help fix your car or do work in your apartment. If it's not about Jarod, I don't need you to call me for anything. I will always be thankful to you for giving me such a beautiful son who means the world to me, but you my dear, need to grow up. Unfortunately, becoming a mother didn't grow you up. Your behind will be twenty-six years old in two weeks. You're a telemarketer with a damn bachelor's degree in business and a minor in journalism. What a joke. When do you plan on getting your life together, Charise? What will it take for you to grow up? Life is not a game, and I certainly am not your toy."

"Oh, Arnold, please kill that shit! You are not my fucking father, and I don't need you telling me what I should be doing with my life. You are Jarod's father and nothing more. Just because you are some big company executive, that doesn't give you the right to think you can run my life. Run that company and shut the fuck up!"

Charise remained lying on her side with her head held up by her hand, looking unfazed by the same argument she had encountered many times during the past year with Arnold.

"Yeah, okay. You just remember that shit while you're sitting at that wedding by yourself today. I'm out!" Arnold stepped off the bed that he and Charise just finished having sex on, snatched a sheet from the messy bed to cover his nudity, and headed to the bathroom to shower.

"Okay! Okay, wait, Arnold. I need you here with me today. Please don't leave me, baby. Baby, please. I'm sorry," Charise begged as she stumbled off of the bed, trying to run behind him before he slammed the door in her face.

Arnold would not respond to her banging on the locked door. After his quick shower, he packed his clothes in silence, preparing to leave

Cancun, while Charise continued pleading for him to remain by her side for her sister's wedding. She tried rubbing her large breasts against his back and fondling his manhood, attempting to lull him back into bed with her, but nothing was working as it usually would. Arnold had no idea when the next flight to Houston would leave, but he knew he had finally reached his breaking point with Charise's emotional abuse.

After a one night stand more than a year and a half earlier, Arnold learned that Charise had given birth to his son Jarod. Charise went her entire pregnancy believing her baby belonged to her sister Sandy's husband Lewis. When she learned that Lewis was not the father of her child, she tracked Arnold down. Arnold gave up his happy life in Bethesda, Maryland to go to Houston and be a good father to his only child after Charise moved from DC to Houston so she could be with Lewis. He had hoped that after jumping through hoops for Charise for about a year now, he would have won her heart and she would want the three of them to be a family. No such luck.

A 6'2", caramel colored, muscular, 210-pound Global Operations Manager, Arnold knew he was an ideal catch for any single woman, but having been raised by two parents who provided a strong family unit, he wanted the same for his offspring. He had always taken precautions not to produce any children up until his one reckless night with Charise after a night at the club. Now at thirty, he was trying to be the man he was raised to be by accepting his responsibility.

He couldn't begin to understand why he went along with Charise's scheme to play this charade on her own family for the wedding, but this reality check was just what he needed to finally come to terms that Charise could never be the woman he'd call his wife. His mother tried to warn him about Charise and her undisciplined ways. His mother also told him he'd do well to pursue gaining custody of their son Jarod, but he had hoped it would never come to that.

The Queen

Charise hadn't exactly been the best example of what a mother should be, but he continually tried to give her credit for the little effort she did put forth, hoping she'd do more for their child. He didn't dare tell his mother about the occasion he knew of when Charise left the baby sleeping at home alone, while she ran to the store. She said it was too hard for her to manage with the baby while trying to shop in the rain. The only reason he learned about her deed was because she got into a minor car accident on the way back, and since she had to wait for the police, she called ol' reliable Arnold to the rescue. He had to leave an important business meeting with clients to help her out. She used sex to disarm him, as she always would when he threatened to report her to children services.

He kept his son anywhere from four to six days per week, because most of the time Charise didn't want to be bothered with a baby. Still, he voluntarily paid Charise $900 per month for child support and provided daycare and insurance.

Charise seemed content working as a telemarketing supervisor, with no plan to better herself professionally. She had outstanding writing skills but wouldn't put them or her degree to work for her. The youngest of six girls with one younger brother, she always felt as though everyone was looking down on her. She was going to therapy at one point, but even her therapist became fed up with her lack of progress and terminated their sessions.

The big kick in the gut for Arnold came when Charise went to court to change the baby's last name from Lewis' last name: Taylor, only to replace it with her own name: Wiggins. She had to get Arnold to help her with the legal process, but wouldn't do the decent thing and give the baby Arnold's last name: Hamilton. It took everything in Arnold to help her when he learned what she was up to, but knew if he didn't help her, his child would carry another man's name forever.

Frankly, Arnold had grown tired of indulging Charise for sex, but he held out hope that she'd wake up, realize what a good man she had, and change her life so they could be together as a real family. Instead, he was wheeling his luggage out the door of a beautiful resort in Cancun, and leaving Charise for once and for all.

"Well go then, you stupid motherfucker! I don't need you," Charise yelled down the hallway as Arnold left the room with his bags in tow.

And then he was gone.

Prologue

2

"Damn baby, what's up with all the noise? Your man ain't fucking you right?" Lewis casually strolled up the hall with his familiar arrogance to the open door of Charise's room. He wore yellow linen shorts and a partially opened Caribbean floral printed shirt, exhibiting his deliciously dark chocolate smooth chest. A raffia straw outback hat and tan sandals complemented his look. Women craved a second glance as he walked by.

"Go to hell, Lewis!"

Lewis walked close enough to Charise to kiss her, but didn't. "It sounds as though you miss Big Daddy," he said, brushing himself up against her hip.

As his Polo cologne tickled her nostrils, Charise felt herself melting at the suggestion that Lewis was making. She gently bit her bottom lip. "You need to get away from my room, Lewis," she said in a soft whisper that let Lewis know he could have her if he wanted.

He boldly ran his fingertips across her nipple, which had become exposed as her robe loosened from her grip. Charise closed her eyes and licked her lips as she allowed herself to get lost in the many memories of her lovemaking with her sister's husband. Lewis let his fingers trail their way down to her pubic area, outlining the patch of hair on her mound.

Charise let out an audible sigh and turned back into her room, anticipating a stolen moment with Lewis. What Charise did not anticipate was Lewis letting the door close between them once she turned around. She was certain Lewis was going to enter her room and make wild passionate love to her as he had so many times in the past. When she realized he was not coming into her room, she reopened the door only to find him gone. She closed the door again and screamed out as though someone was killing her.

She couldn't believe she was about to fall for Lewis again after how badly he'd treated her. He left her while she was pregnant with what they believed was his child, only to return to Sandy, who had just given birth to his daughter. Then he came back around to Charise for one last blowjob and a paternity test. He hadn't been seen or heard from again for almost a year.

According to the discussions at the family dinner the night before, Lewis and Sandy had been going to church and had gotten their marriage back on track. So much for Lewis' redemption. Charise knew by the way Lewis had just touched her that he was the same old dog, but she yearned to have him inside of her just one more time.

There was a knock at the door. Charise took a deep breath and ran to swing the door open, her robe still in disarray.

"Expecting someone?"

"Elaine! Kelly! What are you doing here?"

"Apparently, you were hoping someone else was knocking." Elaine raised an eyebrow while looking down at an exposed Charise.

Charise looked down at herself and rushed to close her robe as Elaine and Kelly barged their way into her suite.

"Funny, I just saw Lewis' ashy black ass going down the hall. Surely that wasn't who you were expecting?" Kelly asked.

Charise diverted her guilty eyes from her big sisters' stares.

"You are fucking ridiculous, Charise. You are here for Harmony's wedding trying to fuck Sandy's husband AGAIN, and don't give a shit that Sandy is here and will beat your little ass before the wedding," Elaine yelled.

"What do you want? Why are you here?" Agitated, Charise began picking imaginary dirt from beneath her manicured nails. "And for the record, I don't give a shit what Sandy has to say."

"Elaine, please indulge me this thought." Kelly took a seat at the small, round, festively decorated dining table while holding her chin. "Could the death of our daddy have caused this child to be so mentally and emotionally off balance? I mean, after all, she was like eight or nine years old when he died. Perhaps his death caused this desperate state that she's in, and her total lack of all self-esteem?"

Elaine pretended to ponder the thought.

"Fuck you!" Charise yelled to Kelly.

"Well, Kelly, I'm inclined to agree, but I think perhaps it was all the drinking at those blue lights in the basement parties Mama and Daddy used to have. Charise was conceived around that time."

Kelly continued in their private discussion as though Charise wasn't standing there. "And you know what the sad part is? This is someone's mother here."

"Poor baby! Thank goodness the boy has a pretty decent daddy," Elaine came back.

"If he has a half of grain of sense, he'll go file for custody of Jarod and flee before the kid grows up just as stupid as his mama," Kelly added before the pair laughed.

Charise charged at Kelly just as she was standing back up, but Elaine grabbed Charise by the back of her neck. "Watch out there, heifer. You wouldn't want me to call in Sandy to handle your simple ass, would you?" Elaine threatened. "Don't forget, I still owe you an ass whipping from when you were pregnant. Remember?"

Charise broke free from Elaine's grip and ran into the bathroom crying.

"Had me all locked up and shit behind her dumbness."

Kelly laughed after the momentary shock of Charise charging at her wore off. "This chick must have bumped her head if she thought she was going to kick my ass. What the hell?"

"You're slipping, sis. She would have had your ass if I didn't grab her."

"Like hell! I wish you didn't grab her. Apparently all those months in therapy didn't give her an ounce of sense."

"That's your sister," Elaine joked.

"She's your mama's daughter." Kelly rolled her eyes then looked around the suite. "Damn, how come her room is so big and I got that little-ass room?"

"Uh, because this is the suite, pea-brain. It's the same size as mine, and you know Arnold must have paid for this, because I know that cheap-ass girl didn't come off of her dollars for this."

"That's a damn shame. The man paid for this room and can't even stay in it." Kelly laughed. "Hope he at least got some punanny before he had to leave."

Elaine shook her head. "He'll learn one day."

"I doubt it. His fool ass will probably be waiting in Houston with candles and a rose petal-covered bed, anticipating her return home."

They laughed and gave each other a high-five.

"Girl, come on. I need to go find me a drink after dealing with this nutcase." Kelly rolled her eyes and shook her head.

"Don't you always? You lush." Elaine laughed.

They continued laughing as they left Charise's room.

Prologue

3

Walking from the outdoor bar to sit at a poolside table, which offered a spectacular view of the ocean, Kelly and Elaine filled Shawnee in on Charise's shenanigans as they carried their assortment of fruity drinks from the bar.

"You have got to be kidding. Do you know if she was actually sleeping with Lewis?" Shawnee asked them as the trio took their seats.

"No, I don't think she had the chance. I just saw her baby's daddy leaving in a huff with his suitcases. I only spoke with him a few minutes before I ran into Elaine. Then a few minutes later, we were heading to Charise's room to find out what was going on, but saw Lewis strutting down the hall like Mr. It wearing that stupid Cheshire Cat smirk on his face. He nodded his head back as though he was signaling us to something. Then we heard Charise scream out, so we ran around the corner and down the hall to see what happened. That hot-in-the-ass girl had the nerve to open the door all happy when we knocked, showing her naked body through an open robe."

"Well, maybe she thought it was Arnold coming back?"

"Shawnee, get real! You can't be that damn dumb," Elaine spat back. "Kelly just told you about Lewis nodding his head back with a smirk. Stop acting like you don't know what time it is."

Shawnee almost choked as she was sipping on her drink. "Don't be calling me dumb!" She shook her head out of frustration. "I just don't want to believe that Charise would use Harmony's wedding day to start a war with Sandy."

Elaine sucked her teeth. "We're talking about Charise. That girl started the war the day she first laid down with that dog-ass Lewis. Sandy is just laying low for the right moment to strike. I know her ass."

"You ain't telling no lie there," Kelly agreed, chugging her favorite mixture of Hypnotic and Hennessey. "There's not one conversation I have with Sandy where she doesn't let me know how she keeps praying God will give her the strength not to beat Charise to a pulp—particularly before Harmony's wedding. You saw how Sandy kept looking at her last night at dinner?"

"Yeah, I sure did. So do you think once Harmony and Todd leave for the South Pacific tomorrow, there may be a fight?" Shawnee looked as if she was ready to put money on that fight.

"I don't know what's going to happen, but after the night Kelly and I spent in jail because of that little snot, my ass is getting on the first plane leaving after Harmony. I'm not trying to get caught out there again when my good sense tells me to leave," Elaine half-joked.

Elaine remembered all too well how she ended up in a rumble with Kelly in a restaurant back in DC that caused them to spend a night in jail. She ended up paying $9000 in damages to the restaurant in addition to her attorney fees.

Elaine was preparing to leave the restaurant that night when Harmony dropped a bomb on them by informing them of their only brother Angelo's homosexuality. The news was so shocking that she couldn't move after hearing it. Charise seized the opportunity to jump bad with

Elaine and Shawnee. Kelly came to Charise's defense since she was pregnant, causing the brawl between Elaine and Kelly. Charise was owed an ass-kicking for that, and Elaine had planned on giving it to her after she had the baby. However, the thought of being locked up again, and in Mexico of all places, was going to be Charise's saving grace.

"I plan on leaving tomorrow as well," Shawnee said.

"Isn't that wonderful? The two of you can head back to New York together on the same flight." Kelly joked. She knew that Shawnee living in New York rubbed Elaine the wrong way.

"There she goes trying to start shit again. You damn lush," Elaine said, playing angry as Kelly was about to nurse her second drink. She switched her attention from Kelly and directed it to Shawnee. "Then again, New York had tons of places to live, and you just had to move on Roosevelt Island in the same damn building as me."

Shawnee sighed. "I already told you that I did not know you were living there when I moved there. How was I supposed to know you had an apartment both in the city and on Roosevelt Island?"

Kelly was cracking up at the coincidence, as she did every time the subject came up. The alcohol made it even funnier.

"That's all right. I'm getting ready to head to LA next month to open my third boutique," Elaine responded. "Instead of this chick, I'll have flaming Angelo and all his flamboyant-diva buddies to work my last nerve."

The ladies laughed as they sipped on their cocktails.

SNAP, SNAP.

"I know I just heard my name, bitches!" Angelo came up the steps to the poolside table where the ladies sat, snapping his fingers and playing his flamboyant gay role, which he knew drove his sisters crazy.

Since coming out of the closet with his homosexuality, his once masculine voice miraculously became high-pitched and feminine. The once masculine attire the sisters were used to seeing him wear had been traded for brightly colored neon striped Capri pants, a pink Ralph Lauren polo shirts, and pink and white Ralph Lauren flip flops.

"Oh, shut up!" Kelly stood up, laughing, and snapped. "Elaine was just talking about her move to Los Angeles, where you will be."

"All the girls are dying to meet the Queen Diva. I can't wait," Angelo said, all excited. He plopped down in an empty seat. "Just don't forget, I'm Angela when we're in LA."

"Oh, Lord, Angelo! Please don't remind me . . . damn!" Elaine said dramatically with her forehand to her forehead. "Gee, I thought I had already met them all when I was there."

"Hardly. You know how many friends I have? You only met my business partners."

Shawnee peeked over the glass she was holding to her face. "So, Angelo, when you say 'the girls,' are you really referring to people born female or what?" She was embarrassed for not knowing.

"Uhm, I didn't say fishes!" Angelo responded. "Picture Elaine getting along with a school of fish. NOT! The only reason Elaine gets the title Queen Diva is because she is bringing us shoes, which means we don't have to personally go to Europe to get them."

"Gee, thanks!" Elaine responded dryly, sipping on her non-alcoholic mixed-fruit drink.

They shared a laugh.

"Us? Angelo, you be wearing women's shoes too?" Kelly looked at Angelo, hoping she was wrong.

Angelo looked at her like she was stupid. "And if I did? What, you got a problem with it or something?"

Kelly busted out laughing. "Lord, if I could see my six-foot-one, lanky-ass baby brother in some stilettos . . . That would be a sight." Kelly laughed so hard that tears formed in her eyes as Angelo gave her a twisted-lip look.

13

The Queen

"And not a pleasant one," Shawnee said, giving a disapproving glare as she sipped her drink.

"ANYHOW, bitches all up in my business, Harmony asked me to round you all up so we could start getting ready for the wedding. She'd like for it to start on time," Angelo said.

"Oh, fuck Harmony! She wouldn't even let me coordinate her wedding. What kind of shit is that? We should all show up an hour late," Kelly half-joked.

Angelo pulled his neck back and did his double snap again. "That was scandalous, wasn't it? She wouldn't even tell us where the wedding was going to be until last month. I almost didn't come, but since she begged me to be the one to give her away and was paying for my trip, I figured what the hell. Oh! And then she's going to emphasize that she needs me looking masculine for the occasion."

The ladies laughed as Angelo pouted, rolling his eyes.

"Come on. We better get going. Somebody needs to go collect Charise from her room." Shawnee stood up from the table, causing the others to follow her lead.

"Send Sandy," Elaine responded.

"Ouch! Not a good idea. I'm surprised Charise ain't already dead from those death glares that Sandy's been shooting at her. I guess I'll go get my sister," Angelo volunteered.

Kelly grabbed Angelo as he was about to walk off. "Warning! She's not a happy camper right now. Her baby's daddy ditched her. He said he's tired of playing this charade with her. Supposedly she brought him as a front for Sandy."

They all laughed hysterically.

"Oooooh! Uhm-hmm. Now that's a scandal. Thanks for the heads up." Angelo grinned. "Now I can go console her and get her to spill all the dirt." He skipped off as his sisters laughed at him.

"You better hope Charise doesn't spill too much dirt," Kelly warned, looking back and forth between Elaine and Shawnee. "You know neither of you want Charise talking about Mandingo. I don't think Angelo would let you live that scandal down."

"I'll be tucked away in New York, but Elaine would have to be the one day in and day out with him." Shawnee finished off her drink and placed the empty glass on the table.

"Mandingo? Mandingo who? I don't know what you're talking about," Elaine joked with a straight face.

"Cute. Real cute." Kelly laughed. "I wonder what ever became of his stalking ass."

"Who cares?" Elaine answered, still annoyed about Mandingo choosing Shawnee over her. "Good fucking riddance!"

As the ladies were leaving their table, a model-like vision of beauty appeared. Standing at a statuesque six feet with a long neck, dark hair swaying down her back, and wearing nylon athletic wear that accentuated her perfectly toned body with curves in the right places, the young woman walked toward the women. Each of their mouths fell open while Elaine raised her perfectly arched eyebrow as the woman approached with an equally dazzling smile.

"Wow, you all are beautiful, so I can't figure which of you is Shawnee," the strange woman said with her Texan accent.

Shawnee hesitantly raised her hand. "Uh, that would be me."

The strange woman walked to Shawnee and gave her a hug. "Hi, Shawnee. I am Todd's sister Tatiana. He told me to find you and meet you since we have so much in common." Then she directed her attention to Elaine and Kelly. "I guess since you look like you're also obviously a part of my new extended family, I should hug you as well." She hugged both Elaine and Kelly as they tensed up.

Elaine turned her nose up and gave her a phony smile, making it no mystery that she already didn't like the woman. She picked up one of her favorite Chanel scents on the woman, and made a mental note to discard her own bottle when she returned home.

"These are two of my sisters, Elaine and Kelly. The others are scattered. You weren't here for the dinner last night, correct?"

"No. I just arrived this morning. Work has been hectic, so I couldn't get away any sooner," Tatiana replied, not swayed by the rude reception.

The Wiggins sisters just nodded with their fake, disgusted smiles. Their veins were filled with Haterade as they were absolutely disgusted with the natural beauty of this woman. They always considered themselves head-turners, but felt this new possible threat may be in a league all her own.

Tatiana continued. "And speaking of work, Shawnee, we work for the same company. I work out of the Houston office and hopefully soon will make it to the New York office."

Over my dead body, Shawnee thought as she looked the woman up and down. "Uh-huh. So you're trying to relocate to our New York office, huh?"

"Yes. I just met with Brad yesterday afternoon about my transfer. He said he would talk with you when you returned to New York. Todd thought this would be a great time for us to meet."

Shawnee could feel her nerves frying and a migraine coming on. This woman called the man Shawnee had been sleeping with for the past year by his first name: Brad. Shawnee felt Tatiana should be referring to their boss as Mr. Neely and not Brad.

Kelly, sensing her sister's tension, intervened. "So, Tatiana, what do you do for The Right Look Inc.? I figure you must be high up on the management chain since you refer to your boss by his first name."

Tatiana laughed, placing her hand to her full, perky-breasted chest. The women's eyes followed and saw her hardened nipples poking through. This further annoyed Shawnee.

"Oh, Brad insists we call him by his first name. Actually, I am Director of Marketing. I am hoping to make it to partner before I turn forty, as Shawnee did. That's why Shawnee is my hero. She has not only broken barriers for women, but for women of color. And when Brad speaks of Shawnee, he speaks with such great admiration and confidence of the direction she's taking the company. Do you have any idea of what a task that is? I would love to work with Shawnee and follow in her footsteps."

Now how am I supposed to hate the woman who looks upon me as a hero? Shawnee thought. *Hmm, maybe it would be a good thing to bring her snooty-ass to New York and keep a closer eye on her interactions with Brad. And I know the bitch has to know her nipples are standing at attention through that thin fabric. That's probably why she tries to hang around Brad. Bitch!*

"If you don't mind my asking, Tatiana, how old are you now?" Shawnee inquired.

"I just turned thirty-four last month. A go-getting Capricorn."

Elaine looked her up and down, sizing her up some more. "Don't you have a husband or family to consider before making such a big move?"

"I've had a few near misses in the way of marriage, but I feel my career is more important at this time. I love Houston, and most of my family is there, but I need to spread my wings and explore life on my own in order to grow. I also understand that each of you is doing well in your lives. Elaine, Todd tells me that you have a string of successful shoe stores, and that Kelly is a big-time celebrity event planner. That is impressive, especially given your ages."

"You just have to love her," Kelly said to her sisters, giving Tatiana a false sense of security. "Welcome to the family, Tatiana."

The Queen

Tatiana flashed her dazzling smile, oblivious to the hell the Wiggins sisters would soon give her. Once again, Tatiana hugged the sisters with only Kelly hugging her back.

"Have you all had the opportunity to meet the rest of my family?"

"Well we have met many, but we can't be certain if that was the rest of them. As you probably know, our large family is going to be a great deal for you to meet as well." Kelly laughed. "But I did meet your cute brothers Kenny and Kyle."

"And their wives, Kelly," Elaine reminded her.

The ladies all laughed, but Elaine cut her laugh short to keep from laughing along with Tatiana. "And for the record, I don't have shoe *stores*; I have shoe *boutiques*."

"Oh, I'm sorry. I stand corrected," Tatiana answered, embarrassed.

"Uhm-hmm . . . I guess." Elaine discreetly checked out Tatiana's perfectly sculpted body. "So, how did you turn out so much taller than your sisters? What are you, about six feet?"

Tatiana uncomfortably laughed. "I am six feet without shoes. I typically wear high-heeled shoes, which angers my sisters. They feel I'm too tall to wear heels. As you saw with my brothers and father, height is something I've paternally inherited. My father's sisters and mother are also tall. My sisters took their height and size from my mother's family. Since I am the youngest of my sisters, they haven't made it easy for me to have my own identity. They even criticize me for letting my hair grow, saying it makes me look like a Hispanic Barbie doll. I try keeping fit and in shape, and they accuse me of looking anorexic. According to them, all of these things combined are why I can't manage to get a husband. I typically avoid our family dinners because I can't stand the berating. And between you and me, work wasn't hectic yesterday. One, I didn't want to get here with my family too soon, and two, when I learned that Brad was going to be in Houston yesterday, I wanted to get the opportunity to speak with him about my transfer."

Although Shawnee felt a twinge in her nerves when Tatiana said "Brad" again, she felt her heart softening up just a bit toward Tatiana. She thought of how they all ganged up on Charise in the same manner. However, Charise and Tatiana were like night and day. Tatiana appeared to have her life together and Charise refused to get her life on track.

"You know, I can't help but think of our youngest sister when I hear you speak. She feels we are always on her case for one reason or another, but I'm glad to see you turned out pretty well despite it all," Shawnee said.

"I have to give credit to my father and brothers. They were always in my corner. I love my mother to death, but she tends to view life the way my sisters do. When I ask her to get my sisters off my back, she reminds me that they only love me and want what's best for me. Not quite the response I am looking for," Tatiana said with slight sadness in her face.

Kelly held out her arms for Tatiana. "Come here," she hugged her. "Again, welcome to your extended family. We might secretly hate you because you're absolutely gorgeous, but we'll treat you like one of ours. You can count on it."

The dazzling smile was back on Tatiana's face. "Thank you. What a kind thing to say. I think."

The ladies laughed, with the exception of Elaine.

"Well, I better get going. I have to start preparing for this wedding. By the way, are you all in the wedding?"

"Our sister didn't think we were good enough to participate in her wedding. We barely received an invitation," Kelly responded with pressed lips. "Oh, but our brother did make the cut. He's walking Harmony down the aisle, giving her away or whatever it is they decided on. Hell, if Harmony allows Angelo to walk with her, Angelo will steal the spotlight."

The Queen

Elaine burst out laughing hysterically. Tatiana looked confused.

"A family joke you'll learn soon enough," Shawnee told Tatiana.

Prologue

4

"Sandy, I have to thank you for not using my wedding as the place to do battle with Charise. I know it wasn't easy sitting through dinner last night with her. On top of getting married, you have no idea of how bad my nerves have been concerning a confrontation," Harmony said, while Sandy worked on her hair.

"I can't believe you worried yourself over this mess. I would never do you like that. Now Shawnee, maybe, but I wouldn't do it to you, ever." Sandy chuckled but then got serious. "You mean the world to me and to my children. I know I haven't lived thirty-five years as well as I could have, but the beauty is that God is a good God, and He allows us the opportunity to make our mistakes and learn from them. He forgives us even when we don't know how to forgive ourselves. And contrary to what everyone may think, I can forgive my baby sister for her transgression against me, but she needs to ask me. She needs to come to me and at least show me that she has an ounce of remorse for sleeping with my husband."

The Queen

Harmony looked at her sister with amazement through the mirror. "I am just floored by this positive change in you. You have been going to church forever, but I never quite saw this humble side of you, Sandy. I am so proud of you. And I agree that Charise should at least come to acknowledge her wrongdoing. Are you still attending Joel Osteen's church?"

"Girl, yes! Lakewood Church has been one of the best things that happened to me. My kids love it as well." Sandy paused and dropped her head down to her chest. "I have something I want to tell you. Something I'm almost ashamed to admit. My minister told me the only way to be free of my burdens is to let go of them through the confessions of my mouth."

Harmony was a bit apprehensive about hearing any confessions on her wedding day, but she was intrigued. "I'm listening."

Sandy closed her eyes and took a deep breath while holding Harmony's curl in her hand. "It's probably no surprise at all, but I don't love my husband anymore, and I'm not sure I can stay with him much longer."

Harmony's mouth was wordlessly opened by the admission.

"The truth is, I realized that I didn't love him a long time ago. When I slept with Eric, I thought if I could give Lewis a dose of his own medicine, maybe I'd feel differently. But not only was he sleeping with my sister, he left me while I was pregnant to be with that sister. I've had nothing but contempt in my heart for him since he came crawling back, but I took him back as revenge against Charise. I took that snake back just because I didn't want him to be happy with my sister. I wanted to give him the boot when we learned that Charise's baby was not his, but I struggled spiritually about whether I should forgive my husband and stay with him or not. Lewis had been going with me to church, and at one point he seemed as though he was capable of changing his evil ways, but a wolf can't wear sheep's clothing but for so long before the tarnishing seeps through."

Harmony pulled her hair from Sandy's hands and turned in her seat to face her directly with her mouth open and no words to escape.

"The bottom line is: I don't love him, and I want to be free of him. I don't want to leave Houston or my church, but I can't be the better person when it comes to him any longer. He makes me lose my religion, and I'm in a fight for my and my children's salvation. I don't know what else to do," Sandy confessed with misty eyes. She went and sat on the sofa, where Harmony joined her.

"Wow! I know that was very difficult for you to admit, but you have taken the first big step by admitting there is a problem. Despite what little I think of Lewis, I don't dare tell you what you should or should not do. Your answers are going to have to come from within. I do know you deserve so much better from a husband, and if you'll hold onto the God that you've found, you'll have better than what you have. Once upon a time, I thought I would never have anyone for me, but here I am about to marry the best thing that has ever happened to me." The tears poured from Harmony's eyes as she spoke with adoration of her husband-to-be.

"God knows if anyone deserves to be happy, you are that one. You have been an angel to me and everyone you've come into contact with. You also couldn't have picked a better career. Your being a psychologist is the best thing that could have happened to all of us. You are truly wonderful, Harmony, and you are an inspiration to me. You make me want to be better and do better. Thank you," Sandy said as she embraced her sister.

"Okay, what are we missing?" Kelly asked as she, Elaine, and Shawnee entered the bridal suite.

"I thought I was going to have to send out the search party to find you all." Harmony wiped away her tears.

The Queen

"Hell, we couldn't be in the wedding. What you looking for us for?" Elaine joked with attitude.

"I figure all of you were too busy to take part. Sandy and Angelo are in it," Harmony defended herself.

"*Whatever!*" Kelly yelled.

Everyone laughed.

"Where's Angelo?" Harmony asked.

"He went to gather Charise," Shawnee answered. "I figured they'd be here by now."

Prologue

5

"Charise, you are older than I am. You are supposed to be setting the example. You are someone's mother now. You can't keep making these poor decisions." Angelo followed Charise back and forth from the bedroom into the suite's living room area as she gathered her outfit for the wedding.

"I thought I could talk to you, Angelo. I thought for certain you wouldn't be trying to judge me," Charise turned and spat back.

Angelo dramatized the headache he was getting from listening to Charise's foolishness. "No one is judging you, but you have to know it's not okay to sleep with your own sister's husband. It's not okay to sleep with your friend's boyfriends, let alone their husbands. Maybe Daddy died at a very bad time in your life. All of our lives. I also know Mama didn't give you the nurturing that you needed after Daddy died. But then again, maybe he wasn't exactly the best daddy, which has you all messed up."

Angelo turned his face up as the words came from his own mouth.

The Queen

"Then, on top of that, you were left to be cared for by cruel teenage sisters. Hell, they were cruel to me, so I can imagine how you felt. But now we're adults, and everything in the past is in the past. We can't change any of it. We have to be more responsible and accountable. This is our life now."

"What's this constant shit about Daddy dying affecting me? Angelo, you're gay. How is that more responsible?" Charise set her shoes down near the dining chair where she'd placed her dress and put her hand on her hip.

"Yes, I am gay and proud of it. But guess what? I'm not screwing anyone's husband!" Angelo shot back in disgust. He wasn't sure why he was wasting his time trying to get through to his hardheaded sister. "You don't sleep with your sister's man. That's all there is to it."

Charise folded her arms across her chest. "Shawnee and Elaine fucked Sandy's ex-boyfriend Eric. You know, that same guy that Sandy screwed and thought was her baby's father?"

Angelo let out a high-pitched howl and fell on the sofa as if fainting. "Stop it! You are lying!"

"No, I am not. And that was going on while Shawnee was still married to Robert. Not only that, they were all sleeping with him at the same time."

Angelo let out another of his high-pitched scream. "Stop it! You're killing me, Charise. I can't hear this." He covered his ears. "La-La-La-La-La!! I'm not hearing you. Please! I've had enough. Let's go! We have to get to Harmony's suite." Angelo stood up and headed for the door. "Get your dress and let's go."

"Wait. I still have to shower. I have to wash Arnold off of me," Charise confessed.

"Uh-uh! Oh, hold up, ho!" Angelo stopped in his tracks and turned to face Charise. "Your skank ass was about to screw Lewis, but you just finished doing Arnold?" He held his hand up then turned his back to Charise. "I'm done! I can't talk to you anymore. I'll see you in the bridal suite." Angelo walked out of Charise's room.

Charise could hear Angelo in the hallway screaming with his high-pitched scream. Then he yelled, "Calgon, take me away from these bitches!"

Charise debated on if she wanted to join her family in the bridal suite. She felt that she had tolerated more than she wanted for this short trip, but then Harmony didn't deserve the aggravation on her wedding day. Charise decided to call Harmony's suite and let Harmony know that she'd see her down at the wedding because she wanted to keep the peace. Thankfully, Harmony was understanding and let her off the hook.

PART ONE

It's a Family Affair

1
Shawnee

Lord, if you're listening, please make Harmony fall down while she's coming down the aisle.

She knows she is wrong as hell to leave me seated as the referee to Mom's sisters Aunt Willie Mae and Aunt Willow, and then Daddy's sisters Aunt Henrietta, Harriett, and Hattie. And if Mom's other four sisters were still around, that would be even worse, since they hated Daddy's family just the same. (Well actually two are deceased and one is serving a double life sentence for murder, while the other is currently serving a five-year domestic violence sentence, for the third time.)

The two families have been feuding since Mama and Daddy first married forty-two years ago. And why would Harmony invite Daddy's drunken brothers, Harry and Hank to a resort in Mexico that feeds you alcohol from sunup to sundown? It is only three o'clock, and Uncle Harry has fallen down twice already. That was the ammunition to get Aunt Willie Mae started about Daddy's drunken family, and how Daddy's drunkenness was what killed our mother. Actually, Mama died of ovarian cancer, some thirteen years after Daddy died. Completely unrelated.

Daddy's funeral was a fiasco, and the last time his whole family

had to gang up on Mama. They blamed her for him being a drunk and dying of liver failure, despite his brothers also being drunks. They even accused her of killing him.

When Mama called Aunt Willie Mae and told her Daddy's family was ganging up on her and talking about reporting her to the police, all of my aunts rode in from Detroit with their husbands, daughters, and sons in tow to do battle with the Wiggins family. They were actually fighting at the funeral. Poor Daddy's casket was knocked over in the church. The police were called to the church, but no one was arrested.

Talk about embarrassed, my boyfriend at the time, Michael Woods, attended the funeral with me and wouldn't have anything more to do with me after he saw I had a crazy family. That would be the Michael Woods I relieved Sandy of so many years ago. She still harbors jealousy of me about him. He didn't even want to be with her. He was my age and wanted me, but she could never accept that.

Grandma Etta, who is Daddy's mother, doesn't help matters. She is eighty-two feisty years old, and mean as hell in a wheelchair, wearing diapers. She started talking crap about Aunt Willow's 21-year-old grandson being a *nappy-headed fool*, because he has his hair in dreadlocks.

Grandma Etta is Native American, and her children all had a good quality of hair. Although we have a pretty decent grade of hair, it wasn't good enough for Grandma Etta. She'd often complain that our mother caused us to have nappy hair. Most of Daddy's family could pass for white, so Mama's bronze complexion only *tarnished our complexions*, according to Grandma Etta. Charise and Angelo were the only two to take on Mama's complexion. The rest of us took on a pleasant mixture, which produced an almond-honey complexion.

The other problem was Daddy only stood at 5'8", while Mama towered him at 5'10". Both Harmony and I took Mama's height at 5'10". Somehow Angelo stands at 6'1". Kelly and Sandy are 5'7" and

Elaine is 5'8". Poor Charise was height challenged by Daddy's side, and is only 5'3". She tries so hard to get Daddy's family to accept her since she's closer in height, but her complexion stands in her way. Grandma Etta would often refer to me and Harmony as "big Amazon women, like y'ur mama." When she gets around Mama's sisters, she also calls them Amazon women because they too are tall and heavy in the hips.

When I married Robert, I didn't bother to invite Daddy's family to my wedding. Aunt Henrietta, who is Daddy's twin sister, felt the need to call me and tell me about myself. She went as far as to tell me that they were all placing bets as to how long my marriage would last. According to her, I was "too hot in the tail to hold on to a good man." I haven't spoken with any of them since then.

When they showed up in Cancun, I wanted to strangle Harmony for putting me in the position of having to face those people and explain why my husband wasn't present. So I lied and said that he had to work and couldn't make it. Kiss-ass Charise felt the need to let Grandma Etta know I divorced Robert. And they still didn't like her because she was *too dark*. They sat right at the dinner table and talked how much of a shame it was that Charise was so sweet, but had to go through life with that *ugly* complexion. Although it was said loud enough for most of us to hear, Charise pretended not to hear. Our cousin Rayvin, who is Mama's deceased brother William's 41-year-old daughter, spoke up. She told the Wiggins clan that they needed to grow up and stop being so hateful. The Wiggins clan just pursed their lips together as though someone insulted them, and said, "Hmmph!"

So I have to sit here in an $1100 Carmen Marc Valvo gown and $1,400 Christian Louboutin sandals, hair all perfectly laid, waiting for a repeat of Daddy's funeral at any moment.

"I smell piss. Do you smell piss, Willow?" Aunt Willie Mae says loud enough for all those seated waiting for the wedding to begin to

The Queen

hear. She sniffs around the area of their seats.

"I smell it too. It's probably that old bat in the diapers," Aunt Willow responds, pinching her nose. She knew it is going to incite a brawl.

"I thought it was her also, but I think that drunk-ass son of hers just pissed on himself." Aunt Willie Mae waves her fan, as if trying to shoo away the odor.

"Who you calling a drunk?" Aunt Harriett stands up behind Aunt Willie Mae with her hands on her hips, speaking properly-country.

"Will the real drunk please stand up?" Aunt Willow never looks behind her. "Oops! She's already standing."

There is a great laughter from both sides of the aisle as Aunt Harriett quickly takes her seat.

"I'll see you after this wedding is over. I came to share in my niece's joyous day, and I'm not going to let you ruin it for her with your foolishness."

Aunt Willie Mae turns in her seat. "Well if you really wanted it to be joyous, the lot of you would have kept your drunken, pissy asses home."

The rest of Mama's family looks on as if they dare anyone from Daddy's family to jump in.

Now I have to step in. It's funny as hell, but I know any minute all hell will break loose. I stand and walk back the one row where Aunt Willie Mae and Willow are sitting, but look at both sides of my family. "Would you please just stop it? When Harmony leaves tomorrow, you all can rip each other's eyes out and find yourselves in a Mexican jail, but right now, everyone is going to put a sock in it."

"Shawnee, I don't see your husband here with you. Charise said he divorced you. I sure hope Harmony knows how to hold on to a husband," Aunt Henrietta says to me, loud enough for many to hear.

I look behind me to see if Todd's family was able to catch her smart remark. They're looking at me as if they had.

"Henrietta, stop that!" Aunt Hattie says. "She can't help that he left her."

My blood pressure has to be through the invisible roof. *Oh, no these battleaxes didn't sit here and try to publicly humiliate me!*

"Oh, go drop dead! You evil trolls! I've had about all that I will of your shit," I yell at Daddy's evil sisters. "Now, you say one more damn word, and not only will this wedding come to a screeching halt, but we're going to all end up in a Mexican jail today. Fuck with me one more time!"

They all gasp as if they are truly shocked. Nonetheless, there isn't another word said.

Lord, could I amend that previous prayer? Please let Harmony trip while coming down the aisle, step on the bottom of her Vera Wang gown, it rips, she rolls down the aisle like a bowling ball and knocks over Aunt Henrietta and Aunt Hattie's chairs. Also, let the locks come off on Grandma Etta's wheelchair so she can roll down into the ocean, for breeding this evil. Oh, and can you make Charise deaf and mute?

Thank you, Lord.

2
Sandy

I peek out of the tent set up for the bride. "Harmony, you better hurry up and get this wedding started. Your family is about to riot out there. I don't know what possessed you to invite both sides of our family."

"I never thought they'd actually show up in Mexico on such short notice," Harmony answers. "I just invited them three weeks ago. I waited until the last minute because I didn't want them to say I didn't invite them, but I was hoping they wouldn't be able to get their arrangements together in enough time."

"Get real! Mama's family showed up at Daddy's funeral with less than one day's notice when Mama called and told them it was about to go down. And you know Daddy's family would show up just so they could have something to talk about," I remind her.

"I don't know! I had so much going on, I just wasn't thinking." Harmony seems frustrated as she does a last minute check of her make up for the umpteenth time.

"You better hope Todd doesn't watch your family interaction and run for the hills the way my boyfriend that Shawnee stole from me did at Daddy's funeral." I soured on the last part of my statement.

"Okay, Sandy, I get it. I fucked up!" Harmony yells, almost teary-eyed. "Please let them know I am ready."

I give the signal that we are ready to begin. I decide to look out at the crowd again and spot Lewis and Charise sitting together, looking all chummy. *Now ain't that a bitch!* If it's not bad enough Charise wouldn't try to make peace with me, but instead she wants to dump the man she came to Cancun with, to take up with my husband? AGAIN!

Hell, Lakewood Church ain't here in Cancun to help her when I lose my religion.

"What's wrong?" Harmony asks when she sees the disturbed look on my face.

"Charise is sitting with my husband, Harmony. Please help me keep it together."

"Oh no! You have to be kidding! Come on and let's get this wedding over with," Harmony says as calmly as she can. She gives the signal for the music to begin.

As I walk down the aisle, I can't help but make it clear to Charise and Lewis that I am watching them. The bitch has the nerve to give me a big cheesy smile and wave.

This better be a quick wedding, because obviously Charise is going to put on a show to antagonize me. I'm not too sure how long I am going to be able to keep it together. Lewis certainly isn't helping matters. Why must he indulge Charise by sitting with her, knowing it would piss me off?

The biggest kick in the behind, almost literally, was when Lewis started harassing me for anal sex, and threw in my face how Charise was completely uninhibited, and I should be more like her. That statement had him sleeping on the sofa for over a month. Then, of course, the church sermon was about wives submitting to their husbands. I still wouldn't give him my booty, but I let him back in the bed.

Knowing Lewis, he didn't miss out on sex. There are two shameless women in the church who always offer to do things for him or need him to fix things at their homes. I spoke with one of the ministers about it, and he said he'd try counseling Lewis. That counsel went in one ear and out the other. Once Lewis was aware that I knew of those two women, he'd tell me I needed to learn to appreciate having such a good man that everyone else wanted. Now that we have a daughter together, it makes it more difficult to just walk away from him. My other three children have different daddies, and I wasn't married to any of them.

When I spoke with the therapist that Harmony set me up with, she informed me that I was in an emotionally and mentally abusive relationship. It's been difficult to accept that because I can give Lewis a run for his money just the same. And he met my mama's family when we went to Detroit, so he knows better than to lift a finger in the wrong way. My therapist feels my tolerance of the situation represents low self-esteem. My church disagrees and feels all marriages have their challenges. Both my heart and mind are leaning with the therapist on this one.

And now I have to watch this fool sitting with the one person he knows to steer clear of. I ought to let my male cousins rough him up before we leave Cancun.

3
Harmony

My legs are about to buckle from under me. I don't remember walking down the aisle. I can't even hear the minister speaking. My mind is racing.

"Fall down before you have to say 'I do,'" my mind is screaming.

My heart is about to beat through my chest. Is my body trying to tell me to run now while I still can, before it's too late? Could this be some type of omen? Could Todd have some crazy side that he's been able to hide from me thus far?

What if Todd turns out like Robert? He started off perfect, but turned out to be a closet freak who generously splurges on prostitutes and was obsessed with Elaine. What if Todd one day decides he wants to sleep with Elaine too?

Or Shawnee? She's a backstabbing, sneaky one who thinks everything is a competition.

Could Todd be weak enough to fall for Charise as Lewis did?

Why am I having all of these crazy thoughts?

What if my siblings end up feuding with Todd's siblings over forty years later? What was I thinking about when I invited "The Hatfields" and "The McCoys" to my wedding? Why must Aunt Hattie sit there like a sobbing fool, crying as though she really likes me?

Why does Charise need to use my wedding to antagonize Sandy?

Damn, my feet hurt. I don't know why I let Elaine talk me into wearing these expensive-ass sandals.

I wonder why Todd is crying. Maybe he's having regrets and doesn't know how to back out of marrying me.

Oh, I'm so thankful Angelo manned up for this wedding. If Daddy's family would have said one word about him being gay, I would have kicked their asses myself.

I wonder if Todd will be pissed when I let him know I left my birth control pills home by accident. He knows I want a baby, but I don't think he planned on starting a family immediately.

I wonder what Todd's family thinks of my family. I should have been told Shawnee that Todd's sister works for the same company. I can already tell she's pissed about the whole situation.

"I do," I say after Sandy drew my attention back with a nudge on the shoulder.

Did Todd already say his "I do?" I didn't hear him. He's putting the ring on my finger. Is it that time already?

Sandy hands me the ring for Todd, and I place it on his finger in silence.

I think I was supposed to repeat after the minister. Oh, this is a disaster. Everything we rehearsed went out the window.

Todd is kissing me. Oh, Lord! Is the wedding over? I missed my own wedding. He's happy. Is he happy we're married, or is he happy the wedding is over? Finally!

All of my crazy thoughts disappear out of my head as I get lost in Todd's kiss. I could kiss him forever.

"Ladies and Gentlemen, I present you Mr. and Mrs. Palmer," the minister announces as most everyone applauds with teary eyes. I say most, because most of Daddy's people are looking with raised eyebrows, turned up noses, and pursed lips as Todd and I walk down the aisle together as husband and wife.

I AM MARRIED!

The one thing I thought would never happen has happened to me. And the first thing I'm going to do when we return from our honeymoon is change my last name with every government agency. I will go to my grave with the name Palmer on my headstone instead of Wiggins.

"Come on, honey. Let's hurry up and get away from here. All hell's about to break loose," I whisper to my new husband.

"Why? What's wrong?" Todd asks.

"I know good and well you can hear my aunt Willie Mae carrying on about someone smelling like pee."

"I heard someone say that." Todd looks at my family, at the onset of a brawl. "Would you like me to go and speak to them?"

"I got this."

I walk over to both Mom's and Dad's siblings. I stand silently with my hands on my hips until Uncle Harry finally notices I am standing there.

"Oh, congratulations, baby girl," he says.

The others all turn around and look at the pissed expression on my face. Then they all try to pretend they've been behaving all along.

I say through gritted teeth, "If you all don't shut the hell up and stop embarrassing yourselves . . . I am so sick of your shit, and then you wonder why you don't get invited anywhere. Say one more stupid thing and watch me come out of this gown so fast and whip somebody's ass out here. I'll be damned if I'm going to let ANYONE ruin my wedding day. Now say something else."

I can see the shock on all of their faces, including my sisters'. I know most people have never seen this side of me, but those folk could

The Queen

bring out the ugly side of a preacher. I fix my smile back on my face, turn, and begin walking back to my husband, who is surrounded by his family. I only take three or four steps before I turn back around and show the family my mean face once again; just to show I mean business. I also point to my eye and then to them, to let them know I am keeping my eye on them. Then I go back to join my husband and new in-laws.

And speaking of my in-laws, I've been finding some serious characters within his family over the past year. I feel bad for poor Tatiana. It's obvious her sisters envy her to no end. Tatiana looks like something that stepped off a page of a fashion magazine. She is career driven, while her sisters are women who traded in their professional careers for husbands and children. Thankfully, Todd doesn't expect me to follow their paths by trading in my career once we have a child.

Todd's 86-year-old grandfather thinks he's the Mack with his 41-year-old wife. Needless to say, Todd's not too happy about it. Todd's two sisters-in-law don't have a great relationship with Todd's sisters. His sisters act like they know everything that is best for Kenny and Kyle. They have yet to act ugly with me. Tatiana told me their feelings may change once I have a baby and try to return to work, leaving our child with strangers (daycare).

My new mother-in-law is a pure hypochondriac. She's always watching reruns of *ER*, *House* or one of those medical shows on television, and then picking up the phone to call Todd or Kenny, who is also a doctor, to find out if she's afflicted with the disease featured on that day's show. Of course, she's not afflicted to the point where she'd accept her sons telling her she's a hypochondriac. She'll do a scene from *Sanford and Son*, telling them they will be filled with regret once she's dead and gone and they didn't try to do anything to make her well.

Other than that, she's as sweet as they come, and she can cook her ass off. I often look at her and wonder if my sisters view me like her, when they say I have no backbone. Momma Palmer, (my new pet name for my mother-in-law) certainly has no backbone when it comes to her first three daughters. She's always trying to accommodate them and their opinions. She personally would never belittle or put someone down, but if her daughters said it was the gospel truth, then she'd do whatever she must to facilitate her daughters' happiness. Whatever the consensus, she'd go in that direction, because she thinks that's the fair thing to do. But she fails to realize how her elder daughters are pushing her youngest daughter out of the nest.

Although we encouraged Tatiana to talk with Shawnee since they worked for the same company, and Tatiana wants to move to New York, I was a bit apprehensive of how Shawnee would receive Tatiana, since Shawnee tends to use her physical assets to excel professionally.

Somehow Shawnee has become romantically involved with her boss. Shawnee had never crossed the color line when it came to dating, but did for this old guy. They have been involved for about a year now, and Shawnee is getting very possessive when it comes to him. She thinks every attractive black woman wants his old ass (and her seeing Todd's grandfather with his young woman didn't help matters).

I could just imagine how threatening Shawnee would find Tatiana. I'd be surprised if Tatiana didn't have old Mr. Neely drooling on himself. Especially since Shawnee told me that he spends a lot of time between Chicago and Houston when he's not in New York. The last thing Tatiana needs is Elaine in Shawnee's ear. You certainly would never see Tatiana and Elaine hanging anywhere together. Elaine doesn't like to be anywhere where she's not the focus of everyone's attention. I think Tatiana's beauty and height would certainly detract from Elaine being the center of attention. Shawnee, on the other hand, would keep Tatiana close just to keep an eye on her when it comes to her old man.

Our reception went over *almost* without a hiccup. Shawnee and Sandy cracked up by the way I handled our family. For a period of

The Queen

time, both Charise and Lewis went missing. Ironically, they resurfaced like five or ten minutes apart. For the rest of the evening, Charise was walking around like *Queen It*. Even Todd picked up on her sudden change in attitude. It wouldn't take a rocket scientist to figure out that Charise slept with Lewis again. I don't want Sandy to go to jail, but Charise needs her ass whipped. Both Elaine and Shawnee also want to beat her down, and she'd deserve it.

~~~

In a few more hours, Todd and I will be off on our honeymoon. I spent the better part of the morning talking myself blue in the face to Sandy, to keep her from jumping on Charise.

What is it going to take for that girl to learn?

I also spent my last few hours making rounds to both sides of my family to thank them for coming and to say goodbye. With the exception of my sisters and Angelo, my family will be in Cancun for an extra day. That's a disaster in the making, but as long as we are gone, I don't care.

4
Charise

Ohhh, the look on Sandy's face was priceless when I returned to the reception with Lewis returning five minutes later. The truth is, Harmony would be more pissed with me than anyone if she knew how things really went down. Yeah, Lewis spent the whole wedding ceremony talking shit to me and trying to get me all hot. At one point, he showed me his erection trapped inside his pants. Nope! He blew his opportunity to get this pussy when he tried to play me outside my hotel room. Instead, I decided to give him an eyeful so he'd think the next time he wants to fuck with me.

I noticed the night before, Todd's older son Andre was checking me out. I had to behave because Arnold was being a bug up my ass. Once Arnold was gone, it was on. Right after the wedding, Sandy quickly came to claim Lewis and gave me her dirtiest look. Andre was still checking me out from a distance. He approached me the first chance he could at the reception, accompanied by one of his cousins, who was just as tall and fine.

Supposedly the cousin was celebrating his 25th birthday while on the trip. I let them know my birthday was also coming up in two weeks. Andre grabbed two bottles of champagne from the bar and suggested we go somewhere more private to celebrate. At first I was a bit apprehensive because this was Todd's son, but also because I had never messed around with two guys at the same time. However, when I noticed Lewis still spying on my every move, I figured I'd give him the show of a lifetime. Andre's cousin, whose name I never asked, found a blanket from somewhere, and the three of us took a stroll along the beach to a secluded area. I noticed Lewis off at a distance following and watching.

It didn't take much time for things to heat up, probably since we all had been consuming alcohol prior to Andre popping open the champagne, which we had to drink without glasses. Andre's cousin, who I'll call Joe Blow just to give him a name, sat straddled behind me when I said it was nippy out. Then he awkwardly started kissing the back of my neck, despite our big height difference. *Amateur!*

Andre was encouraging me to drink more to warm up. Joe Blow rubbed my bare arms, which were covered with goose bumps. Then the rub turned into a massage. Once I felt Joe-Blow's bulging erection poke me in the back, my pussy began pulsating. Andre was sitting off to the side, but he was close enough for me to reach over and pull in for a deep, passionate kiss.

While Joe Blow fumbled with the zipper on the back of my dress, Andre's hand made its way under the front and found a hot, wet surprise waiting beneath my thong. Joe Blow managed to get my healthy breasts out of my dress and strapless bra. He fondled and squeezed them like Charmin bath tissue. Andre's mouth made it to one of my hardened nipples, while he inserted two fingers into my wet pussy. Joe Blow reached one of his hands under my dress as well and began rubbing my clit along while Andre's fingers moved inside me. While Andre's mouth attended to my two nipples, Joe Blow put his tongue deep in my mouth.

I can't be sure at what point I became completely naked on the blanket. I just know I was far from cold at that point. As I lay there with my legs spread far enough to take in the ocean, Andre licked the kitty-kat. I guided his fingers into my asshole, to make the sensation just right.

Joe Blow sat straddled atop my face and guided his long, thin dick into my mouth. I lost count of how many times I choked with him so deep in my throat. I thought his ass was about to knock my sinuses from the back of my nose since his dick felt like it was up there.

I was glad when Andre suggested me turning over and sucking Joe Blow with him on his back. Once we changed positions, I had better control of giving Joe Blow a dick sucking he wouldn't soon forget. While changing positions, I looked around until I finally spotted Lewis at a distance behind a huge rock, watching everything.

Once I was turned over, Andre sucked and licked a bit more, and then his hardened manhood entered my pussy from behind. Again, I guided his hand to my asshole, and he skillfully followed my directive. At first his stroking was slow and deliberate, but as my body reacted to the combination of a dick in my pussy, fingers in my ass, and a dick in my mouth, it didn't take much time for Andre to lose control of his pace. I think the three of us were in sync, because at the time I was having a massive orgasm, Joe Blow's cum was filling my mouth, and Andre's body was convulsing, so I knew he was done. Or so I thought...

After giving me the bottle of champagne to drink from, Andre asked me to suck his dick while his cousin sampled my pussy. At first I was reluctant, but when each of them sucked on a breast and had both of their hands playing in my pussy, I could no longer resist.

But Joe Blow had something different in mind. While I lay bent over Andre, sucking his healthy-proportioned penis, Joe Blow decided he wanted the booty hole. Since we were without any lubricants, he used the juices from my pussy. This two-man thing was an absolute

first for me. I could barely concentrate on Andre, while Joe Blow had his lengthy dick dug deep into my ass. He was stroking my asshole as though it were pussy, trying to hit it from different angles. I was trying to let him hurry up and get his, so I could refocus on Andre, but Joe Blow was taking forever. Andre had to settle for a hand job instead of a blowjob. When Joe Blow *finally* came, I orally finished Andre off.

My body was so exhausted and hurting, I didn't know what to do. And once again when I thought Andre was spent, he laid me on my back, climbed on top of me, and fucked me mercilessly. He had my legs up, down, spread, twisted—whatever they would humanly do. He turned me backwards, forwards, sideways, upside-down, sat me on him, then back down again. At that point, I wanted to cry because I wanted this shit to end, as it seemed to go on for an eternity. He made me wonder if he was anything like his father when it came to fucking or dick size.

I silently prayed that Joe Blow wasn't going to follow up. My prayer was answered when I heard Joe Blow say, "Yo man, there's some peep-freak over there watching us."

That stopped Andre mid-stroke. Andre yelled, "Yo, what the fuck you looking at?"

Lewis stepped from behind the rock where he was hiding, holding his dick through his pants, and yelled back, "Just enjoying the view, young blood."

Andre and Joe Blow collected themselves and dressed quickly before taking off and leaving me naked in the moonlit darkness with a man they didn't even know. It could have been a stranger for all they cared. When they were gone, I continued to sit half back on the blanket naked, waiting with my thighs parted.

Lewis walked over to me smiling. "You think I could get one of those blow jobs?"

I asked, "And what are you going to do for me?"

He said, "I saw you fucking both of those clowns and didn't see condom the first. I don't want any of that pussy. Now that I think about it, I don't want that blow job either."

He stuck two fingers in his mouth and then used those two fingers to play with my nipples. Then he laid me on my back and started sucking my breast. His fingers massaged my clit as my legs opened wide anticipating the entrance of his fingers into my awaiting pussy. Then he suddenly stopped, wiped his fingers on the blanket, and said, "Sorry, but not tonight. Maybe some other time." He got up and walked away.

Somehow, after I put myself back together, I made it back to the reception hall before Lewis. Andre and his cousin were already back there as if nothing had happened. Even worse, Joe Blow had two attractive Hispanic girls sitting on his lap, while Andre was hugging on a third girl who appeared to be of mixed ethnicities. None of them were with the wedding party. Perhaps they were guests at the resort.

At first, the sight infuriated me, but when Lewis made his entrance only five minutes after me, and the look on Sandy's face appeared, my mood shifted like a pendulum. I saw Sandy going off on Lewis and pointing in my direction. I flashed these thirty-two pearly whites to agitate her even more. Then I pretended to be adjusting my bosom, which needed no adjusting. I wondered at what point Sandy would make her move, but surprisingly, she never did.

What was even more annoying this morning is that I saw Andre flaunting around one of his new bitches from the reception last night. He wouldn't even acknowledge me. *Fuck his punk ass!*

Now that Harmony and Todd are off on their honeymoon, I only hope that my adventures with my sister's new stepson never make it back to her. Then again, I don't give a shit. So what if it does?

Since Sandy is leaving today, I'll hang around one more day and enjoy Cancun without the stress of my sisters. I'll deal with Arnold's bullshit about me being an unfit mother tomorrow when I return. I need

The Queen

to enjoy my life now while I'm young and still can.

5
Shawnee

"Shawnee, I have something very disturbing to tell you. I'm not quite sure what to do with the information," Sandy said when I answered her call.

Damn, I have been back in New York a total of two hours and already getting hit with the bullshit I rushed home to get away from.

"What's wrong, Sandy?" I tried to sound as if I cared.

"I know you and everyone else can't stand Lewis, but he told me something quite unsettling."

"Sandy, you know I don't want to hear shit about Lewis."

"I know, but this isn't really about Lewis. It's about something Lewis witnessed."

I admit I was intrigued, but I tried to mask my piqued interest. "What?" I asked.

"Well, you know how I was furious about Lewis hanging around Charise at the wedding? When we were in our room, I went ballistic on him. However, while on the plane, he explained to me why he and Charise were both missing from the reception."

"Oh, I can hardly wait to hear this shit. He actually told you he went off to fuck Charise while you were only yards away? And you're not in jail, why?"

"It's not what you think, Shawnee."

I was so disgusted with Sandy at this point I didn't want to hear anything else.

I know this girl is not about to defend that sorry-ass nigga to me about anything.

"You know, Sandy, I really don't want to hear you defending that piece of shit to me. If you want to live your life like a fool, then leave me out of it. I have to go!"

"No, Shawnee! Please don't hang up. You are so far off base. I didn't believe him either until I started putting everything together, and then it made sense," Sandy pleaded.

"What? What did you put together?"

"True enough, Charise and Lewis left the reception moments apart, but do you remember everyone searching for Todd's older son?" she asked.

"Yeah, I remember. They said he was somewhere with his cousin." I was still puzzled about the direction of this conversation.

"Exactly!" Sandy said as if I'd said something worthwhile. "Todd's son and nephew were off together for quite some time. Someone said they saw the boy get two bottles of champagne before he left. I remember seeing Charise talking to the two guys shortly before she and Lewis disappeared. Lewis told me he was taking a stroll along the beach until he came upon two guys screwing one girl on the beach. He said he hid behind a rock and watched. He eventually realized the girl was Charise and the guys were Todd's son and nephew. He said he then left, but wasn't sure who to tell. He said he had no idea that Charise had just returned minutes before him. I also remember—"

I cut Sandy off because I didn't want to hear any more. "Okay, that's enough. Sandy, Lewis has sold your ass the Brooklyn Bridge. How naïve are you? Because if you remember correctly, Todd's son and nephew returned with a bunch of scantily dressed girls they picked up from somewhere. And as I recall, I saw the boy with one of those girls this morning at breakfast. I didn't pay any of them too much attention, but Charise was nowhere around them when they returned to the reception or at breakfast. Sorry, but I am not buying into Lewis' bullshit, so try again." After a very brief pause, I said, "Better yet, I don't want to hear any more. I'm sorry you are going through this crazy shit with Lewis, but that is a decision you made and continue to make. Call me when you're ready to dump the no-good lowlife."

"Why, so you could have him too?"

"Goodbye!" I hung up before Sandy could say another word.

This is not the shit I need immediately upon arriving home.

Then, my phone rang again. I thought for certain it was Sandy calling back until I saw Brad's number on my caller ID.

"Hello, my sweetness," Brad said when I answered.

I lit up. I don't know how and when I became so smitten by this old man. I knew when we talked outside of the office, I got all happy inside. Some might even call that love, but I'm still in denial.

Brad and I had started with constant flirtation in my effort to climb the corporate ladder, but once I moved to New York a year ago, that flirtation evolved into a full-blown relationship. Although many in the office may suspect that there's something going on between us, we maintain a totally professional relationship at work.

Funny we have become so professional in the office, because prior to the consummation of our relationship, we were anything but professional. I used to think that Brad was only fascinated by being with a black woman. But that changed, and I believe this man is genuinely in love with me.

Him increasing my salary another 20% beyond the 60% increase I received when moving to New York helped confirm that thought. Now I am the highest paid Senior Vice President in the company. *Now that's what I'm talking about!*

"Hey, sweetie. I'm glad to hear your voice," I responded.

He chuckled. "That makes my old heart happy to hear."

"Oh, Brad, you're anything but old. You know I know first hand," I say, stroking his ego the way he likes.

The truth is Brad's old ass can hold it down in the bedroom. I actually look forward to fucking him. And besides a couple of quick flings last year, I haven't fucked any other man during my year in New York.

"You don't know how much I miss you," he tells me. "I have some things I need to discuss with you when you get here. Some good, some maybe not-so-good."

"That doesn't sound too good. I don't know if I want to hear the not-so-good part."

"I am sending my car to pick you up, if that's okay with you. I know you are just making it home and haven't quite settled in yet. I was trying to catch you before you got too settled."

He was right about not yet settling in, but I needed to hear what he had to say. Particularly after meeting that Tatiana.

"Brad, you know I always want to see you. Just tell me how much time I have so I can be ready," I answered.

"Say in about an hour? And plan on staying over tonight," he said.

That sounded good to my ears. "I'll be ready."

Then we hung up. I went to find something sexy to put on. I settled on a red teddy that provided easy access. Since it's the middle of February, I decided to top it off with the white mink Brad gave me for

Christmas. We missed spending Valentine's Day together because of the wedding, but a day later will do.

When I arrived at Brad's mansion, he had a fire going in the fireplace of the large foyer area, and had romantic candles burning throughout the way he knows I like. I noticed the candles were all either red or white. He greeted me with a glass of my favorite wine and a quick kiss before leading me to his masculine decorated great room filled with custom made dark cherry leather seating and another lit fireplace.

"Have you eaten yet? I have a salmon salad in the kitchen. Let me get your coat." Brad reached for my coat, which I had yet to open. I was hungry for that salad, but knew once this coat opened, food would have to wait.

I opened my coat and Brad looked at my half-naked body as if seeing it for the first time. Without saying a word, he placed his mouth on my breast while pushing my coat off and onto the floor. Thankfully, I had put my glass down already; otherwise, it would have hit the floor also.

He then released my nipples from the teddy and sucked each one so tenderly. His stubby fingers found my clit and gently massaged it. My knees became so weak, I thought my legs would give any moment. Instinctively, Brad stopped and led me in front of the fireplace, where he laid me on a waiting blanket laid atop of the Oriental rug used as a centerpiece.

He removed the straps of the teddy from my arms, and pulled it down under my breasts. He just stared as the reflection of the fire bounced off of them, and my nipples hardened as he pondered his next move. His gaze left my breasts and found my eyes.

"Shawnee, I love you. I hope you know that by now," he said solemnly.

"I know you do, Brad," I whispered, still anxious for his touch.

I still haven't been able to bring myself to say, "I love you," back to him. I know he needs to hear the words from my mouth, but I just can't say it. Instead, I reached up for Brad's face and brought him in for a deep kiss. It was easy to make love to Brad, but saying the words was a whole other demon for me.

Brad seemed content with my kiss as a substitute for the words. His mouth left my mouth and kissed and nibbled his way down to my clit. His tongue tantalized me. His hands held my thighs apart while his tongue rotated between my clit and opening of my wet cave. When his tongue found its way deep inside my cave, I tried to find something to grab to muffle my scream. Too late. My scream was out, and my pussy was squirting like there was no tomorrow.

Brad stopped long enough to turn me over onto my stomach. Again he spread my legs, but then lifted my ass to his face. As he buried his face into my ass, I lifted myself onto my knees to give him better access to my pussy and clit. His fingers stimulated my clit while he licked my asshole. Then his mouth worked its way back to my pussy. He licked and sucked all the juices that were now pouring out.

At some point, he worked his lounge pants off and his hardened cock eased its way into my pot of honey. His hands held onto my hips as his rod went in and out, and in and out. Eventually one of his hands reached around me and found the unattended breast to play with, as I fondled the other. His other hand reached around to massage my clit. Brad grunted and moaned as he kissed my back while stroking me. Brad's dick isn't the biggest I've had, but when he has me in this position, he always manages to hit my G-spot.

Even better, Brad would not allow himself to release until he knew I was thoroughly satisfied. When he realized I got the first big orgasm out, he turned me on my back. While he sat up with his feet folded under him, he opened my legs and brought my hips up into his lap. He slid his penis back into my pussy. While his thumb massaged my clit, I worked my hips to maximize the wonderful feeling I was getting.

When Brad raised himself onto his knees, he lifted my hips with him, as a wheelbarrow. Now he was fucking me all too good as he continued to massage my clit. He totally controlled the pace and the strokes. Sometimes he'd go slowly, and then he'd go fast, and then slow it up again. Some strokes were harder, while others were gentler. His fingers squeezed my thighs, letting me know each time a sensation shot through his body. He lowered my hips back to the floor and leaned over to tantalize my tits with his tongue before coming up to kiss me in the mouth.

Now he was lying on top of me, and this time it felt as though he was making love to me instead of fucking me, as his body seemed to melt into my own. He reaffirmed my feeling when I once again heard him say in my ear that he loved me.

After our lovemaking, I went to clean myself up. My red teddy was a mess from all of my wetness. The whole time we were at it, the teddy was still partially on. After I got cleaned up and put on one of his robes, I joined Brad in the kitchen to finally eat that salad and drink that glass of wine I was first greeted with. I noticed a watch box gift wrapped on the counter. He picked up the box, handed it to me, and said, "Happy Valentine's Day, Shawnee."

I laughed.

He looked confused and asked, "What's so funny?"

"I have a box in my bag for you," I answered as I went to retrieve the gift for him.

He opened the box and saw a watch, and then also laughed before kissing and thanking me. However, when I opened my gift and found the diamond watch that didn't compare to the one I bought for

The Queen

him, I cried. It was absolutely exquisite. Certainly the best watch I've ever owned.

He killed the moment by saying, "Shawnee, we need to talk."

Those dreadful words scared me. I'm not sure why. Somehow, the thought of losing Brad is disturbing to me, and by the somber expression on his face he couldn't possibly be about to say anything good.

"I don't know why I get this sinking feeling in the pit of my stomach when you say that," I confessed.

"Well, you shouldn't," he said and smiled warmly. Then continued, "Shawnee, you are an absolutely beautiful woman, and I feel like the luckiest guy in the world to be with you, but sometimes I have to question whether you realize how beautiful and intelligent you are."

He could tell by the puzzled look on my face I was confused.

He went on, "I will admit, when I first laid eyes on you all those years ago, I was drawn in by your beauty, but when I actually had the opportunity to experience your creative genius and your brilliance in business, I was even more captivated. Although I will be eternally grateful for being the beneficiary of the sensual side of you, I want you to understand that Shawnee Wiggins doesn't need to use her sexuality to advance in her professional life. Your intelligence got you where you are, and that same intelligence will take you as far as you want to go."

I was feeling somewhat hurt by his words. Yes, I have used my sexuality to climb the corporate ladder, but I hardly think I would be a Senior Partner and Senior Vice President of any company that I didn't create myself, before I turned thirty-five.

Is he about to dump me? That's what this is sounding like.

"I know you've mentioned that you would like to travel to foreign countries. Is that still one of your desires?" he asked.

I couldn't even answer. Instead I cried at the thought of Brad about to ship me off somewhere just to get away from me. Did he want Tatiana?

Will I go away only to return and find that she has taken my place in his life?

Brad rushed to me and hugged and consoled me.

"Why are you crying?" he asked.

"You don't want to be with me anymore," I childishly said through my tears.

Brad broke out into a roaring laughter.

So much so, my tears instantly dried up and were replaced with anger. "I don't understand what's so funny," I said with attitude.

"Sweetheart, I love you. I sometimes wondered how you felt about me, but just at this very moment, I know you love me also." He kissed me on the forehead, and then continued, "I would never try to get rid of you. Not personally or professionally. I want to promote you. That's what I wanted to talk to you about."

My mouth was wide open with shock. How do you get promoted from Senior VP while he is President and CEO?

"Shawnee, I want to create a position but I wouldn't feel comfortable with anyone but you in it. I certainly don't want to create a position where someone ends up being your boss, and then creative differences may arise, resulting in a mess."

"But Brad, how do I go up from Senior VP?" I asked.

"I said I want to create the position. You'd become President of Foreign Affairs. Your home office would still be New York, but it would require a great deal of international travel. I'd travel with you about 25% of the time, as long as I have my health. We could arrange most of your travel during times when I have to travel to various domestic offices. That way we would still have time together and our relationship won't suffer," he told me.

I stood shock for a moment. "Wow! I don't know what to say," I finally responded.

"Say yes! You know how I have talked about creating a division to run our foreign offices. I feel you are the best-qualified person for the job. This is not about our intimate relationship. However, because of our intimate relationship, I don't want to bring anyone else into that position that would create any conflict for you. I'd fire any person that gives you a hard time, on any level. This brings me to my next point: a very necessary point ..."

I was stunned by Brad's extraordinary level of commitment to me. He would fire someone for me? Wow!

Brad continued, ". . . Shawnee, you know there's a sizeable age difference between us, and you know I'm getting up in age. Although I don't plan on going anywhere anytime soon, I'd like to start grooming you to be my successor. I'll admit that decision is not only based on your professionalism, but our relationship as well. The way I feel about you, I would take you out to marry tomorrow, but I don't want to put that kind of pressure on you. Particularly with you having just come out of an ugly marriage last year. It's obvious you still have trust issues to sort out. Hopefully before I get too old, you will feel the level of comfort that you need to become my wife. No pressure, though. Nonetheless, you will be fully taken care of, and I'd take comfort in knowing the company I started from nothing all those years ago, will go forth with the ingenuity that you bring the company even now."

"Brad, why are you talking about dying?" I finally asked after my brain got stuck on this man telling me he wants me to be his successor.

Did he say something about marriage? I thought I heard the word while he was talking.

"Honey, I'm not just talking about dying. I might want to retire and live on an island somewhere," he joked.

"So you're going to go live somewhere without me?" I teased back.

"Never," he answered before taking me into his arms. "But please give everything some thought and give me your answer as soon as possible."

"I will give you my answer now, as long as you can promise that this position is not going to compromise our relationship," I said, looking into his hazel-green eyes.

He kissed me and said, "Then I guess this makes you the new President of Foreign Affairs. I would never let anything jeopardize our relationship. I can't imagine anything that could. When we get back to the office, I will make this offer official and on the record, minus the part about our relationship." He chuckled.

I wrapped my arms around Brad and just held him with my eyes closed. It was a perfect feeling.

"Oh, by the way, that watch was just one part of your gift. The other is waiting for you in the bedroom on your pillow," he told me.

I raced upstairs to find my diamond earrings in a cute little box on my pillow.

Damn! I'm going to be a President of something in my life. I'm a month shy of forty. Shit, don't tell me it doesn't pay to fuck your way to the top.

True enough, I have the brains and intelligence, but that intelligence let me know that I had to use my sexuality to outshine my competition.

6
Kelly

I'm pretty certain Sean slipped something in my drink. I have a three-month waiting period before I give up the goodies to any man. Once they reach that three-month period, I run a background and credit check on them, which tends to eliminate most. When I still had Harmony around, I'd let her meet them and give me a psychoanalysis on the guy. Now that my psychologist sister left DC and started her new life in Houston, I've been on my own when it came to my dates.

I met Sean Greene about a month ago while coordinating an event for an entertainer in Los Angeles. It was a job I got through Elaine, who always throws business in my direction. Sean is a fine-ass 30-year-old with a 6'1 frame loaded with muscles. He owns a record company and produces new artists. He has a huge house outside of Beverly Hills and a fleet of cars lined up outside.

In the month that we've been seeing each other, he has flown to DC to visit me—six times. I was half tempted to take him with me to the wedding last week, but decided against it when I thought of the interrogation I'd get from my family. I wasn't quite ready for him to meet the whole family just yet. I felt I needed more time to feel him out for myself. My sisters know I have always been one of the more sensible ones when it comes to men, so I didn't need anyone questioning my decisions.

During our time together, he has never pressed me for sex. That's why I'm not sure how it is I am laying butt naked right now, next to his sleeping body. He flew in yesterday evening and we enjoyed a very nice evening out at Blues Alley. Despite the cold weather, we enjoyed a romantic stroll through Georgetown. The beautiful sable coat he brought me yesterday helped keep me warm. Each time he comes to see me, he brings nice gifts, so I'm always anxious to see what's next.

Having my own successful event planning company doesn't leave me much of a social life. I informed Sean of this when I met him, but he was adamant that between both our hectic schedules, we'd find a way to make it work if we both want it. I greatly appreciated the sentiment.

With the upcoming opening of Elaine's new shoe boutique in L.A., I'll be spending a lot of time there in preparation for her grand opening gala. During that time, I'll be staying at Sean's house. The plan is for me to stay in a separate bedroom, as he does when he comes to my house.

But now here we are sharing my bed. What went wrong with my three-month plan? The only thing I can come up with is that he put something in my drink.

The messed up part is that I can't remember how we ended up in bed together. It's obvious that we had sex, but I can't remember that either. I did have plenty to drink last night, but that's never caused me to breech my three-month rule in the past.

Damn, if I could remember if the sex was good, then I'd know if I should be fixing him a breakfast fit for a king or not. I know one thing: my pussy is sore as hell right now. I can't even say how big his erect dick is. I tried to size him up while he was covered up. I also felt a nice sized bulge when we went out dancing on one of his previous visits. I

The Queen

guess I could reach my hand around him and just feel it, but then he may think I'm trying to wake it up for another round.

What am I going to do? How do I now tell this man that we can't have sex again because I didn't mean to sleep with him the first time? I mean, I do like him a lot, and he seems to be a good catch. But what if he really did drug me? What kind of piece of shit do I have in my bed?

Damn, I am horny and I have been celibate for almost two years now. Well, I guess I "was" celibate. So then it shouldn't be such a horrible thing to fuck him while I'm conscious, right?

I need some answers.

"Sean, baby." I gently shake him to wake him up. "Sean, wake up."

"Hmm? Hey, baby. What time is it?" he asks in a groggy voice, while trying to adjust his eyes to the daylight.

"It's seven-twenty," I answer.

"You're up early. Do you have an appointment this morning?"

"No, my calendar is clear for today. I just need to ask you a question. I'm a bit confused about what happened last night. We're in the same bed naked."

He raises himself up in the bed. "Oh, Kelly, that is so not cool," he answers with a genuine look of disappointment.

"I don't mean to hurt your feelings, but I really can't remember how we ended up here like this. You know how I feel about my three-month waiting period." I hide my nudity with the sheet.

"Wow! Now I feel like a rapist. Like someone who took advantage of you," he said, shaking his head. He sat fully upright. "I guess I should have known you had too much to drink, but we've been together when you were drinking before and nothing happened. Then I just thought when you came and straddled me and started grinding on me and kissing me, you were ready."

Oh, Lord. This man is telling me I initiated things?

"I don't remember doing that!"

"This is not good." He shakes his head with frustration. "I take it you don't remember opening my shirt and belt buckle either?"

Oh, Lord, how could I have done this? Yeah, that sounds like a move I'd make when I'm sober after the three months, but . . .

"Please tell me you at least used a condom? I am sorry, but I don't remember anything. Imagine my shock to find you here in the bed with me."

"Yes, Kelly, I used a condom each time."

EACH TIME! How many times did we do it? Oh, Lord, this is not good.

"I think I need to leave. I'm not too happy about this. The last thing I would ever do is try to make you feel violated in any way." He gets up to go collect his clothes, which are scattered around the room.

I watch his uncovered body naked for the first time as he moves about. Talk about a work of perfect art. His ass and chest are perfectly chiseled, and his limp manhood has to be hanging at least seven or eight inches.

No wonder my pussy is sore. I'll be a damn fool if I let that walk out of my door.

"Wait, Sean," I call out as he walks into my living room.

He comes back to the bedroom door.

"Please don't leave. I didn't mean to upset you. It's just that this wasn't quite what I had in mind for our first time together. I do remember the beautiful evening we spent out last night and I also remember lying in your arms, listening to some nice jazz and a bottle of wine."

"So you don't remember upgrading to Hennessey?" he asks with a raised eyebrow. "I figured then you were about to make a move, but was nervous, so you pulled out the Hennessey."

The more he talks, the more mortified I become. It sounds sounded like a typical Kelly move when I'm about to consummate a relationship. I just don't understand why I have no memory of anything that happened after that. Why did I abandon my three-month waiting period?

I'm having a hard time concentrating with his ding-a-ling dangling while he holds his clothes under his arm.

"Well, I'm fully awake and sober now. Do you think you could help me regain my memory?" I ask while removing the cover I am clinging to for dear life.

Hell, I already did the damn thing, I may as well go for broke now.

Sean's face lights up, along with all ten inches of his fully erect penis. He drops his clothes and walks back to me. I stand up at the edge of the bed to greet him in my arms. He lifts me up and wraps my legs around his waist. He kisses me so damn good, despite neither of us brushing our teeth yet. Then he lays me down on the bed and makes the best damn love I have had in all my 27 years. He didn't leave anything undone.

Damn, I love him! I loves me some Sean! I'd cut a bitch for this dick, tongue, fingers and all. WHEW! This man feels so good, he's going to have to get a restraining order if he tries to leave me.

"I hope this means we are now an official, exclusive couple," Sean says three rounds later.

"Well it's a bit sooner than I had planned, but that's what my goal was."

"Do you believe in love at first sight? That's how I felt when I first laid eyes on you." He strokes my hair as I lay in his arms facing him.

I smile. "I never believed in love at first sight, but then I hadn't met you." Sounded like a good comeback line, without crushing his ego.

He shows all of his beautiful white teeth. "You know I hate for this moment to end, but we better go grab something to eat before I go catch my flight back to L.A."

Well maybe my nose is wide open, because my heart just sank when he said that.

"I don't want you to go," I say pouting.

"I have a business to run, baby. I want to be able to give you nice things. I'll fly back out here later in the week and then when you come out to L.A., we'll be able to spend even more time together."

"I guess that'll have to do."

I can't believe my ass is whipped after only a month of knowing this man.

Sean gets up and pulls my hand. "Come on and join me in the shower. I might need help washing my back."

I give him a big grin and follow his lead.

7
Angelo

I am a fine-ass brotha who most women would kill to have, but sorry bitches, Angelo is 100% gay now. I love the titties, and I have struggled with the pussy, but when I started wrestling at UCLA, I found myself getting turned on by the lovely bodies I came in close contact with. Umm, umm, umm! Delicious! The feeling I'd get was sensational. It didn't take much convincing to convert me.

My first gay encounter was with a former classmate, Andrew Peterson, in my freshman year. A massage here and a massage there, then it was on. Andrew was a 'BIG' act to follow, if you know what I mean. He set the standard for all to follow.

Being so far away from my family, I was able to keep my newfound lifestyle a secret. When Mama died, I felt guilty and questioned my decision. I was relieved when I finally talked to Harmony about my sexuality.

Sometimes I want desperately to talk to her or one of the others about my thoughts of Mama killing Daddy. I always felt his dying was my fault. They said he died of liver failure, but I know he was never sick before. His illness seemed to begin right after that time Mama walked in on him messing with me. I just can't understand why he would mess with his own son. I know I always saw him touching on Elaine and Charise in ways that a father is not supposed to touch his own daughters. I know Mama would see how he would handle Elaine, but instead of confronting him, Mama ended up being mean to Elaine. Me, she took and coddled for dear life when she caught Daddy, but never treated Elaine in the same manner. My sisters and I have never talked about any of that stuff. I think it's just been easier to let the memories die with him, but I still feel guilt because I'll always believe that Mama killed him because of me, and aside from his perversion, I can remember him being a fun dad.

Although Harmony was disappointed when I told her of my homosexuality, she told me it was my life to live, and I had to live the life that made me happy and not worry about what other people had to say or what they think. From that point on I became proud to be gay. I make it a point to attend any and every gay pride function there is, and will hop on a bus, train, automobile or an airplane to get there. Yes, it is very worth the trip. Whew! I'm getting excited thinking about it.

We each received $100,000 after Mama's death, which helped me to focus completely on finishing my degree in business. In my social circle, I've come across many talented designers and hairstylists. Since I am the business mind, we've talked about trying to open up some business that would incorporate our talents. I have just a couple more months to finish my degree.

Elaine asked me to manage her new L.A. boutique. The problem I had with that was, it wouldn't be my own business, nor would my friends be involved. Somehow, Elaine was able to find a property that will individually house her shoe boutique, a hair salon with day spa, and a clothing boutique that will feature the fashions of my designer friends. She would only own the shoe boutique, while my friends and I would own the other two businesses. In exchange, I have to manage her

The Queen

shoe boutique, and she'd have a small claim to our business. After discussing it with my partners, we felt it was an opportunity of a lifetime.

While I finish up with school, Elaine will manage her shoe boutique herself. During my summer and winter break, I stayed in New York with Elaine and worked with her manager Jason, to feel out the operation. I was highly impressed and proud to have Elaine as my sister. Jason even gave me tips on being a true diva such as he.

Once upon a time in my confused state, I thought of getting a sex change later down the road in my life. After spending time with Jason, I've decided against it. Jason says he is totally proud to be a man, and said that I should be as well. He said I don't need to have any operations to be a gorgeous gay man. Since he is very well respected and received in the industry and gay world, I value his input and experience. He is supposed to fly in for the grand opening gala. He's going to introduce me to his people. He's also going to be promoting our fashions in New York to help get us some business. Jason is my idol. Him and Wendy Williams.

All of my sisters, minus Charise, will be in town for the grand opening. I'm hoping Sandy won't use that opportunity to tell Harmony about Charise possibly screwing Todd's son and nephew. I begged Sandy not to say anything to Harmony, but she said she couldn't promise. She said she tried to tell Shawnee, but Shawnee wouldn't believe her because of the contempt she feels toward Lewis. I'm not sure what to believe myself. I do remember checking out Andre's fine ass myself, and I saw him with Charise before all of them did their disappearing act. However, I saw Andre return with that other skank ho, so that created the doubt about him being with Charise.

I know Sandy is not just going to let it go because she wants to believe that whoremonger she's married to. I can't believe Sandy would take him back after he dropkicked her ass to the curb—while she was pregnant— to go be with her sister. I love drama as much as the next person, but that's what the Lifetime Channel is for. That's drama I'm too embarrassed to tell my friends about. I have to keep that to myself or will only tell my best friend Antwan. I didn't want any of my friends in Cancun at the wedding because I was too afraid of what was going to happen. Oh, and my heart dropped when Charise gave me the scoop on Shawnee, Elaine, and Sandy's ex-boyfriend. What is wrong with those bitches? I thought Shawnee could do no wrong. Elaine? That's another story. I wouldn't put anything past her.

I'm hoping Shawnee doesn't come to L.A. being all critical of my friends. She asked how I became gay. She figured it had to do with being surrounded by all girls. I told her I didn't grow up with any intentions to be gay. It was just one day I realized I was more attracted to men than women (and maybe the possibility of my momma killing my daddy scares the hell out of me when it comes to women). Now I hear about all this mess with my own sisters? That would make any man think about becoming gay. Or maybe my sisters think they need to share men because all the good guys, such as myself, are gay or in jail. Something to think about.

I guess if I was into fish, I'd have four or five different girls lined up. Not! Angelo is a lover of the dick!

8
Charise

"Arnold, who is that bitch you have around my son?"

I roll up just in time to catch Arnold about to go into his house with some trick-looking 'ho.

"Go home, Charise. You don't have any right to just come popping up to my house, and you certainly don't have any right to dictate who I can have in my life."

I am furious. When did Arnold start seeing this bitch? Bitch ain't as cute as me.

"So I'm sure that she doesn't know about you and me?" I say, looking her up and down.

"There is no you and me, Charise. You made that perfectly clear the other week." Arnold turns to the tall, attractive, well-dressed woman with him. "Samantha, you can go inside the house. I'll be right behind you." Then the bitch has the nerve to kiss him and go into Arnold's house. But not before looking me up and down with a smirk.

"I want to know who that is and where is my son?" I demand.

"My sister picked up the baby earlier this afternoon from daycare. As for *who* that is, that's none of your business."

"Any bitch you have around my baby is my business. And what about you and me, Arnold? We were just together in Cancun at my sister's wedding."

"No, Charise. YOU were at your sister's wedding. I was on my way back to Houston alone after you made it clear there was no you and me. Then it was another four days after the wedding before you came to see or inquire about Jarod. You dropped him off yesterday. Why are you here today?"

"I can come and see my son whenever I want. I don't need to make appointments," I yelled.

"Again, NO! You can't come to my house whenever you want. You can tell me which days you want to have him with you and then when I have him, you will not be coming over anymore," Arnold says very calmly but firmly.

"I want to see my son every day, and you will never change that. Where did all this selfish bullshit come from? Are you even thinking about the negative effect this will have on my son's life? He needs to be able to see his mother every day."

"What the fuck? You are the negative effect." He laughs. "Charise, you didn't see him every day before Cancun. Where the hell are you coming from with this 'every day' bullshit? Do you want to keep him with you every day, and pick him up every day from daycare? You can ride by my sister's house and pick him up right now if you want him."

"I know that bitch you have in there put you up to this shit. You don't have a mind to think for yourself. You know damn well I have to work every day and can't keep him every day," I argue.

"First of all, you need to stop referring to my date as a bitch. She's a woman. She's one with class and a very promising future. Second, I work every day, more hours than you do or ever would. And third, if you really wanted to keep Jarod, you would see that he could be picked up from daycare or from my sister, who also works, every day. But to

The Queen

be honest, I don't want him with you because you have repeatedly proven yourself an unfit mother, and the only solace I had was knowing I could come around when he was with you, as my guarantee that he'd be safe. You want to be with your sister's husband or whoever, then go be with them. Jarod will be fine. I won't deny your spending time with him, but you won't be just showing up on my doorstep, unannounced, as you have done this evening. So on that note, we'll talk tomorrow about when you would like a visit, but now, I'm going to rejoin my date inside my home." Arnold turns and walks inside his house and closes the door.

I will beat that prissy-bitch's ass! I know she put him up to this shit. Arnold would never act this way with me otherwise. Who is she, and where did she come from? I heard him call her Samantha. Damn, I need some dick. Maybe if I cause a scene, she'll leave and I can get some from him. What if she tells him to call the police?

Maybe I should hit a club and see what I can find. I don't have my reliable Arnold, so I'm going to need some back-up dicks. I wish I could figure out what part of town Lewis is in. That's the dick I really want to track down. Where can I go on a Wednesday night to find some dick? I gotta begin my birthday celebration. I can always find a bar. I need to find out who that smug bitch is in there with my man. She has to go. That trick ho!

Warren isn't the greatest looking, but he was the best looking thing at the bar. His one lazy eye and crooked teeth were somewhat of a turn off. He said he's 6'5, so I figured he must have a pipe packed in those jeans. He bought me three drinks after I told him it was my birthday, so I let him think he was getting me drunk enough to take home to fuck. Other than the fact that I'm not drunk, the plan worked. I decided to bring him to my apartment. He's 39 years old and works in construction. He has a decent body for a man his age, but I can't wait to see what's really underneath those clothes.

When we get into my apartment, I offer him a drink. When I bring his drink, he gulps it down and then pulls me onto his lap. Dude isn't trying to waste any time. He starts kissing me deeply and rubbing my breasts through my T-shirt and bra. He pulls my shirt out of my jeans and his hand makes its way underneath and unfastens my bra. When my tits are free from my bra, his mouth find its way to my tits. He's sucking the hell out of my breast. While sucking, his hand opens up my jeans and works its way deep inside to find my clit. He uses his middle finger to tickle my clit while I try to reposition myself for easier access. This man is getting me wetter by the minute.

I maneuver to pull his T-shirt off of his slender frame. I then return the favor by sucking on his dime-sized nipples. I can feel his pipe growing under me. He pulls me to my feet and peels my low-rise jeans off of me. He takes a couple of seconds just staring and admiring my body. Then he removes my T-shirt, bra and panties.

"Wow! You are a beauty. Much better than what I expected," he says, grinning.

I'm not sure what to say to that, so I just say, "Thank you."

He gets down on the floor and lifts one of my feet onto the sofa. He uses his middle and forefingers to rub my pussy. He examines it as if he were a doctor. Then his mouth covers my pussy and his tongue goes inside to explore. My legs collapse from the sensation, but he keeps me held in a standing position. Warren is eating and sucking my pussy wonderfully. The more I squirt, the more he sucks.

Then he lays me on the sofa while he unfastens his pants. He strips down to his plaid cotton boxers. I can't believe my eyes when I see his dick hanging past his boxers. His mouth zones back in to my pot of cream soup. He spreads my legs as if I am doing a split. Then he inserts two fingers inside while his mouth continues to suck. I am in seventh heaven. To hell with Arnold. Lewis too for that matter.

When Warren stops, he gets up, pulls his boxers off and dangles a dick the length of my lower leg before my mouth. I'm not even sure how to suck a dick this long, but I am going to damn sure give it my all. His fingers continue to fuck me while I suck him.

Then he stops me and says, "Small Fry, we're going to have to stop. I just realized I don't have any condoms with me."

"I have condoms," I volunteer. I'll be damned if this dick will elude me on this night.

"Now really, do you seriously think any condom you have is going to fit this?" He points to his extra long penis.

"Please, baby. I need to feel that big dick inside of me. Please don't take it away from me," I beg like a fiend trying to get her next fix.

"I don't need any extra babies or any diseases."

"Trust me, I don't need any babies either. We are protected on that. Believe me, I don't make it a habit of picking up men in bars. I've been in a relationship that ended a few weeks ago. I need you right now. I need to feel like a woman." I wrap my hand around his dick and use my other hand to play with my pussy. "My kitty-kat needs you to make her purr. She wants you inside of her." I take his hand and guide it back to my pussy to assist my hand already in it. Then I take his dick back into my mouth.

That is the end to Warren's resistance.

Minutes later I have that raw pipe inside my kitty. Happy Birthday to me!

He sits on my sofa and straddles me on top of him. There I go up and down on his pole. I try to take it in as much as my pussy will allow. When I work him from that direction, I turn my body away from him, while maintaining his dick inside of me. Then I give him a nice view of my ass as I lean away from him while still stroking him.

Eventually, he lays me facedown on my sofa. He positions himself behind me and places his pole back inside of my wet pussy. His thumb massages my anus before its entry. He is in full control of each powerful thrust. He goes so deep inside of me that I can feel my internal organs readjusting.

He leans over me and says, "I want you to take this back in your mouth."

I do as instructed and suck all of my creamy cum off his big black dick. A few strokes later, he is relieving himself in my mouth. I didn't quite want that part, but Warren was sensational. He deserved that. This is someone I wouldn't mind seeing again.

Warren starts dressing.

I ask, "You're leaving so soon? You've only been here like thirty minutes. I was hoping we could spend some more time together."

"Sorry, Small Fry. The Missus will be looking for me soon," he answers.

The Missus?! When the hell did this bastard say he was married?

"Oh, you're married? I didn't know that," I say, disappointed because I wasn't sure how this was going to impact our future.

"Yep, been married eighteen years now."

"Eighteen years? Wow!" I am at a loss for words. Desperate for an opportunity to do it again I ask, "Well does that mean that this is our first and last time together?"

"Well I don't want anyone causing my wife any grief, so I don't need any attachments. Maybe if I see you at the bar sometime, we could get together. I do like how you handle this here dick. Not many can handle it."

"I loved the way you made my kitty-kat purr. She would hope to feel it again," I try to say as seductively as possible.

Warren leans over and kisses me. "Take care, Small Fry, and have a happy birthday."

The Queen

Next thing, he's out the door. Damn!

9
Elaine

I am three weeks away from the opening of my third store. I opened my first shoe boutique in Georgetown about three and a half years ago, and then opened my second store in the heart of New York a little over a year ago. My third and final location will be in Los Angeles. I only sell high-end shoes and accessories. I have buyers circulating around the world to bring in some of the top named high quality shoes. I have a long list of celebrities who frequent my boutiques, which prompted the opening of the L.A. store.

Business has been very good from the first store in Georgetown. Most of my customers are politically affiliated. I stepped up the quality of merchandise with the New York opening. I hired a publicist for that opening, and the grand opening was phenomenal. The New York location has two floors. The upper level is for VIP's only by appointment. The calendar stays booked at least a month to six weeks in advance. The L.A. store has yet to open, but people have been calling the New York store to get an appointment in L.A.

My financial wealth began accumulating from high school when I converted giving away free pussy to pay-for-play. Growing up in DC gave me easy access to many politicians and other wealthy men as cli-

ents. I had to keep my money on the down-low because my family had no clue how I was living. Well, that is with the exception of Sandy, who was turned out herself after she tried to blackmail me with her discovery. Her stint was short-lived because she was looking for love. Thankfully, she never said anything.

When Mama died and left each of us $100,000 that provided me the front to open my first shoe boutique. Because the shoe boutique is a very expensive business, as well as my love for sex, I have continued my prostitution. My clients are absolutely great. They helped me obtain the connections I need for the success of my boutiques. They helped me find prime locations for the stores and everything else I needed. I have three "sponsors" covering the costs of my three-quarter million dollar grand opening gala in L.A.

Since I have been in L.A., the number of female clients I have has increased. I'm trying to tell you, these are some of the best pussy-eating, clit rubbing, fake-dick fucking women I have ever encountered in my life. I started wondering if there was some special school these women attended to learn such skills. And their money and connections are long as hell. I've even gotten into the group women thing. I get so into that experience, I forget I'm there getting paid. Truth be known, I feel like I should be paying them.

Don't get me wrong now. I still prefer to be with men. As a matter of fact, more recently I have been considering retiring from prostitution. Well maybe not 100%, but perhaps I'll just hang on to my highest bidders. Trying to juggle three boutiques is definitely going to consume all of my time. Time is scarce already. Now with the addition of Angelo's business merged with my boutique, I have to keep a watchful eye there as well. I can't have them ruin my reputation. In order for me to get Angelo, whom I trust completely, to manage my L.A. boutique, I had to accept his package deal. I understand his dream to have his own business, so I really didn't want to take away from that.

One other thing that has me evaluating the prostitution is how I felt all alone in Cancun. I felt like I wanted someone there with me, for me. I want someone to be into me, for me. Not because that's where the money is at. Once upon a time I had Russell, who was totally into me, but he was broke with no ambitions. I couldn't see myself settling with that. I feel like I have achieved a level of success with no one to share it with. Of course the person I have to share my success with needs to also have their own success to bring to the table. My three sponsors (clients) are also trying to encourage me to retire. They are trying to help me build success through my boutiques, so I won't have the need to prostitute any more.

Prostitution has been a very lucrative business for me. How do you just end it like that? I honestly don't need the money. I have made some wise financial decisions over the years. I own three rental properties in Maryland, as well as my condos in D.C and New York. I never told my family about my assets because they'd really start doing the math and find that $100k doesn't get you all that I have. I have nice sized financial portfolios. One of my sponsors found a nice house for me in Beverly Hills. It's a mini-mansion. He said that I need to look like wealth if I'm going to cater to wealth. He covered the cost of its rent for one year. He said I should know where I want to be after that.

My last date with Shawnee's ex, Robert, was four months ago. That last time together was more than I could stand. I've done threesomes before where I had two men. However, that second man wasn't there for me. He was there for Robert. In the past, Robert got into this thing of me strapping up and fucking him. Of course, by his standards, that didn't make him gay because he loves pussy. After our last rendezvous, he can no longer deny his gayness. I basically got paid $65,000 to watch. I did get my tits fondled by Robert, but his overly possessive new partner wasn't going to stand for Robert showing me too much attention. I had to watch the two men have a duel with their dicks before penetrating each other's asses. Just watching the two of them kissing made my stomach turn. All I could think about was my own brother.

When Robert called me last month to get together, I told him I couldn't see him any more because I was relocating. I didn't dare tell him where. What's been even harder is not having anyone to tell about Robert being gay. It's one thing for my family to find out about my prostituting, but it's a whole can of worms for them to find out Shawnee's ex-husband is one of my clients. When Robert started offering up $20,000 a pop, I had no ability to resist.

Money is my weakness. I'll be the first to admit this. While some women are happy spending money, I am happy having and keeping money. I don't spend my money on anything. That's what my sponsors are for. If anything, I want to provide the items that women spend the most money on: shoes.

When Angelo and his crew made their business proposal, I was secretly doing cartwheels. I ran the idea by some of my celebrity friends and they loved the idea of having everything right there together. They are looking for the same exclusivity that I provide in my New York boutique. When I ran it back to Angelo along with my request for a seven percent ownership in their business for the usage of my clientele, they were game. Once they were on board, I had one of my more generous sponsors shopping for the perfect location to house the plan. I won't lie. I'm excited myself by the thought of running next door to get my hair done, get a massage, facial, pedicure or whatever, and then find a nice outfit to go with a pair of my shoes.

In the past, I have accumulated many of my sponsors/clients through my boutiques. Going forward, I will not be collecting anymore tricks. I will reprogram myself to go on legitimate dates. Of course he better have more dollars than I have, and maybe in another five years, I'll be ready for a totally monogamous relationship. And I don't think this makes me gay, but I'm not quite ready to give up my girl-group. Whew! I get excited just thinking about it. And these are all wealthy married women. Maybe I could still do that after I marry? Maybe?

Damn, it's three o'clock already. Kelly's flight is supposed to arrive at 5:10. That is the height of horrible traffic. I was surprised when she declined staying with me. I know she's been seeing some guy she met out here in L.A., but I can't imagine she'll be staying with him for the next three weeks until the gala. Kelly would never stray from her silly three-month rule. He could pull a twenty-inch bronze dick out of his pants, and she wouldn't budge. So why wouldn't she stay at my home that she loves so much, and where is she staying? I guess I'll find out at our late night dinner tonight.

10
Sandy

"Hi, may I please speak with Sandy?" the strange voice said when I answered the unknown number on my cell phone.

Hmm... He sounds kind of sexy there. Even got my coochie tingling.

"This is Sandy. Who may I ask is calling?"

"Please don't get angry, but this is Arnold. Arnold Hamilton. The father—"

Damn! What a disappointment.

"I know who you are," I snapped. "I'm just a bit thrown that you are calling me. How did you get my cell number?"

"I ran into Lewis earlier today, and kind of filled him in on some things and he said that I might try talking to you about some serious problems. I mean, I know you and Charise don't have a good relationship, but right now, I'm at my wits' end. I still am unable to get hold of Harmony," he answered.

Now you know I don't give a flying fuck about that damn Charise. Oops! I'm supposed to be saved now. I can't be cussing and thinking all those evil and lustful thoughts. However, I couldn't sit there and pass up an opportunity to get dirt on that little tramp. Okay, so I still need help in the "saved" department. What the hell?

"Well, Arnold, you do know I have major problems when it comes to Charise, but don't ever feel I have anything against you personally. I guess you are just as much a victim as anyone," I said sincerely. "What's going on?"

He took a deep breath before he began. "Okay, here it is. I've had deep feelings for Charise from the beginning. I was happy when I learned about my son, and I was happy to have an opportunity to try and make a family with Charise. The problem is Charise not only told me, but showed me time and time again, that she didn't want me the way I wanted her. For my son's sake, I hung in there and held on to hope. Cancun was the final straw. I finally got it. On my flight back to Houston, I met this solid sister who happens to be an attorney. More specifically, a State's Attorney. We've been kicking it since then. One night Charise rolled up to my crib and caused a scene. That was right at her birthday. She carried on about my friend. From that point on Charise has been on some whole other mess that's going to get her locked up, and I'm going to take full custody of my son from her."

"What kind of scene did she cause, and what has she done since?" I had to ask.

"When she saw my new girl, she flipped out. She was loud and ghetto, and kept calling my friend the 'b' word. I sent my friend into the house to prevent a volatile situation. Now Charise is stalking us both. But if you think that is crazy, night before last, she picks up Jarod—"

"Jarod? Is that your son's name?" I asked, trying to refrain from busting out in laughter.

"Yeah. That's my little man," he answered so proudly. I could hear him smiling through the phone.

The Queen

Nah! I won't dare pop his bubble by telling him that was Charise's old boyfriend's name. He'd be crushed.

"Oh, I never knew," was my response. "Go on; continue."

"Like I was saying, she picks up Jarod from daycare, and then calls me to pick him up from her place. I get there and the door was not fully closed. I knocked, but no answer, so I walked in. I could hear her screaming and moaning. Obviously she was having sex. Some stocky, baboon looking dude was doing her with Jarod watching in his playpen. They both looked right at me coming in to collect my son, and didn't even stop. Instead, she gave me this big smile. The guy acted like he didn't give a damn."

Wow! I am blown away! This is a new low for even Charise. In front of her baby? Wow! No class at all!

Arnold continued. "Then, yesterday morning, my girl came out of her place to go to work, and Charise was parked down the block. She attempted to follow my girl, but my girl pulled up to the police department and Charise sped off. Now I don't even know if she's working or what. She seems to have way too much time on her hands. My girl is ready to file charges against Charise, but trying not to put me in a bad situation. She suggested I try speaking to Charise, but we both know that is useless. So now I need to figure out what to do, and consider the all-around effect.

"I know I haven't known my friend that long, but I am looking for something stable, as is she. She's even okay with accepting my son. I'm not trying to replace my son's mother, but the truth is, Charise has never been a mother. If I told you some of the crazy stuff she's done over the past year, you'd say I was crazy for putting up with it for as long as I did. Now I feel it's time for me to take her to court and get full custody. Any visit that Charise gets, I would request it be under supervision."

"Arnold, you have to do what is best for your son and yourself. You deserve to be happy, and you have obviously shuffled your life around to accommodate Charise and her childish ways. Not because of my animosity toward my sister, but you do need to get full custody of that boy. Especially if you have a good family life to offer him. If you need to get restraining orders, then do what you must.

"Lewis told me of some craziness that happened with Charise after you left Cancun. Obviously Charise is nowhere close to growing up or changing her ways. Me being unbiased and objective, I'd say go for custody and restraining orders for you and your friend. And if Charise violates that, then lock her up. That's what the law allows."

Maybe that last statement wasn't me being objective, 'cause that bitch deserves everything that's coming to her.

"I can't thank you enough for taking the time to hear me out. I'm still hoping one day my son will get to meet your family, but I'll understand if you're not ready for that," he said.

"That might be possible after you finish with the whole custody battle. I don't want her anywhere in the picture. And although I really don't know you too well, I'll try to do what I can to help you with getting custody. Anybody would be an improvement to the poor child's mother."

"Sandy, I really appreciate that. Hopefully my phone number showed up on your phone when I called. Please keep in touch."

"I'll do that, Arnold, and good luck."

"Thanks," he said before hanging up.

Ooh, ooh, ooh! I have got to call somebody. That bitch is going to get hers. Kelly. I'll call Kelly. She likes to hear dirt. And this time, I have my info from the source and not from Lewis, since no one wants to believe him. Fucking some strange man with her son watching? That's some shit there. She probably didn't even know his name.

And the wicked bitch had the nerve to name another man's son after her ex-boyfriend. She probably wished he did father her child. But since she couldn't stop being a whore even after the man forgave her twice, he finally kicked her to the curb. Then she was all devastated and broken up. We all were ready to kick his ass for upsetting our sister so bad. Then we looked like fools when he told us that was the third time Charise cheated on him, and he couldn't forgive her or trust her anymore. He was right and she was wrong. Charise hasn't had a serious relationship since then, although I don't know if you could call that serious.

I hope I can catch Kelly. She's always so busy.

11
Charise

I knew my stalking Arnold would eventually bear some fruits. Who did I see him with yesterday? None other than Lewis. I didn't expect that, but I decided to follow Lewis instead of Arnold. I finally found where he works. When I figured it was time for him to get off from work, I started hanging around. Today I decided to go into the bar I saw Lewis and some others go into when they got off the day before. I was hoping he'd come in today. If not, I saw plenty of other fine-ass guys. They were certainly checking me out. As quick as I sat at the bar, one guy came over to buy me a drink. After he paid for my drink, he let me know he'd be at the pool tables if I wanted anything else.

Now he wasn't the greatest looking in the place, but after the ugly ass guy I had to fuck the other night to piss Arnold off, anything is an improvement. That guy was the first thing I could get. After I picked up Jarod, I went by the grocery store. I saw this ugly creature watching me. He wasn't much taller than me. He started making conversation about how cute Jarod is. Then he said he was surprised the father let my fine ass out of his sight. That's when the idea hit me to let Arnold see someone else fucking me. I flirted back with the ugly guy. I don't remember if he ever told me his name. I just know I told him to follow

me back to my place. While in the car, I called Arnold and told him I needed him to get the baby from me.

When Ugly was in my apartment, I slightly opened the door so Arnold would just walk in. I figured it would take about twenty minutes for Arnold to arrive, so I had to get things started quickly. I gave Ugly a drink after I put Jarod in his playpen with a Barney video playing. Before Ugly could get a good gulp, I was all over him. He was trying to slow things down, but I told him he was part of a program that he needs to get with. Otherwise, he was going to miss out on a grand opportunity to have this pussy. Of course, I hiked my leg up for him to see under my miniskirt.

His erection wasn't coming as quick as I needed it, so I had to help it along. After sucking for dear life, I found his dick wasn't growing beyond six inches. He couldn't fuck worth a damn. He acted like a dog in heat, and had absolutely no rhythm. I didn't want Arnold to see me being fucked by someone who couldn't fuck. I wanted him to see me being fucked properly. Unfortunately, there wasn't much I could do at that point, so when I heard the knock at the door, I let out some phony screams and moans. At the very least, he might be under the impression the guy had a big dick.

When the guy heard Arnold, he was about to pull away from me (although I couldn't feel him inside of me in the first place). I had to reach back and grab him to keep him inside of me. He stayed inside, and went along with things. Arnold was in and out of my place in less than two minutes. He called me every slutty-whore name he could think of. I just laughed.

The ugly guy had to leave shortly thereafter. I told him he better go before my boyfriend comes back with his gun. He hauled ass when I said that. Fucking him was like fucking a super tampon. You know how you can go the whole day without knowing it's up in there? That was the ugly guy. I barely noticed he was inside of me.

Just as I had hoped, Lewis walked in the bar. I spotted him out of my peripheral view. I pretended I didn't know he was there. I was flirting with the bartender, who gave me another free drink, when Lewis walked up behind me.

"Charise?"

I turned as though surprised. "Lewis! What are you doing here?"

"No, what are you doing here? When did you start hanging on this end of town?" he asked, almost serious. "And then you are here by yourself?"

"I was supposed to be meeting this guy here," I lied. "I've been here about a half an hour now, and he hasn't shown up or called me to say he's running late. I got here a little late, but I can't imagine he left that quickly."

"Did you call him?" Lewis anxiously asked.

"Several times. I keep getting his voicemail. So what brings you over this way?"

"I come around here every now and again." He clearly left out that his job is across the street. "Why would he have you meet him here in this rundown place? You know this is not a good part of town to be hanging in, don't you?"

"This is just where he told me to meet him. I didn't know it was a rough area until I got down this way. He said he was getting off of work and wanted me to meet him here."

"He works around here?" Lewis asked, looking concerned—more for himself than me.

"I guess so. I didn't ask for the name of the company. He does electrical work or something." I tried to look disappointed from being stood up.

He looked me up and down with that hungry look in his eyes. "I see that little come-fuck-me skirt is going to go to waste."

The Queen

"Why is that?" I asked, happy that he took notice of the skirt that barely covered my goodies as I sat on the barstool.

"If your boy stood you up . . . and it seems as if you've been stood up," he said, still unable to take his eyes from my thighs.

"Well, I guess it's not a total waste. As soon as I got here, some nice guy back there playing pool bought me a drink, and told me to let him know if I want anything else. I told him I was waiting on someone. Even the bartender gave me a drink. To be quite honest with you, I wouldn't mind hanging around here more often. There are a lot of fine-ass men in here, and the women are scarce. This is my kind of spot."

"Charise, Charise, Charise," he said, looking at me and shaking his head. "Well, have fun. I'm going over here to have my drink and then I'm out."

Hold up! That was not the response I wanted. I grabbed hold of his hand before he could get away and discreetly put it between my legs. "So I can't get you to bite?"

His finger got around my thong and quickly made its way into my cavity. He caught me slightly off guard with that. Just as quick as it went in, it was out.

"I think I'll pass this time," he said while wiping my wetness from his finger with a napkin off of the bar. "I have a wife at home waiting for me."

That bastard! Why won't he fuck me? I know he wants to. Damn him.

Like someone once said, "If your man starts acting up, then you take his friend." And then he wants to talk shit about his wife at home after sticking his finger in my pussy? Oh, it's on now.

I dismissively waved my hand at him. "No problem, Lewis. You go have your drink and get on home to your broke-down wife. Maybe I'll see you around sometime," I warned, because I did plan on returning.

I climbed off my barstool and went to find the guy who bought my drink. I acted like I was way tipsy, even though I only had the two drinks. I told the guy I was ready for my next drink. I told him that I got stood up. I knew I had him when he turned in his pool stick to return to the bar with me.

"Have you ever tried white lightning?" he asked when we sat at the bar.

"No. What's that?" I asked like I really cared.

"It's the hard stuff. It'll make everything in this bar taste like water. I have some in my car if you want to try it."

Oh, now I am supposed to be SSSOOOOOO stupid that I don't know he's trying to get me somewhere he can fuck me? I'm game. I know Lewis is still watching.

"You're not going to try and get me drunk, and then take advantage of me, are you?"

"Baby, I wouldn't take advantage of you."

"Okay. Let's go to your car and try this white lightning."

The damn fool was salivating. As we walked out snuggled together, I was certain to make eye contact with Lewis. He didn't look too happy.

When we got in the guys Chrysler 300, he pulled out this clear bottle of liquid. He opened it to let me smell it.

"You know, if I drink that, I'm probably not going to be able to drive home. Do you want to go somewhere?" I asked, knowing full well by that smell, I'd find myself somewhere I didn't want to be after drinking the stuff.

"I don't mean to be too forward, but there's a motel up the street. Would you feel comfortable going there? I promise I won't take advantage of you. That way if you feel like you can't drive, you can just sleep it off," he said with his baritone, Texas accent.

The Queen

So I played naïve. "Okay, we could do that. You want to drive me to my car, and then I'll follow you to the motel?"

"No problem, Sweetie." He looked me up and down like a pork chop sandwich while flashing his gold tooth.

When we got to this motel, which was a far cry from being a Hilton, he went in and got a room for us. We went into the room with white lightning and two Pepsi's in tow.

The room was so dim, even with the lights on. I'd be surprised to learn that the light was any more than a twenty-five watt bulb. The bed looked sunken in the middle and the rustic colored bedspread made me wonder had it EVER been changed. I was nervous sitting on the bed, for fear of what might jump off of it. Instead, I sat at the piece of table, while my new friend, whose name I hadn't asked, poured two cups of this clear liquid.

"Now let me warn you, it's going to burn going down. You might want to start off chugging it down. You'll have a hard time sipping at first. Maybe your next one you'll be able to sip it better."

"Are you going to pour in the Pepsi?" I asked, really not having a clue.

"Naw! You don't mix white lightning. I brought the Pepsi just in case you want somethin' to drink after."

I picked up the cup, took a deep breath, and chugged down the shot as he instructed. Oh, he wasn't lying about the burning. It felt like my entire digestive track was on fire. My sinuses were wide open, bringing tears to my eyes. He handed me a cup with some Pepsi in it. I drank it, hoping to soothe the burning. Pepsi wasn't working. Somehow, despite it all, I worked up the nerve to ask for another shot.

Probably three or four shots later, I found myself laying on that nasty bed, skirt hiked up around my waist, thong off, and this man's face in my pussy. I don't know if it was him or the white lightning that had me feeling so damn good. I especially liked when he had me get on my knees at the edge of the bed, while he knelt on the floor, and ate me from front to back with his large hands holding my butt cheeks apart. When he came up from downtown, he sucked on both of my tits with such attentiveness. I'm not sure when my halter-top was removed or where it had gotten to. I didn't even see what his dick looked like, but I was begging for him to put it inside of me. And when he did, I was happy.

I don't know how long we were in this room drinking and fucking. I know it felt like an eternity. I was disappointed when he said he had to leave, but told me to stay and get some rest. I don't think I could leave if I wanted to. My ass was officially drunk. Wasted is more like it. I can't even say how long it was that he walked out of the room before I heard knocking at the door. He must have left something, I figured. It took me forever to make it to the door only about five feet away. The knocking was persistent. He should know my drunk ass can't rush to the door.

Finally when I foolishly opened the door naked, and not even checking the peephole to make sure it was him, Lewis pushed his way into the room and closed the door.

"Come here and suck my dick!" he demanded, pulling a stiff dick from his pants.

I was in a stupefied state. "Huh?"

"I said, bring your nasty ass over here and suck my dick, bitch," he said, pulling my arm toward the bed.

I snatched my arm away from his grasp. "I'm not sucking your dick and you won't even fuck me."

Then I looked and saw his hard dick standing waiting for me to give it some attention. Lewis stood stroking his dick right near my face as I sat at the edge of the bed . . . Fell, more like it.

"Please, Lewis, can you fuck me? I need you. No one else can make me feel as good as you do. Please, baby, fuck me," I begged.

"Suck my dick, and then I'll put it in your ass," he said softer, but in a bad-boy way.

That's a deal I could live with. I took Lewis in my mouth and sucked that dick as if my life depended on it. I was blissful when he kept his word and anally fucked me. Oh, how much I missed being with Lewis. I was even more grateful when he told me to meet him back at this hotel in three days at eight pm.

He told me I better not fuck anyone else otherwise he'd never touch me again. That sounds like a promising future to me. If I could get Lewis back, Arnold would never have to worry about hearing from me again, and he could have his bitch. Oh, and Sandy? I would love to take Lewis away from her ass again. Apparently she can't satisfy him the way I do. Otherwise, he wouldn't be right back here in this ass.

And if Lewis dared to stand me up, I'd be at that bar every night picking up a different man for Lewis to have to watch me leave with. I know now, that would drive him crazy. There ain't shit he could do about it because he works right across the street, and don't know that I know it.

As if reading my thoughts, he said, "By the way, don't let me catch you in that bar again. When I'm going to see you, I will meet you here at this motel. And you'll wait for me to tell you when I'll see you. But like I said, fuck some other nigga and we're done."

Boy was I happy as happy could be.

I noticed the clock read 11:08 pm when Lewis left. I'd totally lost track of all time. It was only eight when I arrived to the room. Somehow time moved slower than I thought. Although I felt a lot more alert, I didn't know if I felt up to driving back across town. I didn't feel comfortable sleeping on that bed half sober either.

As I was lying on the funky bed in the dimly lit room, completely uncovered, and contemplating my next move, I noticed a small hole on an oddly hung picture across the small room. I lay staring at the hole until I saw a quick light before an eye appeared in the hole. The human eye was blended in the painted trees of the picture. I stood up and approached the picture. I guess when the person spying on me through the hole in the wall saw me approaching, they hurried to run for cover.

Oh my goodness! Some pervert has been watching me this whole time!

My head was still spinning from the white lightning. I knew driving was going to be out of the question. Now I felt creeped out, but not so creeped out that I didn't give the pervert a peepshow. I turned on the clock radio to any station I could find with reception. I started dancing seductively, as though performing for an audience.

After one or two songs, I lay with my pussy opening facing the strange eye, and began masturbating. Insanely, I saw a tongue poking through the hole, causing the whole picture to move. I got up and removed the picture from the wall, where I saw the hole was even larger. I placed the wooden chair just below the hole, stood on the chair, and put my nipple against the protruding tongue. The tongue tickled my nipple, obviously happy for the bone I had provided this dog. I was getting so turned on by this. I stepped away so the eye could see me. I placed my fingers in my pussy, then came back to the hole, put my fingers through the hole one at a time, while the mystery mouth on the other side sucked the pussy juices off. When he was done, I placed my nipples back to the hole for more teasing. Now my pussy was so excited, I actually wanted this nasty pervert to come lick me, suck me and fuck me.

Suddenly, this outlet down below the hole, closer to the floor, fell out of the wall, and onto the floor. I was like, "what the hell?" but then I saw an old man's hand come through the hole. At first I wasn't sure what to do. Then I moved the chair to bend down and put my large breast in his hand. He seemed to appreciate the privilege. Since he was turning me on so much, I decided to get on my hands and knees, and

The Queen

backed my ass up to the wall until his fingers were able to find my wet pussy. Those fingers felt good in me. I actually squirted all over his hand. It was killing me not to be able to fuck this person.

For all I know, this could be some impotent old man on the other side of this wall.

That thought was quickly dispelled when the head of a thick, hard dick came through the opening. I reached in the hole and was impressed by the feel of its full length.

I just wish more could fit through this hole.

I tried to get my pussy as close as I could to the head of that dick. I wanted his dick to at least feel my hot wetness. My ass made slight contact, but hardly enough for my liking.

I can't believe I'm breaking my promise to Lewis as quickly as I made it. I have got to get this dick in me before I leave here tonight.

I gasped when I saw a super long black dildo come through the opening.

He wants to fuck me through a wall with a big black dildo? Why can't he just come over and fuck me?

So I asked through the wall, "Why don't you come on over and let me feel the real thing?"

His hand came through the hole, summoning me to come near. He wouldn't speak. Then he put the dildo back through the opening. That time I decided to let the dildo find my wet pussy. I masturbated as I guided the dildo inside of me. It was working. The man was stroking me well with that inanimate object through the wall.

I wanted a different position, which was difficult. So I went and pulled the mattress onto the floor near the wall. I propped some pillows underneath my hips to raise my pussy more in line with the wall opening. This time I was able to lie on my back. I saw he was watching as I set everything up. When my pussy was in place, his hand came through and massaged my clit. I kept my legs up and open to facilitate his access to my pussy or asshole if he wanted. He fingered me some more before replacing the mega dildo back through the opening. I guided it inside of me as he controlled each stroke. This man made me cum so many times. Maybe it was the perverted thrill.

Unfortunately, when I finally left the motel at 12:40 in the morning, I didn't get to see who this person was. This is definitely an all-new experience for me that I'll never forget. Hopefully when I meet up with Lewis in a few days, I can try to get this same room and have a double thrill of knowing this man is watching me.

Before I left the motel, which had the light missing from the "M", reading "OTEL," I went to the front desk to reserve the room.

The woman behind the desk was surprised that anyone would want to reserve a room there in advance.

Can't leave anything to chance.

12
Kelly

"Well, aren't we just-a-glowing?" Elaine asked when I finally arrived at the restaurant. She was already seated at the table to where I was escorted by the hostess. The place was dimly lit but elegant. I would have preferred someplace with more lighting because I'm already tired from that long-ass non-stop flight across country, followed by some good loving from Sean, which still has my legs feeling like rubber.

I hate L.A. traffic, and getting lost at night doesn't help. Sean wanted to drive me, but I wasn't ready for him and Elaine to meet just yet. Honestly, it makes me nervous for Elaine to meet anyone I'm involved with. Somehow, Elaine can turn heads quicker than the rest of us. Maybe it's her level of confidence or something. I don't know. Elaine makes a room stop talking when she enters it. I'm scared to see Elaine have that kind of effect on Sean. What's worse is, we all know that Elaine had no problem sleeping with Sandy's ex-boyfriend—Mandingo, Eric or whatever his name was. Besides that, I needed to discuss some things in private with Elaine, and I don't need Sean all up in everything.

"I can't imagine that I'd be glowing after the hell it took for me to get here." I hung my purse on the seat I was taking. "Maybe it's the candlelight in this restaurant. Look around; everyone's glowing. Even you."

I quickly picked up the leather-bound menu to hide behind as Elaine continued trying to search my face for some clues for my glow. The short, stout waiter came to fill my glass with water and to take my drink order. I peeked at Elaine over my menu and thought against ordering alcohol, so I ordered a glass of cranberry juice, as she was drinking. When the waiter left, I tried to act as if I was still studying the menu, although I already knew what I would order.

"Kelly Wiggins, don't think for a minute you are going to sit in front of me, your big sister, and think I'm not going to know you are fucking somebody," she said in a loud whisper as she leaned over the table to snatch my menu from my hands. "It must be that new guy, isn't it? But wait, you haven't known him three months, have you?"

I fidgeted with my cloth napkin before I placed it across my lap. "Whatever!" was all I could shoot back.

Then I tried to change the subject to shift the focus from myself. "Girl, I have so much shit to tell you. Some stuff you may already know."

She eyed me suspiciously, knowing full well I was attempting to divert the attention away from the subject. "Well, let's order. I am starving," she said when the waiter returned with my juice.

We gave our food orders and I excused myself to go to the ladies room to escape from Elaine's glare. Thankfully, as I was returning to the table, the server was bringing our starters, allowing me a momentary reprieve.

Over dinner, I filled Elaine in with the details Sandy told me about Charise.

The Queen

"You know, as much as I can't stand Lewis, I believe he did see Charise on the beach with Todd's son and nephew. Lewis would be all too happy to tell that. He probably left out the part where he was on his way to fuck Charise, but those other guys beat him to it," Elaine said.

"Uhm-hmm. I think you may be on to something, but what about the girls Todd's son was hanging with? That's the part stumping me."

"Kelly, you are the damn private eye in the family. That just seems like classic Charise. She has to have what is forbidden."

"Aren't you one to talk?" I asked.

"Mandingo doesn't count. I thought that situation was long history for Sandy. I'll admit I was wrong for that. Anyway, changing the subject . . . So what's the deal with this new guy? He must be something if you violated your three-month rule"

Damn! Why'd I have to press my luck shifting the unwanted attention to Elaine?

I took a deep breath, already anticipating the worst from Elaine. "Okay! I'll admit, the first time I got so drunk, I don't even remember, but after that . . . Girl, I loves me some him! He is so wonderful. He's gorgeous. He showers me with all kinds of gifts. He's a music producer. He has a big, nice-ass crib." I was getting warm just talking about Sean and beamed with excitement from every word.

She looked at me, raising her eyebrow. She stopped eating and set her fork down, wiping the corners of her mouth with her napkin. I knew something was coming. I got quiet and picked at the food on my plate to avoid her piercing eyes. I figured I must have said something I shouldn't have said, giving her the ammunition to despise my man.

"Kelly, you sure that nigga didn't drug you up?" she asked dryly. "When have you ever gotten so drunk you have no memory? Especially of sex? That shit doesn't even sound right."

Elaine underscored my initial thoughts from that first time with him. I wanted to talk to someone about it so bad from that day, but I guess I didn't want to believe that he'd do something like that. Besides, all of that is behind us now, and everything is great.

"At first I thought the same thing, but when he gave me the details of my blocked out memory, everything sounds like my typical move when I'm ready to give up the goods," I defended.

Elaine gave me the "stupid" look as she folded her arms across her chest. "You can talk 'til you're blue in the face. I haven't even met ole dude and I don't trust his ass. And the fact that he got my sister all bamboozled makes me not like the sneaky motherfucker even more," she said in her rawest, un-sugar coated form.

"Damn, Elaine! Do you think you could at least meet someone before you make up your mind about them? Do you think you could let me enjoy this for however long it may last? I mean, it's not like I am Charise, bouncing from dick to dick." Tears filled my eyes, and I fought their release. She really hurt my feelings. She's always hurting my feelings.

She could see my hurt and decided to lighten up. "Look, Kelly, I know you want to be happy, and Lord knows you deserve to be, which is why I always try to look out for you. And I certainly don't want to hurt you. I've known you your entire life. I know you when you drink, when you're sober, when you hurt, when you're happy. I would have been okay with the guy if you told me, 'Girl, I was horny, he was fine, and I decided to go for mine, despite my three-month rule.' And because I know you when you're drunk, I know you wouldn't waiver under any circumstance. Particularly when you have no memory of it. Hell, you have Daddy's, 'Wiggins' high alcohol tolerance level' in you. 'Cause you know those damn Wiggins' can drink." She slightly chuckled, then shook her head. "I just don't trust the situation, and for that, it makes me not trust him."

I sat at the table, unable to find any words. I really like Sean and don't want to believe that he'd stoop to such a level. I hear everything

my sister is saying to me and she does know me to the core like no other.

Elaine continued. "I'll tell you what . . . you always run all these background and credit checks on guys. Run them on this guy. Harmony will be in town for the gala, and she'll have the opportunity to do what she does. See how he interacts, and if he can pass all your normal hoops and tests you put your guys through, and then you will have my blessing. I will eat my words. Hell, I'll even pay for your wedding dress."

"Vera Wang?" I asked with a semi pout and semi-smile, as I wiped away the few uncooperative tears that had fallen.

"David's Bridal, $99.00 rack, bitch!" We laughed. "No, whatever your little heart desires," she answered seriously and then reached around the table to give me a big hug. "Little Sis, don't ever forget that I'm going to always have your back."

Elaine could be so harsh and evil, but she's like the best big sister.

"Okay, enough of that mushy shit. Let's talk about what you put together for the gala." Elaine fell back into her seat, suddenly switching gears in a business tone. "But first you need to take your ass back to that ladies room and handle that cheap-ass mascara that's running around your eyes. I don't know why you insist on using that cheap shit."

As she heartily laughed at my expense, the horror of my raccoon image chased me from my seat, taking me to the ladies room in record time, and not a minute too soon. Not only was my mascara running; I had broccoli embedded in my teeth.

We talked about some of the plans for the next half an hour or so. It was well after midnight by the time I reached Sean's Santa Monica house. I gave a lot of thought to what Elaine said on the ride back. I slept with him and threw all caution to wind. I didn't even think about running any background or anything.

At this stage, I'm almost afraid to learn anything bad about him. I don't want to believe that Sean would ever do anything to let me down or hurt me. I guess I'll learn a lot over the next few weeks here with him. I know everything is going to check out on him.

PART TWO

More, More, More

13

Harmony

"Todd, you know full well any call from Arnold means problems." I peeked into a pot on the stove, causing Todd to swat my hand again.

The delightful aroma of Todd's Cajun seafood boil had me bouncing from my seat on the other side of the maple-colored granite-top island, checking his pot for the third time in hopes of stealing a taste. He gave me a chastising eye without speaking, which sent me back to my seat.

Once I was firmly back on my stool, he answered. "Maybe he was just calling to see how our trip went. Or maybe he wanted to apologize for not staying for our wedding."

"I know you don't really believe that." I laughed.

"Okay, you're right. Maybe we shouldn't call him back. Then again, I'm not like you. I'm curious as hell." He walked to pick up the cordless phone from the wall. "I want to know what new dirt has been going on. Hell, you're probably dying inside to know what we've been missing."

"You know, I could call Sandy. How about you call Arnold and I'll call Sandy?" I shot up from my seat to grab my cell phone from my purse on the table. "We could call Kelly tomorrow to fill in any blanks."

Todd laughed as he set the phone back onto the base, shaking his head. "I knew you couldn't help yourself." He came and took my phone from my hand. "No, dear. We are not calling anyone on our first night home as Mr. and Mrs. Palmer. I already compromised with your checking the voicemails. Besides, you'll be in L.A. next week, and can get all the dirt firsthand."

"But, can't I at least call my sisters to let them know I'm back in the country safely?" I asked with a playful pout.

"Sure you can, Sweetie. After we eat this dinner I prepared for you. I want you to eat while it's nice and hot," he answered, wrapping his arms around my waist and kissing the back of my neck.

His kisses caused an electrical sensation to shoot through my body. I wanted him right here, right now. To hell with dinner. And to hell with my family and their drama.

We finally ate the dinner about three hours later. We tried to do the quickie thing so we could hurry up and eat, but that didn't happen. Damn, I married a superb lover.

The next day I was able to track down Sandy to fill in the blanks for me. I decided to meet her downtown for lunch at one of my favorite Italian restaurants, which Todd had introduced me to when I first came to Houston. I typically like going there during the lunch rush and observe people, but I was more anxious to get all the 4-1-1 on my nutty family.

"Where's the baby?" I asked when Sandy came rushing to the table out of breath. She was carrying only her large pocketbook, typical of a contestant on the *Let's Make A Deal* show, never lacking necessities. "I thought you'd at least bring my niece so I could see her."

"Please, I took her bad behind to the babysitter." She took a gulp of the water the waiter had placed in front of her, then dipped her fingers in the glass to sprinkle her sweating face. "I have too much to fill you in on, and I didn't want any interruptions. Besides, that girl is running now, and I don't feel like chasing a one-year-old."

"I would have chased her."

"I know you would have; that's why I left her. I told you I don't want any interruptions."

"Okay, so what did I miss?"

"Do you think we could order something to eat first? I'm starving."

"That's fine," I said before calling over the waiter.

The waiter took our orders and returned quickly with them since it was still during the lunch rush.

As we ate, Sandy filled me in on Charise's shenanigans. I was most put off by the possibility of Charise with Todd's son and nephew. I'm going to have to get with Charise to get to the bottom of that one. For her sake, I hope Sandy is wrong. Then again, if Sandy is wrong, that means Charise is still messing with Lewis.

"I'll tell you, Harmony, Charise makes it hard for me to be saved. Every time the minister speaks about repentance, all I can think about is kicking Charise's behind just once, so I could go on and repent, and be free of that sin. Maybe I should take a month off from church, go beat Charise down, go out and celebrate with some booze and men, then return to church and repent," Sandy said as if she might be seriously considering all of the things on her *church sabbatical to-do* list.

"Sandy! I don't think that's a good idea. How about you let me find out for sure she was screwing around with Andre, and I'll beat her down?" I said, half-joking.

"That just might work. Uh . . . Nah, I don't know," Sandy stammered. "I think I owe her this beat down myself. Remember how she did me at your wedding and everything before that? My love for you was the only thing stopping me from leaping over all those chairs and snatching her by her neck. Even now, you have no idea how hard it is to trust my husband. Thank the Lord that the hussy has no idea where we live or how to reach Lewis anymore."

"Are you sure he's not reaching out to her?" I asked, not sure if I was going to fuel Sandy's mistrust in her husband. Hell, if I have to choose, I prefer Sandy's husband to be the object of Charise's desires, rather than my newly acquired stepson. Neither are okay, but just saying if I had to choose one.

"Lewis has been pretty much on the ball since we last spoke. He works a lot of hours, but thankfully he's paid hourly and has a paycheck that matches up. Every once in a while, he goes to play pool across the street from his job, but he'll talk to me on the phone most of the time he's out. He also encourages me to come to his job anytime I want. Every now and again, he makes it to bible study with me, and we've been attending regularly on Sundays. I don't think Charise is even on his Doppler at this point," Sandy said almost proudly.

I eyed her, not buying it.

"For both of your sakes, I hope you're right," I said, still not convinced. That sneaky-ass Lewis can find a way to make time.

Sandy stared out the window, looking at the busy traffic. I could tell she too wasn't convinced, but didn't want to admit such.

Changing gears, I asked, "Why would Charise be stalking and harassing Arnold and his girlfriend if she doesn't want to be with him?"

Sandy came back to life once the focus was off of her Lewis.

"You know that foolish game, 'I don't want him, and I don't want anyone else to want him either.' Honestly, I think Arnold was a prize catch for that silly fool. Obviously, she wouldn't know a good thing if it bit her in the ass. Don't get me wrong, but I would prefer to have an Arnold as my husband over a Lewis."

"Ooh, Sandy! I'm surprised to hear that come from your mouth. He is a cutie, though." I laughed. "I do think Arnold was an excellent catch for her or any other woman. Her biggest problem with him is his name.

Things are going to be awkward if he gets custody of that baby. From all you have told me, as well as what I already know, Charise doesn't need to keep mixing that child up. He'll grow up all crazy, and have no respect for women."

Sandy lightly banged her fist on the table. "And speaking of names, why didn't you tell me the nut named her son after her ex-boyfriend Jarod? Remember the one we were going to jump that time when she was all broken up?"

I was about to take a sip of my lemon water, but stopped to answer, "I didn't think..." *BLUUGHH!!!*

Oh my God, I can't believe I just threw up in mid-sentence, into my glass, in the damn restaurant.

BLUUGHH!!!

Now vomit was splashing into my plate, onto the table, and soon the floor.

Oh, Lord, it won't stop. My undigested Calamari Ripieni was everywhere.

"Are you all right?" a manager ran over to the table asking. "Please, can we help you to the ladies room?" he asked nervously, looking at all the on-looking customers and the many moving away from my mess.

"I'll be—" *BLUUGHH!!!* I tried to say, but more vomit flew out stopping my sentence.

Sandy stood looking on in horror as she tried to wipe the yellow and red splatters of my mess from her blue tunic top. I was too messed up to tell her that she missed the puke that was still on her exposed cleavage that she had yet to realize was there. I tried to point to it, but she couldn't understand my sign language.

"Oh, my Lord! I think you all have poisoned my sister. Look at her, she's gasping for air and flailing her arms all crazy." Tears started pouring down her face as she became more concerned by my uncontrollable vomiting. "What have you done to my sister!" she screamed for all of Downtown Houston to hear. "Call a damn ambulance! You poisoned my sister! That damn Calamari whatever the hell that was. I knew it as soon as I looked at it." Sandy turned to me crying, "Damn, Harm, why couldn't you just order the lasagna like I had? Girl, now they done poisoned your ass."

I was so embarrassed. I didn't know which embarrassed me more: the throwing up in public or Sandy's dramatic scene. I couldn't even get myself together to make it to the bathroom. At this point, I am sweating, short of breath, and a total mess. It wasn't too long before I heard an ambulance quickly approaching.

When the paramedics arrived, they asked if I had this happen before. Sandy answered "NO" for me, but I couldn't get it together enough to tell them it happened once last week. I figured I ate something bad then. They took my blood pressure, which was now high, and tried to give me oxygen between my throwing up episodes. So the decision was made for me that I was on the way to the hospital.

In the midst of all my suffering, all I could think about was paying the restaurant bill. I managed to get my credit card out, but Sandy snatched it, yelling, "We are not paying for poisoned food! They're going to be paying us when we finish suing them."

Needless to say, Sandy's many comments about the poisoned food caused most of the customers to leave as I was being wheeled to the ambulance. Well, maybe I killed everyone's appetite with the vomiting.

I had Sandy call Todd from my cell phone, because I didn't dare give her his phone number, for fear that she'd use it every time I decide to ignore her phone calls. He was already waiting at the hospital when we arrived.

When it was just Sandy and Todd in the room with me (where they isolated me from other patients until they could determine my ailment), Todd asked, "Baby, why are they thinking you may have been poisoned? The same thing happened in Bora Bora last week. You've been fine since that one day, so it can't be a stomach virus."

I whispered, "Sandy told everyone I was poisoned by the restaurant. I couldn't catch my breath long enough to say it happened last week."

"Harmony! You are pregnant! Oh, my Lord, you are pregnant!" Sandy said in a loud whisper, getting tickled by her revelation.

"Sorry, sis. I haven't missed a period. Try again," I laughed.

Todd suddenly looked pale. "Harmony, your period only lasted a day and a half. Remember? You figured it was because your cycle was thrown off by you missing your pills and the travel."

"Todd, and Sandy for that matter, if I were pregnant, I'd be throwing up every day or nauseous by the mere thought of food. Once last week, and once this week doesn't qualify."

"Last I checked, your doctorate degree didn't qualify you as a medical doctor. And take it from a mother of four, pregnancy has its own set of rules," Sandy answered with hands on her hips. "Not only that, don't think I didn't notice how you swallowed down all of your food and half of my lasagna too."

Todd gave me a strange look. "Hmm, and I thought she just worked up a big appetite when she ate up all of the food I cooked last night, which I was expecting to take for lunch today."

Just then, the doctor walked in the room and looked at Todd. "Are you Dad?" Then he faced me, "This is your husband, right?"

Sandy screamed for all the hospital to hear. "I told you! I told you!"

Before the doctor could complete his official pregnancy announcement, Sandy was on her cell phone. "Kelly, Harmony is pregnant! Yes, she is! I'm here with her in the hospital now."

The doctor turned from watching Sandy in action to Todd and me. "We're going to need to get you a pelvic exam and ultrasound to see how far along we are. Congratulations! Or so I hope are in order."

The Queen

Sandy repeated every word verbatim in the phone. She called herself trying to whisper after we all looked at her and I gave her an evil eye, but with Sandy's whisper, I'm sure the people in the hallway could hear her. She's loud!

When the doctor left the room, Sandy was still gossiping on the phone, despite the "No Cell Phones" sign. Todd came and kissed me.

"Wow, we're going to start our family off sooner than we had planned. I guess all those other exotic vacations we planned are going to have to be traded in for Disney instead." He laughed.

I lightly laughed back because that seemed like the polite thing to do, but I wasn't sure how to feel. I wanted to at least enjoy one good year married before starting a family. I also wanted time to be certain I didn't make any mistakes in choosing Todd for a husband, let alone father. I guess fate made the choice for me. Seeing the little 'lima bean' on the ultrasound monitor made me feel slightly happy. Sandy was broadcasting the play-by-play details of my pregnancy and ultrasound to the now four-way call including Kelly, Shawnee, and Elaine. Not long after, Todd was on his phone calling God knows who to give them the news.

In the midst of their private celebration, there was a knock at the door. This meek little Italian guy from the restaurant entered my room. "E'cuse me. Mr. Guido want me to get payment for dis if you not sick from food." He held out a bill for our lunch.

Todd snatched the paper from the guy's hand. "Get lost! Damn you!"

The young man scurried out the door.

"Would you believe the nerve of Guido?" Todd said angrily. "Harmony, I don't care how much you love their food, we're not going back there. That was just tacky."

Sandy was Todd's 'Amen Choir' in the background, providing the latest development to the Wiggins Sisters.

Arriving home that evening wasn't too much better than being in the hospital with Sandy on the phone. The whole Palmer family was at our home waiting with balloons, stuffed animals, and flowers. You would have thought I was actually bringing the baby home in my arms.

Lord, help me! This is going to be a long pregnancy. They are treating me like a helpless fool already. You would think I was giving birth to our Lord and Savior.

The next several weeks included the nonstop throwing up and the babying by Todd and his family. It killed me not to be able to stop throwing up long enough to make it to L.A. for the grand opening gala. Everyone says the throwing up will eventually stop. What do they know?

14
Angelo

What was I thinking when I agreed to work with Elaine? She's a beast! Poor Kelly took a lashing at the grand opening celebration. Elaine was worse than a Bridezilla, but once those cameras were flashing and the place was packed with celebrities, she looked like she pulled everything off effortlessly.

I have to hand it to Kelly. She pulled off the gala of the century. Elaine was looking fierce in my friend Nicky's one-of-a kind, original designer gown. The food was good and the champagne was plentiful. The place was filled with some tasty-looking specimens. Even that Sean guy was hot. We were looking for the slightest inkling that he was a DL man. Although Kelly barely spent any time with him, he didn't attempt to ogle another woman. He did seem to know a lot of people at the party. For whatever reason, both Elaine and Shawnee don't trust the guy. He does seem a little suspect, but Kelly will run her background on old boy.

"I wonder what Charise's message was about. I hate to call her back because she keeps so much mess going on. The last time I spoke with her, she was bragging about some super tall, married guy with the super long dick, she was messing with. You know I was only listening because I wanted to hear more about the super long dick," I said to my best buddy and business partner Antwan while I comfortably lounged on the office sofa in our new day spa.

Antwan laughed. "Chile, I'm half tempted to jump on a plane to Houston to see for myself. I'd probably be stalking him myself."

"That's not the one she was stalking. She was stalking her baby-daddy and his new chick," I corrected.

"Well, obviously he must have a big dick also. Why else would she be stalking him knowing she has a Jolly Green Giant!" Antwan reasoned.

"Never mind! I can't talk to you about anything. You're just stuck on dick," I said, frustrated.

Hand over his mouth, Antwan gasped as he stood up from his desk. "Oh, no you didn't! You brought up the man's dick. I was just agreeing with you, Angela. Go on with your story. I won't say another word." Antwan pretended to zip his mouth and sat on top of the desk.

"You know, I'm really thinking about telling Sandy that Charise is fucking her husband AGAIN and on a regular."

"Why? She should have ditched his ass when he left her the first time. Some women just have to have a man for the sake of saying they have one. Yes, it's wrong, and I know you feel caught in the middle, but it would seem to me that Sandy prefers living life like an ostrich, with her head buried in the sand. I'm sure Sandy has to know something's going on but doesn't want to face reality. She will in her own time."

"Well, what about that other freak that Charise is mysteriously fucking through a damn wall of all things, each time she finishes with Lewis? I know she's going to end up with some kind of disease and get it back to Sandy because of Lewis. I know he's not covering up when he's with Charise, although Charise insists he is."

The Queen

"What I want to know is what the hell is wrong with that girl? Does she get a thrill out of the danger?"

"Your guess is as good as mine," I answered. "I'm really worried about my nephew. She is the world's most unfit mother. For Jarod's sake, I hope she does lose custody. Otherwise, that boy will end will end up dead and Charise will be in jail. Lord knows she couldn't handle a day in jail."

"Now that would be a sight. She'd probably be in there screwing all the prison guards." Antwan laughed.

I shot him a dirty look to let him know he was overstepping, talking about my family like that. It's one thing when I do, but hey, I can do that. "I better call her back. I know she has some new mess that she's making. That's the only time she calls me."

"You better take your ass back next door in that shoe store before Elaine tears you a new one."

"Fuck that bitch! I'm not even supposed to be working there until I finish school. This is what happens when you try doing family a friggin' favor. First it was 'could you work one day a week, Angelo?' then it was 'you think you could stop in a couple of days during the week to give me a break?' Now it's 'Angelo, where the fuck are you? I need a break! Get your ass in here!' every day. Every fucking day she's blowin' up my phone with her bitching."

"Angela, you need to let her know you have your finals and final projects coming up. She graduated from college. Surely she would understand what you're up against if you tell her."

"There is no reasoning with an Elaine," I said, sitting up on the couch. "Elaine worked her way through college and was living fabulous even then. I know she ain't trying to hear my woes."

"She's cool in my book. I just crack up with how she acts with you. Oh, I can't forget the beating Kelly took to put the gala together. Speaking of Kelly, have you heard any more on that tricky-dick she's got? There's something about him that doesn't sit well with me," Antwan said.

"I think you've been talking to Elaine too much. Sounds like something she'd say. Elaine can't stand him. She barely calls Kelly anymore because she's always bragging about how wonderful Sean is and how perfect he is." I stood up and collected my man purse sitting beside Antwan on the desk. "I'm out. I better get back over to the shoe boutique. Not shoe store, but *shoe boutique*," I mimicked Elaine.

"Angela, I need you to tell Elaine I gotta have one of those bags. She keeps telling me it's a one of a kind from Sao Paulo."

"She told you Sao Paulo? The bitch told me it came from some village in Africa."

We broke out in laughter. Elaine is notorious for playing up the exclusivity of her merchandise. It wouldn't surprise me if she found a box of bags on Crenshaw Boulevard, and passed them off as high class.

Antwan stood up excited and clasped his hands together in front of his chest. "Oh, I forgot to ask you, did she say anymore on carrying Raphael's shoe line in her store? You know he is so excited about having his own shoe design collection that will be worn by the who's-who. I know Elaine was digging the pieces he did design."

I rolled my eyes. "She said she was going to try them out in her VIP section and see how the buzz is. But you know I don't like that sneaky-ass Raphael. I think the only reason he's been kissing up to you is to get his shoe collection off the ground, and once he blows up, he's going to give you his dung to kiss."

"Angela, your claws are showing. Stop being so pessimistic. Regardless of how you feel about him, we could all benefit from this business deal."

"Which is why I've been biting my tongue. He's your friend, not mine. Keep him away from me and we'll all get along just fine," I rebutted. "Well, let me get going. I have to call Charise and update Elaine on the latest drama."

"Does Elaine know about Charise and Lewis?"

"Did you think I wouldn't tell her? She thinks Sandy deserves what she gets, like you do. She promised not to say a word."

"Not say a word to Sandy or to your other sisters?" Antwan inquired.

"We're talking about Elaine here. You know full well she was going to tell Kelly and Shawnee. They already figured as much."

"Has anyone told Harmony about Charise's escapade with her stepson?"

"I don't know. I'd be surprised if Sandy wasn't waiting on the tarmac to run and tell Harmony the minute her plane landed from her honeymoon. I don't know what Harmony would do if she found out about that. I don't think anyone wants to upset her now that she's pregnant."

"Do you think Elaine is going to let you have time off for us to go to New York in June for the Gay Pride Festival?" Antwan asked.

I looked at him like he was stupid. "Uh, that shit was stipulated before I agreed to work for her. And she knows I'll be going to the events here in L.A. as well that month. She knows the rules: don't mess with my money, my time, or my parties, and we'll get along just fine. Shoot, don't act like you don't know."

I walked to the door and pulled the door open.

Antwan laughed. "Say what you want, but we both know who really calls the shots around here, Miss Thang."

"Whatever!" I said, rolling my eyes at him. "Well, I'm out."

15
Shawnee

"Elaine, what is wrong with your sister? How did the woman show up at Charise's apartment?"

"I guess she's been following her husband, and that's how she found Charise. You know I haven't talked to Charise. I got the latest scoop from Angelo. He called her yesterday from the boutique. I sat there listening. She is off her rocker."

"I think we need to tell Sandy about Lewis. I feel wrong for keeping her in the dark. I did finally tell Harmony about Charise and Todd's son. She was so pissed off even though Sandy wasted no time telling her upon her arrival back in the States. She doesn't want Todd to ever find out about it," I advised Elaine.

"He won't hear a word from me," Elaine answered. "Speaking of Todd, how is Tatiana working out? Is she still trying to be your best friend?"

"Best friend, my ass," I answered with total disgust. "This bitch must be under the impression that she's going to take Brad from me, and take my position in the company."

"I told you I didn't like her ass when we first met her. What is she doing now?" Elaine asked.

"Every time I issue a directive, she needs to privately meet with 'Brad.' I guess she doesn't know Brad tells me everything." After a brief pause and new thought . . . "Oh, my goodness! I didn't tell you, that he told me she came in his office trying to expose her boobs to him. She told him if he liked that, there was much more that she'd love to show him. He told me that he told her that he's going to pretend that never happened because she is an excellent Marketing Director, but he will not tolerate that behavior ever again. He also reminded her that I am her boss and he trusts my decisions, and she needs to do the job she was hired to do. He asked me to not bring it up to her since he already handled the matter."

"Ooh! Oh, no she didn't! Wow! I like Brad. He really has your back on everything. I wish I could find someone like him. That's a good man, Shawnee. Don't fuck it up."

I chuckled. "If you're talking about me fucking up my marriage with Robert, I think he fucked it up long before I did. Sometimes I actually find myself wondering what he's up to. I wonder if he's gotten over his hooker obsession."

"Stop wondering about what Robert's doing with his fruity life," Elaine yelled.

"Fruity?" I asked. "I'd say he's far from fruity. Robert was all about the pussy. All he went through by hooking up with that ugly-ass Renee, just to get to you? No, that's a man all about pussy." I laughed at the thought of Robert thinking about being with a man.

"I'm just saying. Some things you just never know. Some men have wives and children and have their men-lovers on the side. And then they want to run around talking about they're not gay."

"Robert had hookers on the side, not men." I was getting both annoyed and disgusted by the thought. "I don't want to talk about Robert anymore."

"I understand," Elaine responded sympathetically. "So how are you going to handle that Tatiana ho? That bitch needs to go. I could find some crackhead in New York to slice the bitch's face up. Maybe then she'd keep her face away from Brad."

"Trust me, the thought crossed my mind. Brad might feel sorry for her and end up spending more time with her," I answered. "I'll find a way to deal with Tatiana. When I told Harmony, she told me that Tatiana's will always rear their heads in Brad's life. She said I need to just learn how to trust Brad, but don't ever be anyone's fool. That's easier said than done. Trust, that is."

"Shawnee, didn't you tell me a while back that Brad wants to marry you?"

"Yeah. Why?" I asked.

"Well, maybe it's time you give that some serious thought. It's not like you don't love that old fart. He treats you perfectly. And if he decided to ever fuck up, at least you'd walk away wealthy as hell," Elaine said.

"I don't know if I can marry Brad. Our age difference still makes me a bit uncomfortable when we're in public together as a couple. Not to mention the fact that he's white. Even you refer to him as the *old fart*."

"So fucking what, Shawnee!" Elaine fussed. "Stop being so shallow. You love that man, and would be more devastated losing him than you were with Robert."

"What if something happens to him because he is older? How do I deal with that?" I asked my "got-it-all-together" sister.

"So deprive yourself of a possible life of happiness because you're afraid of losing it. Is that your philosophy? That's just ridiculous, Shawnee. Brad is going to realize he's not getting any younger, and a bitch like Tatiana will be sitting in the wings, waiting for Brad to leave your ass because you were dragging your feet."

"What about all the traveling we do? We spend so much time apart now that I have this new position."

"That's all the more reason to solidify your relationship. You'd also be solidifying your position in the company. If Tatiana were to have her way, she'd take Brad from you and have you booted out of the company. That, or have you permanently relocated overseas just to make sure you can't get near Brad again."

"Elaine, you're a genius. Girl, you just gave me a brilliant idea on how to get Tatiana out of the picture. I'm going to have her shipped to Europe permanently. I'll tell Brad I need her more in Europe than in New York. At least when Brad is in Europe, I'll be there too. There she could use her sex appeal to charm those European men, and leave my damn man alone."

"I say have that bitch's face cut up, and then ship her ass to Europe so one of those other European men could feel sorry for her."

We laughed. I love talking to Elaine sometimes. As harsh as she can be, she always makes good sense.

"Shifting gears, how are the stores coming along"

"If you meant to say 'boutiques,' they are doing well. Business has been very good. A lot of work, but very good. Even the day spa and clothing boutique are doing well. They have more appointments and clothing orders than they know what to do with."

"Well, I hope I'll be able to get an appointment when I come in for Angelo's graduation. Hopefully family counts for something."

"You're going to have to take that up with Angelo. I try not to interfere with their business. I just ensure that they are keeping our joint customers happy and satisfied so there won't be any backlash to my shoe boutiques, or my percentage." Elaine laughed.

"Any plans for a future location?"

"None at all. I'm already trying to figure out how I can make time for a social life. I can't think of the last time I've saw a concert or movie. Hopefully when Angelo comes aboard full time, that'll free up some time for me."

My phone beeped.

"Hey, Elaine, I have another call coming in. I'll catch up with you later."

"Okay, Sis. Love you."

"Love you too," I said before clicking over.

"Hello," I said when answering.

"I can't believe that you left me like you did," a familiar voice responded.

"Who is this?"

"It's been that long that you don't know your man's voice anymore?" he answered.

I hope this is not who I think it is. My eyes widened from a combination of fear and grief as my heart rate increased.

Oh, my Lord. Mandingo?

"I'm sorry, I don't know who you are, but this is certainly not the voice of my man. His voice I know very well, as I hear it EVERY night," I told him, angry and confused as to how he got my new cell phone number.

"Ouch. That wasn't nice. Shawnee, this is Eric, a.k.a Mandingo."

"Eric?" I tried to ask as if I didn't already know who he was. "Eric from DC? What are you calling me for? How did you get my number?"

"Damn, I thought you'd be happy to hear from me. I thought you lost my number with your moving and all, and I have been trying to track you down for over a year."

"Why? And again, how did you get my number?" I asked, pissed off beyond reason.

"Your girl gave me your number. She said you'd be happy to hear from me with your being so busy with work and all," he answered.

The Queen

"My girl? Who would that be? When have you ever known any of 'my girls'?"

"Well, that's what she said when she called me back. She said she was your girl and you both work together."

"What do you mean she called you back?"

"I left a message at your job a couple of weeks ago, which is how I finally tracked you down, and she called me and said you were out of the country and would be back yesterday. I waited until today to call so you'd have some rest time."

"And what was this friend's name?"

I asked hoping he wasn't going to say Tatiana.

"I think she said Tatiana or something like that."

My heart sank into the pit of my stomach.

I'm going to kill that bitch. She's checking and intercepting my messages now? Has she been intercepting other calls as well? Oh, this means war now! This bitch has got to go.

"Well, what all did the two of you discuss?" I asked, trying to gauge the amount of ammunition my new nemesis now had on me.

"She asked if I was the boyfriend that you bragged so much about from DC. That did my heart some good to know you still talked about me. She said you still missed me and talked about me all the time. I was kind of surprised myself being you left and never tried to call. She told me you were upset because you lost your phone and had no way of contacting me anymore."

My blood was boiling as I listened.

He continued. "She said you live on Roosevelt Island, and have a big position now. She suggested I come up and surprise you, but I thought against trying to surprise you. I didn't know what your relationship status was and I didn't want to get my feelings crushed. But she insisted you haven't been able to move on into a new relationship because you were so hung up on this mystery guy in DC. She said that's why you keep so busy with work—to try to help ease the pain."

"So what did you tell her about us, Eric?"

"I told her that we were in love and were really close, but that asshole ex-husband was causing you so much grief that you had to leave DC. I told her we were almost inseparable before you left. She said that was all the more reason I need to come to New York and reclaim my love. So when can I come and see my baby?"

I was flabbergasted. I couldn't believe this was happening to me. Not me!

"Eric, I hate to burst your bubble, but that person is not any friend of mine. I have never mentioned you beyond the day I left Maryland. I am in a serious relationship, and you don't stand a chance in hell," I shot with every ounce of venom in me.

"Damn, that's some cold shit. You think you could have kicked me a little harder?"

"I'm sorry if your feelings are hurt, but you set yourself up for that one. You sucked up every lie that bitch told you and believed what you wanted to believe. I am happy and have moved on with my life, not stuck on yesterday."

"I mean do you think there's any way that we could sit down and talk about this over a cup of coffee or something?"

"I don't think so. Maybe in our next lifetime, but not this one."

"Shawnee, I know you have to miss the way I made love to you. I know how much I miss you."

I can't lie; my pussy was contracting at the mere mention of the memory. No man has ever made me feel as good as Mandingo. Not even Brad. Damn, the thought of a 6'8 Mandingo dick inside of me. WHEW!! Now I'm sweating from the thought.

No, Shawnee! Down, girl!

The Queen

"Eric, I appreciate that you miss me and all, but if you have ever cared anything about me, you'll let me go and be happy. I am happy right now, and want to stay this way."

"Your friend said you're not happy."

Once again, anger took over. "That bitch is not my friend!" I yelled. "She only tried to use you to interfere with my happiness, because she wants my man for her damn self. And thanks to your call, you just gave me grounds to fire the heifer. Now I can be extra happy. Thanks!"

"Aw, man, I wasn't trying to do all that. I just wanted to see you again. To make love to you again. I wanted to be able to hold you in my arms again. Taste your love juices again. Can I have that? I would do whatever humanly possible to make you happier than you are now."

Now why he gotta be talking about tasting and all? Damn, I miss his large hands all over my body. Oh, how I miss the way he'd try all kinds of new sexual tricks, and would dance for me. I still get turned on each time I hear Johnny Gill or R. Kelly songs. And don't let it be a Keith Sweat song. Oh, my!

"Shawnee, I know whoever you're with now don't have a tongue that can tickle your cervix like I used to do to you."

He sure ain't told no lie there.

"I bet your pussy is juicing up right now at the thought," he said, exposing a truth. "Why don't you meet me just one time and if you can look me in my eyes and tell me you don't ever want to see me again, I won't ever bother you again. Just one time, Shawnee."

I am so confused. Why is he doing this to me? How can he still have this kind of effect on me? What am I going to do?

"Eric, please don't call me again!" I said before I hung up on him.

I have to tell Brad before Tatiana can do any more damage. She has to go. To hell with trying to send her to Europe. She needs to take her evil ass back to Houston, and away from this company. No wonder her own family doesn't like her. After I tell Brad tonight what she did, he'll agree that she needs to be terminated from the company. I'll tell him right before I give him some pussy. That way he'll definitely comply with my wishes.

I'll also have to let Harmony know before she gets blindsided by Tatiana's warped version. Perhaps I just may let Brad know that I would consider marriage if and when he'd propose. Elaine made some valid points. I do love him.

Damn! Why did Eric have to call now? How am I going to make love to Brad without thinking about Eric? I wonder if I could fuck Eric just one last time before I marry Brad. Then I could feel guilty and know for certain I should marry Brad.

Stop it, Shawnee! Come back to your senses, girl. No more Eric. He's like a drug. You can't hit it just once and walk away.

Oh, my pussy is aching. Damn that Tatiana!

I certainly wasn't going to let Tatiana leave town without confronting her. I caught up with her ass outside of her fitness center. She didn't even seem the least bit stressed or worried about having just lost her job. She almost seemed as if she were expecting me to catch up with her.

"So how exactly did you think you were going to get away with doing the shit you've been doing?" I asked as quick as she stepped out the door. All kinds of thoughts were running through my mind... particularly to *kick her ass*. "Didn't you think by giving him my phone number, he'd call and let me know what you'd done?"

"I figured, 'may the best woman win'," she callously responded looking unfazed as she sauntered down the street as if she didn't have a care in the world, with me close on her heels.

"Huh?" What the hell is she talking about?

The Queen

She stopped and turned to face me with her hands on her hips. "You don't love Brad, and I think you need to be exposed for the fake you are. You're nothing more than a tramp and a user who has fucked her way to the top. I'm the one Brad really wants to be with, but he can't just get rid of you without having corporate backlash. And yes, he told me this when we were together, after we made passionate love."

WHOO!!!!!!! OH LAWD!! OH NO THE HELL SHE DIDN'T!!! Okay, this should be the part when I pop her in the eye. I spied my busy surroundings as I searched for someone to save me from myself, or to see if I could get away with it. My mind raced with thoughts of dropping her bony ass to the ground in the middle of Manhattan. She has to know all of these people passing by are her saving grace. Why else would she talk shit to me like that... now?

She continued taunting me. "And a truly wonderful lover he is. He enjoys every inch of this perfectly toned body, being as you're not all that toned anymore since you're getting old and busy. Too busy for the gym these days, huh, Shawnee? Or did you think Brad wouldn't appreciate this?" she said pointing to her perfect figure.

Now see, this bitch wants me to go to jail. That, or she has a death wish. "Only in your imagination would you fuck Brad. Brad wouldn't want you because you're too stupid. Don't you think I'm smart enough to know that Brad would not have let you move to New York and work day in and day out with me if he wanted to fuck you? He would have kept your dumb ass in Houston on the down-low. You dumb bitch!" I chuckled, knowing I had one up on her.

"Well, I guess that's where you are the dumb bitch. He brought me to New York so I'd be closer to him and able to spend more time with him. He sent your dumb ass overseas so we could be together more. I've probably spent more time in Brad's bed this year than you have. And he loves when I come into his office for one of our private meetings." She sensually closed her eyes and hugged herself then looked me coldly, straight in the eye with a smile. "That's usually when my tits are in his mouth and his fingers are in my pussy digging for honey. And when we're out in public together, he can't keep his hands off of me. Unlike you, I don't have a problem with us being seen together, affectionately in public. And if you don't want to take my word for it, check with the horse carriage workers in Central Park that catch an eyeful each time we ride."

Her lying ass! Please let this girl be lying. I know she's not standing in my face telling me that MY Brad shipped me overseas so he could fuck her at will. Shit. The timing was right when she came to New York. And how would she know about my inhibitions of being publicly affectionate with Brad?

She continued to lay it on. "I mean get real, Shawnee. Did you think you had the only game in town? You may have a lot of tits, but Brad prefers perky—like mine. And you may have a lot of junk in your trunk, but this is the kind of ass that turns Brad on—a toned one that doesn't jiggle. And while you insist on keeping your hair cut shorter and dyke-ish, Brad loves running his fingers through and pulling my hair while we are fucking. And he eats this tight pussy marvelously, unlike your overused pussy. As long as Brad wants it, I'm going to keep giving it to him, because I really do love Brad, which is more than you can say. I have no problem telling him I love him. What about you, Shawnee? When's the last time you told him you loved him, or have you? So he had to terminate me from the company as a matter of policy for what I did to you, but trust that we will still be together whenever and wherever we can, and you can't stop that. When we get married, since I know Brad is quite anxious to marry at this stage of his life, you must know that your trampy ass will be booted from the company so fast you won't know what hit you.

"Oh, and I'm dying for you to confront him about what I just told you. That way you could get the fuck out of the picture and let us be

The Queen

happy together. After all, I don't want him fucking you anymore, anyway. I've only tolerated it because I knew he was in a complicated situation with the company and all. And I can see the heat in your pathetic eyes and bawled up fists that you want to put your hands on me. I wish you would. I really wish you would so I could have your fat ass locked up and away from my Brad and his company."

Oh my goodness! I can't believe this shit. Does this bitch know I would kill her with my bare hands? She's got to be trying to push my buttons. That's it: she's just fucking with me. Oh, fuck this, I need answers! How long has this shit been going on? Is she serious or is she trying to play mind games? She's saying just what Elaine said, about her taking Brad and getting rid of me. That cheating motherfucker! Why did I know that Tatiana would be the one bitch he'd go for? Or is she lying? How can I know for sure? If he fucked her, I'd marry him just to take everything he owns. Then he could have her ass. The bitch!

I tried to maintain the composed front so she wouldn't know she rattled me. I went one better and even forced a smile. "Tatiana, I'm glad you really believe in that warped fucking brain of yours that you could ever take Brad from me. Keep believing that shit. Obviously, you haven't received the memo about who really runs shit around here. I run it, bitch! And I'd highly suggest you get your bony ass back on the night plane to Houston, before you have to find out the rude way who runs this shit. As far as putting my hands on you, I don't have to. I know too many people to make your ass disappear, and become part of some permanent foundation on a construction site, not to be seen or heard from ever again. Not even a decent funeral or burial, because you'd just be 'missing.' Maybe you're fucking Brad, maybe you're not, but whatever the case, you won't be ever again. Now you have a choice: you could leave, go back to Houston voluntarily and see another day, or you could hang around and call my bluff. Your choice."

"Are you threatening my life, Shawnee? I think I could have you locked up for that." She tried to act all innocent with her southern accent and placing her hands to her chest. "Oh, my goodness! Imagine how Brad is going to feel when I tell him that you threatened me. You threatened my life just because I love him and exposed you and the deception you have been playing with him. And he'll believe me because you're here at my gym stalking me right now." She wickedly smiled. "Then when you're locked up and out of the company and Brad's life, he can have all the pussy he wants, whenever he wants, and he won't have you to be worried about trying to sue him or his company. 'Cause you do know that's the only reason you're still around. He doesn't want to get sued by you. He put you overseas because he wants to be with me without any complications, and I am so very grateful to him for doing that for us. For our relationship. For our love." She laughed. "And silly you, I will still be with Brad in Houston if I move back. Oh, but you've never been to his home in Houston, have you? That's where we've made so many wonderful memories. How do I know you've never been? He's told me that as well. Everyone in Houston knows we've been a couple for some time before I came to New York to be with Brad. He was only worried about how you'd deal with my being here. He said you were a bit rough around the edges, and didn't want us to have any confrontations."

I laughed when I had a thought that I knew would surely shut down her gibberish. "Since he's so into you, why would he let me know how you tried to flash your tits in his face, but he had to admonish you for your behavior? Doesn't sound like much of a relationship? Like I said, you sound delusional."

Tatiana laughed hysterically. "Oh, you silly girl. Is that what he told you?" She laughed harder and then got serious as she folded her arms across her bosom. "Surely that must have been the time that I was sitting on his desk with his fingers in my pussy and his mouth covering

my bosom. His secretary walked in unannounced and saw my uncovered tits right before his face with one of my feet propped up on the arm of his chair, which allowed him access to my pussy. Unfortunately, she didn't get to witness his hand under my hiked up skirt or his mouth on my breast. Oh, and she also missed the part when he put his face between my legs and was licking my waxed clit. She had to have seen my bare ass on his desk, since my skirt was pushed up. What she did see made her close the door quickly and kept her nosey ass out ever since, when she knows I'm in the office with Brad. Perhaps that's the story he told you because he thought you might get wind of my having my tits in his face. The tits he had just been sucking on." Tatiana laughed again. "That Brad, he's something else. That was clever of him. And he admonished me?" she laughed.

That lying bastard! He lied about her tits being exposed? He didn't mention that she was right in his face with them.

"Shawnee, we fucked in his office that same day after his secretary left. He said his erection just wouldn't go down from earlier that day, and he was going to burst if he couldn't get his dick into my tight pussy. He also didn't want to be alone that night, so we spent the rest of the night together at his house, where we fucked for several more hours. If you need me to describe his big dick to you in detail, I can. I can also describe his bedroom. You still seem a bit unconvinced.

"So obviously while you think you're running game on him, the game is on you. You are the game, Shawnee. A fucking joke is more like it. I was just trying to be nice by helping you hook back up with your ex. That way you'd have somebody when Brad and I marry, after he kicks your ass to the curb."

I stepped right in Tatiana's space. "I'll just tell you this one fucking time, keep your ass here in New York and see what happens to you. Fuck with Brad one more time, and it'll be your last day breathing."

Tatiana didn't flinch one bit. "Well actually, since you're scheduled to head back out to Holland tomorrow morning, I'll be fucking him then. Apparently you're not enough woman for him, so we already have plans to get together. Thanks to your having me released from the company, I have a bit more time available for Brad now."

I laughed this time. "I guess he forgot to tell you he's going out of town tomorrow as well?"

She laughed back. "An eight pm flight to Chicago. You do the math. Your flight leaves at six am and his at eight pm. Do you know how many orgasms we'll have in that amount of time? So, Shawnee, don't think for a moment that your hollow threats mean a thing to me. And if I choose to return to Houston, that will be mine and Brad's decision. Not yours. Now if you'll excuse me, I'm due for my bikini waxing appointment. I like to keep the pussy straight for my man."

Then she turned and stepped away smiling with a wink of the eye. I wanted to just snatch her ass by her hair and swing her to New Jersey. She knows our flight schedules. Did he tell her?

Of course when I confronted Brad with this revelation, he completely denied everything and said Tatiana was obviously trying to get under my skin. Those sounded like facts, but then most crazy people tend to have all their facts from stalking and breaking into files and shit. We already know she somehow was able to intercept my phone messages.

Let me come back from Holland and find out she's still in New York. If she's fucking him, she better get her last fuck in before I return. Otherwise I will let Elaine know to find a crackhead to slice her ass up.

I wish I had let the bitch give me details about Brad's dick or bedroom. Then I'd know he is lying to me. But if I give him the boot, she'll move right on in, marry him as she said, and try to push me out of the company. That shit ain't ever going to happen. You can believe that! I don't know why I stood there and let her tell me all that shit. Glutton for punishment at its finest. Once upon a time, she would have gotten a quick beat down. I think I just needed to hear what I suspected would be, once I saw her ass in Cancun.

I don't know what to believe right now. Wilhelmina Wiggins didn't raise any fools. I have to look out for Shawnee: Number One. That's all there is to it. He's making me the successor of his company. Oh, she can be a piece of pussy on the side if she wants to. Then again . . . No the fuck she won't!

16
Kelly

"Sean, why all the surprises? Where are we going and how did you charter a plane?" I asked pulling a small suitcase from my closet.

"Blah, blah, blah, blah, blah! That's what I just heard. Now be quiet and get packing," he answered.

Sean is so wonderful. Every time I see him, he's surprising me with something.

"What about my clients? You know I have a business to run," I asked, knowing full well I'd cleared some time on my calendar to spend with Sean.

"You'll be back in twenty-four hours."

"Twenty-four hours? Promise?"

"I promise." He wrapped his arms around my waist. "I love you."

"I love you too," I answered before kissing him.

I can't be certain when we got to the "I love you" stage, but it warms my soul each time he tells me. I guess that must really mean that I do love him.

Elaine won't let me mention Sean's name to her. I think she's just jealous I have a man who loves me and treats me like a queen, while her life is empty and only occupied with her shoe stores. Now with

The Queen

Shawnee's career and her old man, I barely get an opportunity to speak with her. Each time I call, she's so busy or out of the country. I hate calling Harmony now because all she does is complain about her miserable pregnancy.

And Sandy, all she speaks about is that low-life Lewis. I'm half-tempted to tell her about Charise and Lewis just so she'll shut up about him. I was enjoying our conversation when she told me about the new church she started attending that her friend told her about. But of course, the conversation had to shift to how much Lewis enjoys the church and how he's so much more active in this smaller church. That was my cue to end the call before I spewed information I had been forbidden by my sisters to share.

I made the mistake of calling Charise to check on her after I heard about some lunatic woman showing up at her house. I was totally disgusted when Charise told me it was her who anonymously got word to the woman that she was screwing the poor woman's husband. Charise said the woman came to her crying and showing *happy photos* of her family. She begged Charise to leave her family alone. Charise told the woman that she needs to take it up with her husband. After all that, Charise is still messing with this married man, talking about how he has the longest dick. As she put it, "You don't throw a big fish back into the ocean when you catch one."

And on top of that, she's fucking Lewis too. Elaine told me that Angelo told her that Charise is fucking some pervert through a wall at a motel where she meets Lewis. Now I'm just trying to visualize this. How do you fuck someone through a wall? That there would take a super-sized dick.

And poor Jarod; Charise didn't bother trying to show up for the custody hearing. She lost all parental rights. Thankfully when I called Arnold, he said he would never deny any of us from seeing our nephew. When I tried talking to Charise about being a mother, her response was, "At least now I can get as much dick as I want." I swear, there is no reasoning with her.

Harmony was pissed when I told her Charise fucked Todd's son and his nephew at her wedding, but both Sandy and Shawnee had already beat me to it, although they made me promise not to say anything. She said she was done with Charise. She said there isn't a textbook she has ever studied to help get through to Charise. Harmony doesn't want Todd to ever find out about it. She feels her pregnancy is hard enough, and she doesn't need any added complications in her marriage. Hopefully there won't be any big family gatherings that will include Charise and Todd's family. Knowing Charise the way I do, she'd let it be known at the function.

Sean had us taken to the airport by limousine. Talk about a class act. When we were many thousands of miles in the sky on this gorgeous private plane, Sean got down on one knee in front of me. He pulled out a small black box and revealed a beautiful, flawless three-carat diamond.

"Kelly Wiggins, I know we haven't been together that long, but I knew the first day I laid eyes on you, that you were the one. The one I wanted in my life forever. I knew each time we were apart and my life went back to feeling empty and lost, that I needed you in my life. And each time you are in my arms, I know I don't ever want to lose you. Please accept this ring as my offer to devote the rest of my life making you the happiest woman on this earth. Kelly, will you accept my hand in marriage and become my wife?" Sean asked with tear-filled eyes.

I was speechless. I didn't know what to say. No one has ever said such wonderful words to me. Hell, no man has ever come close to asking me to marry him. All I could do was cry as Sean placed the ring on my finger.

The Queen

What am I supposed to say? I need my sisters. Help! What am I going to do?

I couldn't speak. Sean kissed me so passionately when he realized I couldn't speak. Suddenly his kiss was more powerful than ever. All I could do was to kiss him back. It seemed like the right thing to do.

When he came up for air, he opened a bottle of champagne as my eyes were hypnotized by the rock on my finger. Then he said as he handed me a glass of champagne, "If you think this has you speechless, wait 'til you see where we are headed." He held up his glass to toast. "To you Kelly, the one woman who was finally able to bring sunshine and joy to my gloomy heart." He clinked my glass before we drank the champagne.

We spent the remainder of what seemed like an eternity in mostly silence. Sean held me in his arms so tightly, like he was afraid I'd somehow slip off the jet.

God, I need to call my sisters. This is a 9-1-1 call situation.

We arrived in Chicago and took another limo to a place called Sybaris. The place was like some hidden paradise. The suite Sean booked for us provided endless lovemaking opportunities. I lost count of the number of hours of pure, passionate, love we shared.

At some point in the midst of passion, I heard the word escape from my lips, "Yes."

"Yes?" he asked stopping mid-stroke.

"Yes. Yes, I'll be your wife. I would love to be your wife, Sean. Just promise me it will be forever. Don't ever let me be someone's ex-wife.

After passionately kissing me, he answered, "Kelly, I promise you will be my wife and I'll be your only husband until the day we die."

After some more kissing and lovemaking we finally found time to eat. Boy, did I work up an appetite. Sean had to order more food.

When we arrived back in DC the following evening, we shared a romantic evening at National Harbor before heading home for some more lovemaking that took us into the morning. I hated Sean having to leave and return to L.A., but then I couldn't wait to get my sisters on the phone to share my good news.

"What the fuck do you mean 'married'?" Elaine yelled for all of California to hear once we were all on a conference call, minus Charise.

"Elaine, stop being so hard on her. Try being happy for someone else for a change," Sandy said in my defense.

"Fuck that shit! I'm with Elaine on this one," Shawnee contributed. "I don't like that sneaky bastard either. I still believe he drugged her that first go-round."

"Kelly, what do you know about this man?" Harmony asked.

"What did you know about Todd when you packed up your life to move to Houston in record time?" I rebutted, feeling totally defensive by their insensitivity.

By her tone, it was apparent that I hit a nerve.

"I'll have you know that I met Todd during my relocation to Houston. Todd is *NOT* the reason I moved to Houston. He was an added bonus. Furthermore, we didn't rush off to get married. Also, I had an opportunity to meet his family and friends to help me with my decision. This guy, on the other hand, hasn't introduced you to anyone. He keeps you hemmed up in bed when you're in L.A. What do you know about his finances or his family? Todd fully disclosed his finances and the family drama to me while we were dating," Harmony shot back.

"Puhlease! He is loaded. Do you know how much he gives me and does for me? Not to mention he has a big-ass house in Santa Monica, his own record company, and several cars."

The Queen

"Okay, so he's a perpetrator who's probably riddled with debt," Elaine's pessimistic ass said. "My goodness! You sound almost as dumb as Charise."

"Whoa! That's the ultimate insult." Sandy laughed.

Shawnee and Harmony also laughed.

"Fuck you and Charise. Don't ever classify me with that nut," I angrily said. "Just because I got engaged, doesn't mean I'm rushing to get married next week."

"Nope, you'll go the week after next," Shawnee said, laughing again.

"Kelly, why haven't you run your typical background check on this guy?" Harmony asked. "I just wish you would keep your head when it comes to this guy. Maybe he could be a great guy, but you don't know a thing about him. Check into his finances, before his debt becomes your debt. Make sure he's not one of those guys using credit cards to buy you all those gifts to woo you, and racking up endless debt, only for you to find out it was some trap. Find out more about his business and be certain his business is flourishing. Also, make sure he's not financially backed by drug money or shady characters. Find out if he has some unclaimed children in the world who will come back and haunt you once you're married. I know you are not looking to be anyone's mother anytime soon, and especially not a stepmother, so just check him out."

"I think that's reasonable, Kelly," Sandy said. "Check him out, and you'll have my blessing."

"I don't think any of you would ever accept Sean no matter how squeaky clean his finances and background are," I said.

Elaine scoffed, "You got that shit right! I don't like him and never will."

"I'm going to second that. I don't think I'll ever like him either. Even at the gala, he hardly spoke to us or tried to get to know your family," Shawnee cosigned.

"Funny, I don't recall ever meeting your old white man," I spat back as I paced my living room floor, angry that I thought I could talk to my sisters and have their respect and support.

"Yes, you did. He was at the New York boutique grand opening. You were busy working. Remember?" Elaine answered.

"Well speaking of my old white man, I have decided that I will marry him when he officially asks me," Shawnee said so blasé.

"Wow! That's wonderful, Shawnee," Sandy said.

"Yay! I am so proud of you Shawnee. You took my advice. I know it wasn't an easy decision," Elaine said with pure excitement.

"Shawnee, that is wonderful. Congratulations!" Harmony added.

"Thank you guys, but it's not official yet. I only let him know that I would accept a proposal from him. The ball is in his court now," Shawnee answered.

"Now ain't this some shit! I say I'm getting married and you all are doom and gloom. Shawnee says she's getting married AGAIN and it's the best thing in the world. You all are a bunch of hypocrites," I said as my angry tears flowed.

"Hold up! And what the fuck is that supposed to mean... AGAIN?" Shawnee asked, clearly annoyed by my statement.

"Kelly, Shawnee knows everything about Brad. Without even being married, he made Shawnee his successor for the company," Elaine interrupted. "Oh, and I can't forget, she has known him more than a few damn weeks."

"I've known Sean more than a few weeks. We've been together for months now," I answered.

"Kelly, I can't put it any simpler: You don't know Sean. Just slow things down and get to know him," Harmony said. "Shawnee's rela-

145

tionship has nothing to do with your need to get to know the man you're talking about marrying."

"And whatever you do, don't give that bitch any of your money. That's probably all he's after since he's trying to move so fast," Elaine contributed.

"You know I don't need this shit from you bitches. Fuck you all!" I said before hanging up.

I couldn't hear another word from them. Why can't they just be happy I finally found someone to make me happy? And then try to classify me with Charise. Hell, I bet even Charise will be happy when I tell her. At least she's not so damn judgmental like the others. She may have her flaws, but she has a heart of gold and accepts people as they are. I'm sure she would like Sean. But then again, I don't think I'd have Sean anywhere near Charise. She has boundary issues. Still, she's not judgmental.

17
Charise

"I don't know if I'm going to make it for your graduation, Angelo. You already know there's going to be some shit. No one wants me at any of the functions."

"Charise, I want you at my graduation next week. You don't have to sit with the others, and you could stay at my buddy's place instead of Elaine's house. I miss your crazy ass. Plus, I want you to meet my friends and check out our new business," Angelo pleaded through the telephone.

"I know this means a lot to you, but I'm really not feeling a whole lot of drama."

"Now you know you keep drama going, girl. Your name is Charise 'Drama' Wiggins." He laughed. "Please Charise, don't let me down. Even Harmony is coming—pregnant and all."

"I don't know, Angelo. I'll sleep on it and let you know. I have a date I'm getting ready for, so I'll give you a call tomorrow."

"Wait. Before you sleep on it, let me give you this tidbit of added info," Angelo said in his 'I've got some juicy gossip' voice.

"What?"

The Queen

"Kelly called your sisters to announce she's getting married, and they ripped her apart," he said.

"Duh, I already know. Kelly told me," I answered.

"Yeah, but Kelly is going to bring his shiesty ass to the graduation, and you know your sisters are going to have a field day on ole boy. So while you are thinking you are going to be the focus, Kelly and her fiancé will be. I wish you could meet him too. You'd probably see him just like the rest of us do."

"Why would I give a shit? If Kelly is happy, I think her family should support her. And if he turns out 'shiesty' as you say, that's for Kelly to determine, not her family. Her family should be there if she's hurt and needs them. Not always trying to put her down . . . or me for that matter. Angelo, I have to go now. I have a date," I said trying to rush my baby brother off of the phone.

"Who are you meeting? Lewis?" he asked with obvious disapproval in his voice.

"No, Ang, I'm not meeting Lewis. His punk ass has been kind of scarce since he's been going to their new church."

"Well, how come you can't tell me who? You always tell me everything else. What's up with that?"

"Angelo, I promise I'll call you tomorrow with all the details, but right now, I've gotta go. Love you, little brother."

"Whatever, you skank ho!" Angelo laughed, hanging up on me before I could get him first.

'Skank ho' is his nickname for me. Coming from Angelo, I can laugh, but those other bitches better not fix their mouths to say that shit.

I didn't want to tell Angelo about my date because I didn't want him to talk me out of it. I also couldn't tell him because I don't know the guy's name or what he looks like. I decided that I want to go all the way with my mystery man at the motel. So now I'm going to just show up and go straight to his room. I told him I would, but he never speaks, so I really don't know if he's going to open his door for me. I'm also afraid of what he looks like. Hopefully he's not some hideous looking creature that will nauseate me. I got to stick my hand in the hole and held his entire fat dick in my hand until he came in it. Ever since that day, I've wanted his dick inside me. When I asked him to come into my room, he didn't respond. He just put his hand through the wall and summoned me to come closer for him to touch me. I always have to play on his terms. Tonight it'll be on my terms. Hopefully.

As soon as he opens the door, I'm going to flash him my tits. I think that'll convince him to let me in. If push comes to shove, I'll have to settle for the wall fuck, and then go to the bar or a club to see what I can find. I'm hoping I won't have to do that. Even Lewis is starting to bore me. I'd prefer Lewis watching me fuck someone else. That turns me on more. Lately, the only excitement I get out of fucking Lewis is the fact that the "wall-man" is going to finish me off as best as he can through the wall with his super sized dildo and hand. I want his real dick inside of me—inside my mouth. Maybe after I get what I want, I can stay away from that funky motel.

~~~

When I arrived at the motel at nine pm (because I wanted it to be dark when he tried to see out his peephole and just open the door), I knocked and heard nothing. I stayed close to the door so he wouldn't be able to get a good look through the peephole or the window near the door. I did see the curtain move, which told me he was trying to see through the window. I decided to knock more persistently. After ten minutes of knocking with no response, I debated my next move. My feelings were so hurt. I don't know why this meant so much to me. Leaned up against the doorframe in frustration, I finally decided to give up. I decided not to get the room next door and give this man any more

The Queen

cheap thrills. Instead, I would just go to a bar and make some poor desperate fool lucky tonight.

As I began walking away I was stopped by the sound of the door slightly opening and exposing a completely dark room. I wasn't sure what to do. I was kind of scared to go in the dark room.

What the hell? I've come too far to turn away now.

I entered the dark room through the narrow opening and was greeted by a stench that made me want to turn back around. As quickly as I entered, the door was closed and locked. It was so dark that I couldn't see him. His hands quickly found my breasts in the darkness. He was behind me fondling my breasts. He hungrily reached under my light sweater and found my bare mounds. He groaned like Frankenstein. Then he was rubbing his groin against my backside as best he could with his six-month-pregnant-like protruding belly set atop of his narrow hips. I figure he must be at least six feet tall. I reached behind me and felt the smelly, threadbare flannel bathrobe covering his naked body.

He guided me through the dark to the bed, where he laid me down on my back with my knees off the bed. After he peeled off my sweater, he pushed up my miniskirt, exposing my naked pussy to the darkness. Without warning, he pushed my legs apart and his mouth was slobbering in my pussy. He made all kinds of animal noises as he slobbered and sucked. He lifted and spread my thighs as far as he could. I felt his tongue deep inside of my pussy. As I was in this deep state of ecstasy, I realized I didn't feel any sort of teeth in his mouth making contact with my vagina. I placed my hands on his head trying to get some type of image of the man the dark was hiding. I could feel the stubble on his face and that his wooly-hairline wrapped around the back of his head only. His head was huge—fat more like it. I put my finger in my pussy and then pushed the finger in his wet mouth. Just as I thought: no teeth.

Eew! This man is really old.

He put his fingers in my pussy, while he continued to suck my clit. He was sucking the piss out of my urethra.

His other hand desperately fondled my tits. Then he brought his mouth up to slobber and suck my tits. I could smell the heavy alcohol as he got nearer to my nose. Hell, I might need a few drinks to fuck him. This may be tougher than I had imagined. But those fingers felt magical in my pussy. He used his free hand to guide my hand to his hardened dick. Then his hand went back to assisting him with the hungry sucking of my breast. It all was feeling so good; even his dick in my hand felt good. I actually wanted to suck it, but his breath was a beast. He has his own agenda. He sat me up and stood before me with his leg up. The scent from between his legs instantly brought the word "homeless" to mind. His dick found my lips. My gasping only invited his dick into my mouth. So I did what I do best—I sucked him senseless. I felt so empowered by the thought of no one having the opportunity to make him weak in the knees as I was doing him. I just did my best not to inhale his rank odor. He pushed his dick way in the back of my throat, while his hands firmly held my neck as if choking me. It was as if he knew I was trying to hold my breath. In no time I was swallowing a big wad of cum. Then he turned me over on my stomach. I wasn't sure what he was about to do. He parted my butt cheeks and dug his tongue into my asshole. Once his face was deeply buried in my ass, his fingers fondled my clit. This stinky old dude has some mad skills. My ass was bucking like a wild animal. The more I bucked, the deeper his tongue and fingers went.

He briefly stopped and disappeared in the dark as I tried catching my breath. Then he reappeared, turning me on my back with my ass off the bed. He held my legs up, raising my ass upwards. He bent enough to insert his dick into my asshole. I wanted to protest. That wasn't supposed to be part of the plan. After he was fully inserted in my asshole,

he slightly parted my thighs and attempted to insert a dildo into my pussy.

Damn this is a freaky old man.

And he used a fat dildo. Although the combination was painful, it felt sensational. When he pulled both the dildo and his penis out, he went back into the bathroom. He still didn't turn on any lights. The abundance of dripping sweat in my eyes kept my eyes from adjusting in the darkness, but I could make out what appeared to be piles and piles of newspapers stacked around the small room. I could hear the water running from the bathroom. I laid there on the bed, uncertain what I should do. I wasn't sure if I should wait for some more sex from him or if he was done.

He doesn't speak. How will I know when he's done?

Mystery man made his way back to the side of the bed. His hand fondled my pussy while his mouth bent in to find a nipple to hungrily chew on. He sat on the corner of the bed and lifted me on top of him with my legs wrapped around his back. He leaned me backward as he worked his fat dick into my aching pussy. Then he slightly leaned back, which caused me to lean forward, as he inserted his thick middle finger into my asshole. I fucked him the best way I could in that position as I continued to talk dirty to him. He picked me up and carried me a few steps away to a dresser covered with papers and dirty smelling clothing. As I lay on my back, his dick continued to go in and out of my pussy. He took me back to the center of the bed and fucked me until I felt his hot explosion inside of me. After he pulled out, he laid next to me, and his hand went back to massage my pussy. I laid on my back with one knee raised to receive his sensual massage. Since he wasn't going to speak to me, I figured I'd have to do all the "pillow talking."

"I just want you to know you really made me feel very good and I'm glad you opened the door. I was really hurt when I thought you weren't going to let me in. All I could think about each time I left this motel is what being with you would feel like. I'd get so turned on."

He started massaging harder and his finger would occasionally peep inside my pussy as he rubbed. I was getting turned on again. I think I was turning him on by my telling him I was turned on from thinking about him.

So I continued to talk. "All I wanted was to have your big fat dick inside me, banging the walls of my wet pussy." His fingers were fully inserted on that note. "I wanted that tongue licking all over these big titties, and I wanted you to suck my whole breast. As much as would fit in your mouth. One at a time."

With that, he granted my wish. I was juicing all over his hand. My orgasm contracted my vaginal muscles around his fingers. I reached over for his dick and rubbed despite our awkward position. He moved his dick closer so I could grip it in its entirety. As he moaned, his mouth was nuzzled in my neck and around my ear, I stroked his dick harder and his fingers returned the favor in my pussy.

We were both moaning and groaning. Then the unthinkable occurred. His tongue was in my mouth. I tried to squirm away, but his mouth locked onto mine. As I tried to squirm away, he seemed to become a bit more forceful and overpowering. His fingers left my pussy and found my asshole. I stopped fondling his dick and tried to push him off of me. He kept his mouth locked onto mine, slobbering in my open mouth. His fingers went deeper in my ass, and didn't feel as good. Then he climbed on top of me, finally taking his mouth from mine. He was making animal noises as he forcefully spread my legs apart. I told him I needed to leave now, but he ignored me. He rammed his dick into my pussy and forcefully fucked me. He kept a strong grip on me to prevent my escape. I had mixed feelings. On one hand I felt like I was being raped by this stranger. On the other hand, it felt good.

The Queen

I was becoming afraid of this man. I figured I should go along with it to help him hurry up so I can get out of here. Thankfully my miniskirt was still wrapped around my waist, but I had no idea where my sweater or purse with my keys was at that point. I needed him to help me find my stuff. I had to get him happy with me. I *oohed* and *aahed* so he would feel like I was enjoying him still.

Finally the bastard came. Probably thirty seconds later, he was feeling around for something. Then he pulled me by my hand, lifting me from the bed, led my topless body toward the door, opened it and pushed me out of his room. He threw my sweater and purse out on the ground. My skirt was still hiked up around my waist. The guys loitering outside the motel witnessed my nudity and started whistling. Three of the guys came and started groping my breasts and ass as I tried to collect the spilled contents of my purse. I grabbed my keys and my wallet and left everything else. I ran to my car, leaving my top on the ground. I got in my car and took off as quick as I could, crying and shaking.

What went wrong here? Things were going so great. Now I have to make it from my car down that long walkway to my building, topless.

Thankfully I'd worn strappy sandals, which remained on the whole time. Otherwise I would have lost those also.

That's the last time I try some crazy shit like that.

When I made it safely into my apartment, I laughed at the experience, and then I found myself getting aroused by the memory of how good wall-man made me feel. I looked down at my still topless breasts as my nipples hardened.

I think I'll take a hot shower and stimulate myself. To hell with going to a bar tonight . . . Well, maybe I'll go take my shower and then go to have a drink. Lord knows I could use one right now. Maybe I could find someone willing to hold me tonight.

18
Elaine

With all the boutiques keeping me busy, I've had absolutely no time for any of my sponsors. Thankfully they understand and haven't placed any pressure on me. I was a bit concerned when I received a bouquet of flowers at the boutique requesting my presence at the Starbucks up the street at 2:00 pm. I started not to go, but curiosity was getting the better of me. After all, we're talking about a public place in the height of the day. When I arrived, I grabbed a juice and pastry to soothe my growling stomach and sat to wait and to see who I was being summoned by.

Lo and behold, Robert sits across from me almost as quickly as I sat down.

"You have got to be kidding? What the fuck!"

"Hello, Elaine. It's been a while, and I miss seeing you. I was hoping you could make some time for me this afternoon."

"Robert, in case you didn't know, I have a business to run. I don't have time for you and your gay activities anymore."

"Well, I think you'd want to make time for me. It would be in your best interest," he cockily responded.

The Queen

"I don't need the money anymore, Robert. I have a good business now."

"I'm sure the IRS would be interested to know how you supported your good business."

I had the *stupid* look on my face as I tried to process what he said. "What did you just say to me? Surely you didn't just threaten me with the IRS."

"I have a room booked, and I want you there in thirty minutes. There's sixty-five thousand waiting for you there. I strongly suggest you be there." He placed a sleeved card key on the table that read "1210," in front of me and walked out.

My mind was racing. All I could think about was going to the hotel to kill him. *What the fuck is wrong with this man? Damn, he won't even bother Shawnee, but he's obsessed with me instead. Why? He's gay!*

I couldn't believe he said the IRS of all things. I guess he knew better than to say my family. He probably figured no one would believe him or listen to him. But the IRS? WOW! That's a whole new one. Double wow! I've never heard that threat before. How could I fight the IRS without implicating my many sponsors? I can't use that *gift* line but so much. What if I do what Robert says and he continually tries to use this to have a hold on me?

Robert has to die, that's all there is to it. He's trying to destroy me for some pussy. Or whatever it is he wants from me. Maybe I just need to buy some time with Robert, and go get an IRS attorney. Hell, he said he has $65 thousand for me. I guess I could indulge him this one time. It's not like I've had any form of dick in four months. Shit! Robert's ass wants a dick, not a pussy.

As I step off the elevator onto the 12th floor, my mind was screaming for me to turn back around and run.

I don't know if I can go through with this. I can't let this man destroy me. I need some time to figure out what to do.

While my mind raced outside room 1210, the door opened. He reached out and pulled my apprehensive body into the room.

"Thank you for coming, Elaine. It means a lot to me," he said as if he'd really left me a choice.

I looked around the beautifully decorated suite expecting to see another man come out any moment. There was none. "No other man this time, Robert?" I asked.

"No, Elaine. I just wanted an opportunity to make love to you. No more men for me. I'm done with that phase. I'm strictly into pussy, and right now, the only pussy I want is yours."

I HATE THE WAY HE TALKS!! He has this nerdy-ass, annoying voice that creeps me out. Robert removes his robe and reveals a gorgeous nude body. He lies on the massive bed, large enough to fit six grown people.

"Take your clothes off. I can't wait to see your beautiful body again."

"Don't you need to get your strap-on or whatever and put it nearby?"

"I told you I am not into that stuff anymore. That was an experimental phase for me, and now I'm over it."

"I need to tell you something, Robert."

"Sure, Sweetie," he responded.

Oh, I hate his voice and that "Sweetie" shit.

"The whole trip here, I thought about coming to kill you for trying to blackmail me, but then I realized I don't have to do that because if you ever blackmail me again, I will call your bluff. And if you dare try reporting me and try to destroy me, I won't have anything left to lose and I'm going to just have to kill you. So if I so much as think the IRS is looking in my direction, I am going to kill you, and you won't be able to hide from me. And you better pray they didn't just randomly select me to fuck with, because then I'll still hold you responsible just for thinking or wishing the shit on me."

Robert looked shocked and violated as I said my piece. He looked vulnerable on the large bed.

I continued as I began stripping. "So I trust that this is our very last time together, Robert. One way or another, you will leave me alone." When I was completely naked, I demanded, "Now get your ass off of that bed and come suck my pussy. I don't have all damn day."

Robert obediently crawled between my opened legs as I propped one foot on a stool. He used his two hands to part my waxed pussy lips and buried his face deep within. It didn't take long before my knees buckled on me, forcing Robert to catch me from falling.

He laid me across the two arms of a nicely cushioned chair. He threw one of my legs over the back of the chair while the cushioned arm propped up my hips. My body slightly dipped into the seat of the chair, while my head rested on the other arm. Once again, his face was buried between my legs. His tongue teased my clit like it was his major in college. Damn, it felt so good. Hell, it's been months since I've had any dick. I tried hard not to enjoy it, but when he put his dick in, I was exploding on contact. Robert was impressively creative with that chair.

Eventually he led me to the bed, where he sucked my tits before burying his face back between my legs. He had me feeling wonderful. For a brief moment, I didn't give a shit about him being Shawnee's ex-husband. I didn't want to enjoy it. I really didn't. I thought of the things that made me miserable in my life to resist allowing myself to be so caught up in the rapture. Somehow I got my mind focused on how much I don't want to prostitute my body anymore, and just want to have one man to love me like my sisters.

"Are you crying?" Robert asked when he came up for air and saw the tears streaming from my eyes.

I tried to wipe the tears, "No."

"Oh, my goodness. Elaine, I am so sorry. I am no better than a rapist. Would you please forgive me?" he said pulling me to a standing position.

When he held me in his arms, it made me cry harder. I couldn't believe how emotional I had become. Robert holding me tightly in his arms and trying to wipe away my tears just underscored how much I want to have someone for me when I feel weak or overwhelmed. My sister's ex-husband should not be the one comforting me. I am no better than Charise sleeping with Sandy's husband. When did I become so consumed by the almighty dollar? I've allowed money to rule my soul to the point where I am standing naked with my sister's ex-husband and enjoying it.

"What is wrong with me, Robert?" I managed to mumble through my sobs. "Why am I so obsessed with money? You are my sister's husband for crying out loud. Well, ex-husband, but same thing."

"Funny, I should be asking myself that question." Robert stepped away from me and covered his nakedness. "I had a wonderful marriage and threw everything good away to indulge in my own selfish obsessions and then I subjected you . . ." His voice trailed off as he broke out into his own sob.

I didn't know what to do. Was I supposed to console him now? Not! I decided to go in the bathroom and clean myself up before I returned to the boutique. I'm wondering if he's still going to give me that money. He didn't get much time, but he got to eat and fuck me. That's worth something. There I go again with the money shit.

After I got myself together, I left Robert to sort out his own shit—but not without collecting my fee. This way I don't have to feel like I was just fucking my sister's ex-husband. Instead I'd look at him as just another trick. I felt too emotionally drained to return to the boutique. I

The Queen

called Angelo and told him I need him to cover for me the rest of the day. It's time for some serious soul searching.

I drove around until I saw the ultimate place to go for soul searching. I came upon a church that had inviting, open doors. I took that as my cue to enter. I can't remember the last time I stepped into a church. I found a seat in the large, almost empty sanctuary. There were others scattered, probably also in dire need of a search for their lost soul.

The more I reflected on my life, the more it saddened me. The tears seemed to flow endlessly. I missed my mother. What I wouldn't give to just have a moment to talk to her. I need to tell her how sorry I am for being such a mean and hateful daughter. I've been so ungrateful for all that she has sacrificed in raising seven children.

Daddy, bless his heart, was not much help to her. And when Daddy died, leaving us to struggle even more than before, Mama somehow managed to have all her debts paid and leave us $100,000 each. Six out of seven college graduates is amazing. I didn't see it until now. I felt like she owed me something for not rescuing my life from prostitution and worthlessness. And now with all my wealth, I still feel worthless. Even in death, Mama is trying to rescue my soul. If she didn't provide that money, I would not have had the front money to begin my string of shoe boutiques. Sure, I had plenty of money from prostituting, but none of it was legitimate to start a business without raising an IRS eyebrow.

I guess that's why Robert's threat shook the core of my soul. And although I am happy to have my boutiques, they don't make me happy. Instead, I am a miserable wretch, always inflicting misery on other people's lives.

Starting this moment, I am going to do whatever I must to learn to convert my ugly ways into something good. I'm going to find a way to do more to help my baby sister. I know she is suffering, and all I have done is to make her feel worse about herself. It's no wonder she behaves the way she does. And what mother gives away her own child, but a mother who has no real desire to live? She feels her child is better off without her than to be stuck with an insufficient mother.

Imagine all of our lives if Mama had given up and let us go more than she did emotionally? We'd be so much worse off. My God, I don't even have any children and just being alone without my own husband and kids sucks the life out of my spirit. I could only imagine how Mama had the life sucked out of her when she lost her one true love. And when he died, she spent all those years having to battle Daddy's ugly family. I hate that their ugliness runs through my veins. I picked up where they left off, battering Mama until she was finally defeated and taken down by cancer.

Oh, Lord, please forgive me for my ugly ways. Please forgive me for helping send my mama to an early grave, and all the hateful things I said thereafter. Lord, please forgive me for the wicked ways that I have utilized my body, and the countless acts of adultery I have committed with someone's husband. And more importantly, please forgive me for making you the lowest priority. I want to change that. Please help me to change my ways. Forgive me for never taking the time to thank you, Lord. Thank you for this wake up call and all you have blessed me with despite myself. Amen.

I'm not sure how much time went by, but for the first time, I felt the weight of the world (more likely the burdens I've been carrying) had been lifted from me. Wow, if I knew I could feel this much better, I would have come to a church long ago. As I lifted my head, a hand touched my shoulder.

"Whatever you are going through will get better. You've certainly come to the right place."

I turned around to see where the strange voice was coming from. Didn't give one thought to how horrible my face may be looking after

The Queen

my sobbing. I guess he must have found my face hideous as well, because he dug into his pocket and handed me his embroidered handkerchief.

"I used to come here to unload, but now I come here to give thanks. So trust me when I say, life will get better," the stranger volunteered. He flashed a dazzling white smile.

When I saw how gorgeous he was, I quickly turned away from him because I didn't want to be seen with runny eyeliner (well, actually, I pay for the good stuff that doesn't run).

"Thank you for the handkerchief," I managed to mumble after trying to clear the nasal backwash from my throat.

"It's no problem. I'm going to leave you to your thoughts. I just saw you and you looked so defeated, and I wanted to let you know that everything will get better from this point on. When I first came here in the same state, someone came to tell me the same words, and they were so right." His firm hand patted me once again on my shoulder as he stood up to leave. "Keep your head up."

As much as I was grieving, it wasn't so much that I didn't notice this gorgeous man stood 6'4, wearing a Hugo Boss suit and no wedding ring.

"Wait!" I called out before he could get away. He came and returned to the seat behind me. "How will I know when things are better? I already thought my life was together. Apparently, it's not," I genuinely inquired, although I wanted him to come back.

"Funny, I thought just the same, but realized there were unresolved ghosts that were still haunting my happiness. I didn't find true joy until I found peace. I had to make peace with my ghosts in order to be free from their hold on me," he answered.

"So you had dead people issues also?" I asked, surprised by his words.

He laughed. "No, they weren't quite dead people. They were the ugly parts of Kevin."

"Kevin?"

"Yes, Kevin. Oh, I'm sorry. I didn't introduce myself. I'm Kevin Dobbs. Sorry I can't introduce you to my ghosts. They're all gone." He smiled. "So I take it you have dead people issues?"

"Kind of, sort of. I have Elaine issues, but the people I need to make peace with are now deceased. How do you make peace with the dead?"

"When you make peace with Elaine. That is your name? Elaine?"

"Yes, I'm Elaine Wiggins." I reached behind me to extend my hand for a shake. "So how do I make peace with myself?"

"Well, the place you're at right now is a start. Metaphorically, that is. Once you come to the realization that something is wrong, you break down and have the opportunity to rebuild. The great part of rebuilding is that you can leave the ugly parts off. And if you don't like that, you can tear down and rebuild again until you have the 'you' that has peace and happiness."

"So how long does this process take?" I asked, fully mesmerized by his wisdom.

"If you're wondering if it's going to be an overnight process, I can tell you that it is not. There were many demons involved to make up the ugly person that you feel you have become. Identify those demons, and then learn of them what you can, and then you release them. You have to know your enemy in order to defeat them. Today you are probably identifying one or more of your demons. The ugliness of it caused you to break down. Not everyone who identifies their demons is willing to let them go. They continue to suffer and find no peace," he explained.

I was so taken by his words. They were real. He was real. This man looked like he'd truly found peace in life. That's what I want.

I asked, "So if money is your demon, do you have to get rid of the money to be free?"

Once again he laughed. "Sounds like we have a lot in common. To answer your question, money per se is not your demon. It's the things you do to get that money which are your demons. One person hustles drugs and earns a million dollars, with no regard for what it costs another's life. A businessman creates a widget, which makes your life simpler, and he too earns a million dollars. It's how the million dollars was obtained that's the problem."

"So does the drug dealer who wants to be free of his demons, walk away from the million dollars?"

"There are many former drug dealers who have turned their lives around and stopped selling drugs who went on to become decent, law abiding citizens and used that million dollars in a more positive manner. Some opened rehab centers. Some started record companies to help up and coming artists. I mean, you get the gist. Me, I was obsessed with the dollar, and stepped on anyone to get it no matter what. I was never a drug dealer, but I was the ugly businessman. Yes, I have obtained financial wealth, but then one day found myself in this very seat, sobbing as I found you. I left the company I made billions for and took some time to deal with myself. I now work for myself, but I no longer manipulate or mislead people as I did prior. I am no longer willing to do 'anything' to get the dollar and am no longer a slave to the dollar.

"Believe it or not, business is very good, but I no longer take the credit. I give all credit, honor, and glory to God. That's where it begins, and that's where it ends. Now that I have God in my life, I can't do unethical things and not find chastisement. And when God is in your life, and you find favor in His sight, you begin to live your life in a manner that you believe is pleasing to Him. So now I make it a point to stop in here daily just to say 'Thank you.' Of course I could say 'thank you' from anywhere, but this is just my personal preference."

"You truly seem to have it all together, and I am usually a good judge of character. There is this glow or something about you that I just wish I could have."

"Elaine, it's called peace, and you will have it soon enough," he so wisely responded.

Kevin heard the grumbling that was now screaming from my stomach since I hadn't eaten all day. I never got a chance to eat my pastry at Starbucks earlier because of the invasion.

"It seems as if you are about due for a meal. Can I offer you an early supper or something? I wouldn't want you to think I make a habit of preying on beautiful women in church." He laughed.

I laughed along with him this time, part embarrassed by my stomach's noise. "I wouldn't want to hold you up or keep you from anything."

"You're not keeping me from anything important. Besides, you seem like you could use a friend right now. There's an excellent diner right across the street. They have the best apple pie. I sure could go for a slice right now," he said, flashing that million-dollar smile.

"Well, I guess you're right. I could use a friend right now, and I have yet to eat today. So lead the way."

I got a whiff of his cologne as we both stood to leave. He smelled so good. He looked good, and he has his own money. Sounds too good to be true. But then again, I am in a church.

We went to the diner, and talked for the next five hours. I learned that he was married at 21 and divorced at 26. He's 36 years old. He's a self employed investment broker. No children. He attends church faithfully every Sunday. He plays golf, likes to fish, travel, and paint. He's written two investment books and he owns rental properties. He has one older brother and three nephews. Both of his parents are also deceased. He was raised by an uncle and the many women his uncle kept

The Queen

as "temporary aunts." His last relationship ended a year ago because of his commitment to abstinence, and she wasn't ready to settle down for marriage and children. He enjoys cooking. He has a little brother through the Big Brother program, and he teaches free investment classes at the church.

I shared tales about my lunatic family. I actually opened up about my relationship with my mother. Even cried some more. I told him about my shoe boutiques. I also opened up about my disappointment with myself having never done anything positive to make a difference in anyone's life. He tried to give me props for helping Angelo and company, but I confessed that it was self-serving. I confessed just about every ugly thing, minus my prostitution.

I have to say, confession felt good for my soul. My whole world felt so much lighter. Kevin challenged me to make Charise my cause. He felt it would help me also make peace with my mother. Charise? I don't know about that. I'd probably do better coaching a girls' softball team. Mind you, I've never played softball.

We talked for what seemed like an eternity. Before I knew it, it was nearly midnight. I felt so at ease talking to Kevin that time seemed to stand still, and I didn't want to leave. I thanked him for the pie and for lending an ear. He said that his calendar was free so spending this time talking to me was a pleasure. He offered to walk me to my car, and I happily accepted.

Kevin called to make sure I arrived home safely, and we talked on the phone until the sun came up. I laughed, cried, and opened up like never before. Kevin was so non-judgmental. Or at least he hasn't seemed to pass judgment on any of the stuff I have opened up about to him. So many times I was right at the edge of telling him my ultimate confessions. That is the one thing my soul wants to be rid of, but yet I can't bring my mouth to release it. I guess it's also a matter of trust. This man is basically a stranger. I only know what he tells me.

Ironically, he shared my concerns regarding Sean and Kelly's relationship. He also challenged me to give up a whole day of sales and donate to some worthy cause without looking for something in return. When I rebutted, he convinced me it was going to be a big step for battling my obsession with money. So I accepted the challenge. I'll ask Harmony to suggest a charity or cause.

Kevin also asked if I would meet him at 3 pm the next day at the church, just to give God thanks. Not sure how I'll be able to slip away from the boutique again, but I agreed.

I'm not sure what it is about this guy, but something just really feels right about him. Time will tell. At the very least, hopefully I finally found a true friend. Besides my siblings, I have no real friends. I used to have Renee, who was the closest thing to a best friend, but when she had her sights set on Robert, she turned out to be my enemy. She's the reason I became sexually involved with Robert. But if I wasn't so obsessed with money, her schemes would not have succeeded.

So in essence, I am my biggest enemy.

Maybe now I can begin to make some adjustments. But helping Charise? Ugh! That's a big adjustment.

PART THREE

Even More Than Before

19
Harmony

Andre came in the house yelling through tears. "That dirty bitch! I knew she was a dirty bitch!"

Todd and I were relaxing on the sofa watching television. We were both startled. Andre has always been a quiet and well-mannered young man.

He walked directly in front of the television, pacing back and forth. "That dirty bitch killed me."

Now we were really confused.

"Sit down, son, and tell us what's going on," Todd told him.

Andre sat for a total of three seconds and jumped back up again. He picked up a figurine and threw it at a wall, breaking it in a thousand pieces.

"Okay, Andre! Settle down now!" Todd demanded. He got up and embraced Andre. "What's going on?"

"Her dirty-ass sister killed me!" Andre said through tears, pointing to me.

I was shocked. All I could say is, "Huh?"

"Don't 'huh' me! That's your dirty fucking sister. You know she's a dirty ho!"

Todd shook Andre. "Now calm yourself. You are not going to speak to Harmony like that. Sit down and tell us what's going on."

"I don't want to talk to that bitch!" Andre pointed to me. "It's all her fault!"

I swallowed hard. It suddenly occurred to me that he must be talking about Charise. She would be the only one he could be talking about. She is the one he had sex with, but that was months ago. And why is he saying she killed him? As many questions as I had, I knew to keep quiet.

"Well talk to me," Todd insisted, failing to correct his son for calling me a bitch.

"That bitch gave me AIDS. I'm HIV positive. I know it was her," Andre blurted out as if I suddenly wasn't in the room.

I felt my heart drop. Even felt the baby squirming, like I had never felt.

Did he just say HIV positive? Charise is HIV positive?

"Andre, what are you talking about? Who are you talking about? And why are you saying this has anything to do with Harmony?" Todd was trying to be firm and not fall apart from the bomb his son just dropped.

"I messed with her sister when we were in Cancun," Andre said again, pointing at me, causing Todd to look at me with evil eyes. "Terrence and I hit it on the beach after the wedding. She's a nasty ho! That bitch killed me! My life is over!"

"Your life is not over. Stop it!" Todd demanded. "When did you get tested? What about Terrence? Is he positive as well?"

"I don't know. I just told him. I went to the clinic a few days ago with the new girl I was dating. She wanted us to both get tested before sleeping together. Now I find out that my test is positive," Andre answered his father.

"Well, we'll run another test. Those test are sometimes incorrect. Why were you having sex with Harmony's sister? Why were both of you having sex with that girl?"

The beast came unleashed. Todd's wrath then turned to me.

"What the fuck is wrong with your retarded family? And what kind of psychologist are you that you can't even talk any sense into any of them?"

Oh, no the fuck he didn't go there!

"Todd, don't do this. I understand that you are upset, as am I, but don't go there with me."

"Why not go there? First the one sister, who fucks her way up the corporate ladder, gets my baby sister fired from her job just because she's threatened that somebody is going to take that old white man from her. Why, because she knew my sister could dance circles around her in looks and brains? Then you have three sisters all fucking the same stripper. Two sisters fucking the one's husband and the one sister who sleeps with everything slinging a dick, and not giving a damn about losing her own child. Oh, and I can't forget about your fruitcake brother. I should have known better than to get caught up with someone that has a family like yours. Now that I think about the rest of them, maybe I should wonder if that is really my baby you're carrying there."

Andre looked surprised by his father's words. "I knew it was that girl. The whole family is nasty. I knew it!"

I was beyond livid and speechless. My heart was racing. My husband turned on me in the worst way. No benefit of the doubt. Just persecute me because his precious son thinks my sister—not me, but my sister—caused him to be HIV positive. And he wants to talk shit about how much better his sister looks than my sister? Then he attacks my profession and questions my fidelity?

I guess I don't know my husband after all.

The Queen

I got up from the sofa in silence and went upstairs to pack a suitcase. There was no fucking way I would spend another night with that motherfucker. And then he blames me for his trampy sister getting fired. Wow!

I didn't like this country-ass looking house in the first place, and he just gave me a reason to leave it. Time to go!

When Todd saw me come downstairs with a suitcase he asked, "Where are you going?"

"What's it to you? I'll be out of your life, so me and my family won't cause your perfect family any more blemishes."

Todd grabbed my arm, and I snatched away. "Don't find yourself being the recipient of a DC-style ass whipping. Baby or no baby, I will drop kick your ass. Don't be a damn fool."

"Well fine! Take your ass on then! I'm trying to talk to you and you want to act juvenile!" he shouted.

I chuckled at the audacity of this fool-ass motherfucker calling me juvenile. "Oh, you've said more than enough." Then I walked out the door.

I got into my car, not really knowing where I was headed. As I was driving, suddenly sharp pains went through my abdomen and thighs. Then, everything went black.

When I awoke, I found myself in the hospital hooked up to all kinds of monitors. I had a massive headache. I touched my head and found a bandage.

"That's probably going to hurt for a while," a nurse said when she realized I was awake and in pain. "We can't give you anything too strong because of the babies. They're doing great, but we're going to have to keep you for observation."

Babies? More than one? Do I have a concussion, and can't comprehend correctly?

"Babies? I only have one baby. Why am I here?" I asked.

"You had a nasty car accident. You and the babies are very lucky. And there is not one baby, but three babies. You sound as though you didn't know," she said with a big smile.

What the fuck? Three babies. I didn't take fertility drugs or anything. My quack doctor didn't mention multiple births.

"How could there be three babies? I only know of one baby. How would my OB miss something like that?" I asked, hoping I was just delirious from the concussion.

"There were three babies on your ultrasound, and you are 15 ½ weeks pregnant. Most people 15 weeks aren't as large as you are with one baby. I'm surprised your OB didn't pick up on that," she answered.

"Even my husband is a doctor. He chalked it up to swelling," I told her.

"Your husband is outside with Dr. Webber. They're trying to track down your OB."

"My husband? Why is he here? How did he know I was here?" I asked both annoyed and confused.

The nurse raised her eyebrow. "Should he not be here? He was called by the police when you crashed. They did mention you had a suitcase, but we assumed maybe you were heading out of town for business or something."

At that moment, Todd walked in looking like death. He looked like he was the one in the car accident. He clearly had been crying. Guilt! It's a motherfucker!

"Oh, baby, could you ever forgive me? I don't know what the hell came over me. Oh, I'm so sorry, Harmony. Please forgive me," he begged, kissing my face between every other word, with his tears dropping all on me. "My God, I don't know what I would have done if I were to lose you."

I was so confused. I just found out I am having triplets. My husband disrespects me to no end, and now I'm supposed to forgive him just like that? I almost lost my own life and more than likely, the babies in addition because of his bullshit.

"I want you out!" I said.

The nurse said, "Okay, I'll be right out front if you need me."

"I'm not talking to you," I said to the nurse. "I want him out. NOW!" The heart monitor started beeping extra fast.

"Sir, I'm going to have to ask you to leave," she told Todd.

"But I'm her husband. I'm a doctor. I'm the father," he answered.

"I'm sorry, she wants you out, and we can't have you in here upsetting her in any way. You're going to have to step outside, otherwise I'm going to have to call security," the nurse advised.

"Please, Harmony, don't do this to us. Don't do this to our family," he pleaded.

"You did it. Now get the fuck out!" I rebutted and turned my head away from him. If it weren't for all the monitors I was hooked to, I would have turned my back completely.

He stood staring for a minute with his mouth wide open in disbelief and then left the room looking like a wounded puppy.

And when I left the hospital two days later, I went and found a fully furnished corporate apartment to stay in until I could decide what to do about my marriage. If it weren't for the babies, there wouldn't be a second thought concerning my marriage.

If Andre really is HIV positive, will Todd later blame me again if Andre were to actually die? It'll be kind of rough, but I think I could raise my babies by my damn self. I don't need to tolerate that kind of shit from any man. Hell, I'd tell one of my patients to leave under these circumstances.

And fuck that Tatiana, with that lame bullshit story she told her family about why she was fired. I chose not to tell Todd what she did concerning Mandingo, because I didn't want the family thinking any more negative about her ass than they already did. A lot of good that did.

How did my sisters create this wedge in my marriage? Or maybe Todd was the ticking time bomb, waiting to show his dark side. I wish I had seen it before babies were involved.

20
Shawnee

I don't know how I fell into this mess again. Damn that Tatiana! Damn Brad! One fucking cup of coffee was all I agreed to, and now I have slept with him four times since that phone call. Then again, Brad opened the door back up.

There is just this way that Eric makes my body feel. He tantalizes my nipples like I have never experienced with any other man. The enormous size of his dick is certainly something to which no other man can compare. The way he sucks each and every toe, and lets his tongue glide all the way through my love cave. His large hand massages my back as he takes me from behind. He can lift and hold me in positions that seem impossible and defy the laws of physics. Eric can suck the ovaries out of a pussy.

Last night Brad flew into Paris to join me and finally proposed marriage. I almost didn't accept, but I can't allow Tatiana an opening to push me out the door. I also realize I still haven't gotten over Eric. I certainly know I would never want to marry Eric. I accepted the proposal more out of obligation than anything. It surprised me since Brad seems hell-bent on fucking Tatiana.

Other than the Tatiana bullshit, Brad does makes me happy, but Brad can't do for me what Eric does sexually. No man can, for that matter. I was so sexually satisfied with Brad before Eric came back on the scene. I guess that was what Tatiana was counting on. Too bad I had the bitch fired and sent her ass packing back to Texas. She obviously didn't realize she was fucking with one of Wilhelmina Wiggins' daughters. Now, thanks to her ass, I'm fucking with Mandingo and Brad. Damn, Mandingo's the reason I lost my first marriage. Well, actually he was part of the complicated equation. Robert had a thing for hookers and my sister. The nasty bastard! Now Mandingo will cause me to lose Brad and everything that goes with him. What's a girl to do?

Ever since that conversation with Tatiana, I've paid more attention to Brad's behavior and patterns. I also made it a point to get the scoop from Brad's secretary about what she witnessed in his office with Tatiana. Although his secretary insisted she didn't want to get involved, nor wanted to lose her job behind this mess, she ultimately confirmed Tatiana's account. She did see Tatiana's leg up on Brad's chair, as well as her naked ass sitting on top of his desk. Some further probing confirmed Tatiana and Brad weren't all that discreet with their affair around the office. In Houston, it was well known news that they had been screwing for at least two years, when Tatiana didn't even have a management position. Brad tried to keep things hush-hush because he didn't want people to think the reason she got promoted was because of their affair. Most of her co-workers hated her and thought she lacked talent and vision. Brad claimed she was so talented. She didn't get the salary compensation that went along with fucking him. Guess he preferred my "fuller" tits and larger "jiggling" ass after all.

I also put Brad's driver on the spot, who ended up confessing that he has driven Tatiana to Brad's house quite often since she's been in New York. Always while I'm overseas. How did I get the driver to confess? He's a damn man. Yeah, it was a big risk, but one that yielded me the answers I wanted.

One evening when he picked me up in Brad's limo instead of the Town Car, I asked that he sit in the back with me to chat. I thought that since he was a brother he might be more inclined to open up to me. He was a bit reluctant at first. I told him not to be afraid, that I wouldn't bite. When he got in, I asked the questions and told him I would not betray his confidence. He denied knowing anything about Tatiana, but I could see in his eyes that he was obviously lying.

I was wearing a see-through teddy under my trench coat. I opened my coat to let the driver get a good look at my body. At first he was about to make a run for the door, but I grabbed his arm. I took his hand and glided it over my breast, then I guided his hand between my legs. The driver instantly lost control. He started groping my pussy through the teddy and feeling up my tits. I stopped him. I told him if he tells me what I want, I'll let him have what he wants. His mouth was like a running faucet after that.

He told me about Brad fucking Tatiana right there in the limo. He said they go out on the town often, and that she often stays at his home. Brad even told him he had one woman too many, and was glad he still had "it" at his age. Brad also told him he wanted to get married so he'd have it every night, all night, but wished he could keep both of us because Tatiana and I made a dynamic combination. He said I was more expensive to have than Tatiana and had more brains, but he loved us both.

That being said, I figured all is fair in love and war. I had the driver park the limo, come up to my apartment, and have his way with me. He let me know that he secretly fantasized about sucking these tits and tasting this pussy from the time he witnessed me and Brad together when I first arrived in New York.

The Queen

He sucked my titties like he may never have the opportunity again. He ripped off the $300 teddy I was wearing for Brad and buried his face between my legs to get that much fantasized about taste of my pussy. When he had me straddle his face, he was able to suck out every bit of cum that was squirting out. When he finally got his dick in my pussy, he fucked up and came as quickly as he got it in. When I realized that he didn't have a quick rebound, I made him wait while I cleaned up and prepared for my journey to Brad's house. Hell, I need more dick than that.

I was hoping my keeping the bathroom door open and letting the guy watch me sensually bathe would get his dick back up so I didn't have to go see Brad at all, since he wants to fuck Tatiana and flaunt that bitch around. No such luck. I even asked if he was done before I let him take me to Brad's. He apologized for crossing the line and said he just couldn't help himself. He ought to be apologizing for that weak ass fuck. He was also worried about losing his job as a result. I assured him that wouldn't be the case. So Brad benefited from what his lame-ass driver couldn't finish.

But that's okay, because Tatiana in all her evilness did give me Mandingo back. If Brad is going to be sneaking off to fuck Tatiana when he goes to Houston, which has been quite often lately, I'll have Mandingo on Brad's dime, and everything Brad wants to give me. The first time I caught Brad in a lie, I called him from Europe and he said he was in New York working from home. He fucked up when I asked him the time and he gave me Houston time and not New York's time. I then called the Houston office and they told me he was working from his home in Houston. Now I have an inside mole who hates Tatiana and lets me know each and every time Brad is in Houston. Since Tatiana no longer works for the company, they can't be certain if he's with Tatiana when he's not at the office.

I haven't confronted Brad ever again about Tatiana because I can't afford to push him away and risk losing everything. If I'm going to risk anything, I'm going to fuck Eric and be fucked in the best way I can be fucked.

You're damn right I'll marry Brad to secure my position and future.

I needed to call Sandy back. She'd left three messages saying it was urgent. This time difference takes some getting used to.

"Hey, sis," I said when she answered. "I didn't wake you, did I?"

"Yeah, but don't worry about it. I need to be up anyway."

"I got your messages. Sounds like something's going on."

"Girl, you don't know the half of it. I talked to Harmony yesterday."

"Oh, good. How's the little one coming along?"

"Try, how are the THREE little ones coming along. She's having triplets. She found out when her car accident landed her in the hospital after she walked out on her husband, who she now has left."

I was in total shock. Sandy just said more than a mouthful. "You have got to be kidding?"

"Oh, no, and it gets worse."

"What would make her leave Todd?" This is very upsetting because I thought nothing would ever destroy that marriage. "What do you mean car accident?" I asked when that part finally registered in my brain.

"Remember when I told you all that Lewis saw Charise screwing Todd's son?" she asked.

Oh, Lord, here we go with this Lewis nonsense. "Sandy, what does Lewis have to do with any of this?"

"Stop being so damn pessimistic when it comes to my husband, Shawnee. This has nothing to do with Lewis. This is about what he witnessed that no one wanted to believe."

The Queen

"Well, it's old news about Charise fucking Todd's son. Angelo already confirmed that. We all know about that," I said, getting more annoyed.

"Would you please let me speak? Based on that time, he decided that Charise is the reason he is HIV positive. Both he and Todd blamed everything on our whole family. Even brought you up because of Todd's Barbie doll sister getting fired. He dumped the whole thing on Harmony because she didn't *control us*. He even questioned the baby's paternity."

The only reason I wasn't saying anything, was because I couldn't. When I could, I asked, "My baby sister is HIV positive?" I asked, choked up.

"Harmony spoke with Charise, but she claimed that she was not. She said she gets tested regularly, and was just tested a month ago," Sandy answered.

This is all so confusing. "So how did he think he became positive from Charise? He was with some other girl at the reception."

"Maybe Charise is lying about being tested, but I'm pissed that Todd would blame this on Harmony. And then say a bunch of horrible things to her while she's carrying his children. Shawnee, we could have been burying our sister over this mess. She could have been killed in that car accident, along with those babies."

"Wow! All of this because Charise just couldn't help her damn self and had to fuck Todd's son. We need to find out if she's really HIV positive or not. And where is Harmony staying? You said she left Todd?"

"She's staying in a corporate apartment downtown. She said she needs to carefully figure out her next move. She really doesn't want to go back with Todd ever again, but she has to think about how she's going to manage those three babies all by herself."

"Damn! I wish I could just drop everything and say I'd be there to help her. But it's a shame that her marriage is wrecked because of Charise." I felt myself getting angrier.

"Well, from what she told me, your feud with Todd's sister was also a problem, but I thought Todd was better than that."

"Last night Brad proposed to me, and I accepted. Now that I hear all this shit, I think I had better reconsider this whole marriage shit."

"Shawnee, you can't base what you have with Brad on any other situation. You have a really good man. He booted that tramp out of the company for you. He handed you the keys to his kingdom, not apartment, but his kingdom. Don't throw that away. And I know you all don't like Lewis, and, yes, he has made mistakes, but he's a really good man. I can't base my marriage on other people . . ." Sandy said before a long pause. "Hold on, Shawnee. Someone's at my door."

I never shared the whole Tatiana story with my family. They might think differently about Brad if I told them he is fucking her. Then I'd have to tell about Eric as my recourse.

I guess she didn't realize this was an international call because she took forever to get back to the phone. I could hear her sobbing uncontrollably before she returned, which scared me.

When she finally came back to the phone, I asked, "Sandy, what's going on? Are you crying?"

She cried some more before saying, "I can't do this anymore. I can't do this anymore, Shawnee."

"Sandy, what's wrong?"

"He's still fucking her. Oh, my Lord, why is this happening to me? I tried so hard to believe and trust him. He's a dog from hell! I can't do this!" she screamed.

Is she talking about Charise? Did she find out about Charise and Lewis?

"I'm going to kill that bitch for once and for all," Sandy yelled out.

"Who, Sandy? Who are you talking about? What happened?"

"That bitch could have spread her AIDS to me if she really does have it. Oh, my Lord. Why? Why me?"

I think that answered my question.

"Sandy, who was at the door? What did you just find out?" I asked, already partially knowing.

"Charise is still fucking my husband!" she screamed into my ear. "Someone dropped an envelope of photos in my mail slot with a note saying 'you need to stop living in the dark and leave him once and for all.' The handwriting looks like my friend from my church. She's been telling me to leave Lewis. But I don't understand why she would drop the photos in the slot and run. Why wouldn't she just hand the photos to me herself? Why wouldn't she tell me about Charise and Lewis rather than send me some damn pictures?"

"Sandy, maybe she felt the only way to convince you would be with pictures. What is in the photos?" I asked curious as hell.

"There's a picture of Charise going into a motel room alone. Then there's a picture of Lewis going into that same room. There are multiple photos because they are wearing different clothes in the photos. It's the same room number in each of the photos. There is one photo of him kissing Charise with a sheet wrapped around her body. It looks like he was leaving the room. Nonetheless, it's clear as hell what's going on," Sandy started sobbing again. "WHY!"

This coming from the person, who just moments ago, made him out to be a saint. Man!

What if Charise is positive, fucking Lewis unprotected, and he's fucking Sandy? That would be a true tragedy. This was definitely a conference call situation. Hell, I'm having difficulty trying to sort out my life by myself, let alone trying to deal with my sisters' drama.

That conference call was a massive mistake. On top of everything else that's fucked up, Kelly proudly announces that she has invested into Sean's company and has a 30% interest in the company that she'll never work in, all for a mere fifty-thousand dollars. She said since they are getting married, Sean wants her to be part owner just in case anything ever happens to him. Why she thinks she could have a 30% interest for only $50,000 in a company that he somehow convinced her is worth over 40 million. Apparently, she missed some of those business classes in college. He must have some dick on him. I can't believe Kelly is so taken by him.

What is wrong with my family? What is wrong with me? I am about to throw away a really good future for a piece of dick. Well, actually, Mandingo is more than a piece of dick, but I'm going to have to put an end to this shit. I'm going to have to stop this Tatiana and Brad thing so I can be happy with Brad as I was before she came on the scene. Even with them fucking for two years, he wants to marry me, not her. I already know she wants to marry him. That should tell me something.

What am I going to do if I lose two sisters to AIDS? I guess I'm no better than Charise. Lord, help me if Sandy were to learn that I have once again resorted to fucking her ex-boyfriend, while Charise is fucking her husband.

Thankfully, Harmony is doing well despite all that she is dealing with. One of her friends has been helping her get well from the accident and trying to help her sort through the pieces of her life.

Elaine sounded so different. She wasn't her normal cutthroat self who always suggests kicking someone's ass as the solution. She even mentioned that she's been thinking about bringing Charise to come live with her in L.A. There's definitely a story here that I am missing. I'll find out soon enough.

21
Angela

"Okay, so my buddy Tyrone found out the room was registered to a Robert Townsend that day."

"Robert Townsend? That name sounds familiar. The actor? Antwan, how did your friend end up following my sister into the Beverly-Wilshire Hotel?"

"Oh, Angela, stop getting your panties in a bunch. And no. Not the actor. Tyrone would have really been all over that. No one followed your sister. Tyrone works at the Beverly-Wilshire and saw her when she came in, and saw her leave looking distraught. In case you don't know, your sister is somewhat of a celebrity herself in this town. Creeping into a hotel in the middle of an afternoon is bound to get some attention," Antwan answered.

I really hate that my friends are now all up in my sister's personal business. I do wonder who this Robert is. He must have been the mystery person who sent the flowers to the boutique, and the reason she left my ass stranded there for the rest of that day by myself. I'm going to have to chat with Elaine about her indiscretions being public information. I know she won't like that.

She looked me in my eye and told me she spent the afternoon in a church. I actually fell for that, since she seems so much calmer lately.

But now I find out she's in the Beverly-Wilshire, getting her freak on with some Robert Townsend.

"So you left me stuck in this store all by myself, with all these overly dramatic bitches, so you could go to church? Is that the story you're sticking to, Elaine?" I asked when I caught her alone in the boutique. I intentionally used the word 'store' to hit a nerve with her. It drives her insane.

"Yes, Angelo, I was at a church, then went to a diner and ate there. Why are you bringing this back up, and why does it seem like you are trying to accuse me of something? And speaking of church, I'm going this Sunday and would like for you to go with me. There's someone I'd like for you to meet, but you'll have to leave the 'girls.' I don't want them all up in my business."

"Church?" I asked totally thrown by that one. "You want me to go with you? Is this Robert Townsend that you want me to meet?

Elaine looked as if she saw a ghost.

"Well, is his name Robert?" I asked when she didn't respond. "And too late; the bitches are already in your business. How do you think I know about Robert? Oh, and the Beverly-Wilshire also. Elaine, I believed you when you said you went to church. Or at least I wanted to believe you. How could you look me in my face and lie? And why does that name sound so —" I had a sudden epiphany. "Shawnee! That's her husband's name."

Tears filled Elaine's eyes. Her eyes would not let her deny it, although her quivering lips were trying. I took my sister in my arms and held her as she buried her face into my chest.

"Oh, Elaine, what have you done? Why Shawnee's husband?" I asked, causing her to cry harder. "Elaine, you all are going to have to stop this craziness. I don't even have to ask if Shawnee knows. I hope she never finds out. Our family would be ripped apart forever."

The Queen

"That's done," she managed to say when she recomposed herself. "And I did go to church that day. I've been going almost each day to say a prayer ever since then. While I was there I met this guy who has been helping me with my spiritual transformation. I really like him, but I don't think he's interested in me romantically."

"You want to go to church because you want some guy to want you romantically? And what, you want me to tell you if he's gay, which may be why he's not into you?" I drilled, annoyed.

"No, Angelo. I'm trying to make changes in my life. I don't want to have this whole secret existence anymore. I don't want to be doing ANYTHING for money anymore, as I have with Robert. I want to make a change, but I'm kind of afraid. I want my brother there so I can hold onto his hand. As for the guy, I think he's a wonderful person, but I don't know if I am so taken by him because he hasn't put forth any romantic advances, as most guys would. Maybe I'm just so messed up in the head. I just want my brother there. I want my family. I want my mother," she said before having a complete breakdown.

Again I took her into my arms. I can't believe what I just heard. Elaine said she wants Mama. Wow! Maybe she is changing. Robert? One more family secret I have to hold onto.

I can't believe Elaine doesn't have a clue that Kevin is definitely into her. I guess she's never had a decent man, so she doesn't know the difference. Church was pretty nice. I hadn't been in some time. I even gave up a fierce party last night to be here this morning. I was very impressed to see my sister was totally into the service, despite all.

"I've decided to send for Charise," Elaine announced after we were seated at the diner Kevin introduced her to. "I've been giving it a lot of thought, and I really feel in my heart that my sister needs me, and I have to be there for her. I think today's sermon confirmed that thought."

I was too shocked to respond, but Kevin responded instead, "Oh, Elaine, I think that is wonderful. I am sure it's going to be a challenge at first, but you'll see the fruits soon enough."

"Uh-uh!" I finally responded. "Oh no, Elaine, you need to give that some more thought. Charise is not someone you can help. Jesus can't help her!"

"Don't be taking the Lord's name in vain," she shot back. "If I could be helped, then Charise could be helped. I feel I am in a good position to help her. Especially with you nearby, and her close bond with you, we could get through to her together."

"Speak for yourself! I don't need 'Charise' drama all up in my mix. It's one thing to talk about her drama, but it's another thing to have to be a part of her drama," I answered.

"I'll try to do whatever I can to help in any way," Kevin offered.

I poofed. "All you need is a dick to help that girl, 'cause all she'll try to do is fuck you too!" I caught myself too late. "Oops. I wasn't supposed to be saying dick and fuck when I just left church." Kevin laughed at my retraction. "But you know what I mean. Elaine, I know you mean well, but I can't even imagine anything that would cause that girl to change. Leopards can't change their spots."

Mr. Preacher Man Kevin threw his holy two cents in. "But see, the goodness of God can wash away any blemish. Elaine, if you ask God for guidance and direction, and then He provides it, you can't just turn a blind eye as though you didn't see. You will feel haunted and convicted because He wants you to do the right thing."

"I say send her a one-way ticket to Timbuktu, and be done with it," I shot back.

Elaine took my hand in both of hers. "Angelo, I know you are concerned, and I'd be lying if I didn't admit that I too am concerned, but this is something I have to do." Elaine's cell phone interrupted her.

The Queen

"Excuse me, it's my sister Sandy. I'd better take this call," she said before getting up from the table.

Mr. Preacher Man and I went back and forth on the pros and cons of bringing Charise to L.A. Then we heard Elaine bawl out crying. She returned to the table trying to control herself.

"Angelo, we have to get to Houston. That was Sandy. Something happened to Charise," Elaine blurted out before breaking down again.

Kevin jumped up and took Elaine into his arms to console her. "Please, let me go with you. I want to be there for you."

I kind of felt jealous seeing this man consoling my sister when I felt it should have been me. "Elaine, what's going on? What happened?"

It must really be something bad if Sandy put aside her differences to make the call. Suddenly I found myself crying as well. All those horrible things I just said. I even felt bad for being so hard on Kevin, when he pulled me up into a group hug with Elaine, as he tried to console us both.

"I don't want to put you out, Kevin," Elaine told him.

"Elaine, it's no problem. I will be by your side for as long as you need or want me there. And I guess Angelo could use someone around to help be strong as well."

He ain't told no lie there! I don't even know what happened yet, but I don't think I could handle losing my sister.

I had to ask. "What happened to Charise? She's not dea . . ." I didn't want to say *dead*.

"Sandy said Charise is in the hospital unconscious. She was badly beaten, raped with objects, stripped naked, tied up, and possibly left for dead. Someone found her barely breathing. The doctors don't know if she'll make it or not because she hasn't regained consciousness. Sandy said her face is not recognizable," Elaine explained before both she and I broke down again.

Kevin seemed like such a rock for us. "Okay, you guys, let's get you going. There's obviously no time to waste. Don't worry about packing. I can get you what you need when we get to Houston. I'll take care of all the arrangements. Let's just get to the airport."

Elaine and I just followed Kevin's lead. He made all kinds of phone calls and had a private jet waiting for us at the airport. I called Antwan to fill in and hold things down at the boutique for us. Elaine called Sandy to get more information. Thankfully Shawnee had just made it back to the states the night before, and was also on her way to Houston. Kevin had a limo waiting for us at the airport in Houston. I'm not sure what he does for a living, but his money seems long.

Maybe he is a really good person for Elaine. At least he wouldn't try to take advantage of her money. And anyone who can get Elaine to turn her life around is all right in my book.

22
Sandy

Who would have thought I'd be the one here for Charise? As many times as I wanted to kick her ass myself, no one deserves what was done to her.

Someone used a pipe in her vaginal area, and a stick of some sort in her rectum. Her face was battered so badly, they had to rewire her jaw. She's still going to need several other surgeries. They had to do emergency surgery to stop the internal bleeding. It's been two weeks now, and she still hasn't regained consciousness. Elaine and Angelo left this morning with Kevin. They're going to get things situated in L.A. and then head back to Houston.

Elaine surprised us all when she let us know she was taking Charise back to L.A. when she gets well enough to go. Angelo said she had just made the announcement to him right before I called her about Charise. That makes me believe that God is going to pull Charise through this. Sometimes we have to hit all the way to the bottom before we get our calling.

Tragedy has a way of turning people's lives around. Elaine's confession of her prostitution to the whole family and Kevin, at my dinner table, was evidence of that. She admitted everything. Even the part about Robert. Shawnee wasn't too happy about that, but she ultimately forgave her. I wasn't too happy when Shawnee then felt compelled to confess her recent affair with Eric. Shawnee also 'fessed up about Brad and Tatiana. That was a big disappointment, given the respect I had for him. I also respect Shawnee's decision to go forth with the marriage. I hate that she won't talk to Brad, but keeps screwing Eric as her payback. That's so foolish. For all that Brad is willing to give to Shawnee, I still feel he's a good thing for her, and she needs to fight for her man. Furthermore, I would greatly appreciate if my own damn sister wouldn't keep feeling the need to screw my ex-boyfriend. That's so not cool.

Kelly annoyed us to no end. Every five minutes she had to call Sean. And the minutes in between, he was calling her phone. Then she'd want to come back and tell us how great her fiancé is. I bet when he starts whipping her ass because she forgot to report in, she won't think he's so great. I'm no domestic violence expert, but that sure sounds like the makings of a butt-whipping in the works.

Personally, I've never understood why some women would think that insecure nonsense is cute. That insecurity is a damn red flag. Run! Run now while you can. And what can you do when you try to warn them and they won't listen? You just have to wait it out until they've had enough. Oh, I know firsthand from my time with Lewis.

I finally put Lewis out of my life. This was my wake up call. I don't know how I let him talk me into letting him stay after I received those photos. I realize that I let some fool come between my sister and me. And although she was wrong as hell, he's supposed to be my husband and not her lover. On top of that, I learned that my so-called friend who had me changing churches was not only responsible for sending me the photos of Charise and Lewis, but she's the one Lewis went to stay with when I put his ass out of my house. The sorry bastard hasn't made one

The Queen

effort to try and talk me into taking him back. I say "good riddance, muthafucka!" Forgive me, Lord, for my language.

I was sitting by Charise's bedside when Harmony wobbled into the room sporting swollen ankles.

"Sandy, come here. I need to speak with you," she said, obviously disturbed.

I followed her to a private area to hear her out. "What's up, Sis?"

"My marriage is over forever," she said before crying.

I was confused, because Harmony had refused to return to Todd since their incident a couple of months ago. "What brought you to such a final decision, Harmony? I thought you were going to at least wait for the babies to arrive?" I asked.

Harmony's tears streamed down her face, but she kept her composure. "All of this is my fault."

"Harmony, this incident is not your fault. We all were guilty of turning our backs on Charise. You have been the one person who has always tried to look out for her."

"No, Sandy! You don't understand! This is really all my fault. It's my fault for marrying Todd and his evil family."

"How so?"

"Todd just came by my office to confess his son's deed. His son Andre did this to Charise, and then Todd wants to rationalize Andre's state of mind since Charise caused him to be HIV positive. He said he would hope I'd understand Andre's state of mind under the circumstances."

I was way past shocked and pissed all rolled into one. "Harmony, did you not tell him that Charise isn't even positive? Did you tell the lowlife bastard that it was his nasty-ass son putting his dick all over the fucking place, and don't have a clue where?" I yelled. "Forgive me, Lord, for my filthy words. Fuck that nigga! Who the fuck does he think he is? The raggedy bastard! Oh, Lord, forgive me again." I was pacing back and forth. My mind was thinking all kinds of evil thoughts. Payback was number one. "Harmony, did you call the police?"

"No! I went to the police. They said it might be hard to prove it if he doesn't confess to them," she answered. "They claim they will 'investigate.' Whatever the fuck that is supposed to mean."

"Well, didn't he just confess to you? Wasn't that good enough?"

Harmony was frustrated. "I asked the same thing, but they told me that Todd could deny ever telling me that and because we are currently separated, it might look as though I'm being spiteful by implicating his son."

My mind was still racing. I had to think of something. Finally a thought entered my mind. "What about Arnold?"

"What about Arnold?" she asked looking confused.

I nodded my head because I knew I'd come up with the right solution. "Arnold said if he could help us in any way to let him know. His girlfriend is an attorney with the DA's office. Surely if we could get them on our side, the police would have to do something. I'm sure Andre has some type of wounds on him from beating Charise the way he did. Maybe if they could bring him in before he's all healed, it'll help."

Harmony looked as though she saw the light. "I remember last week when Todd came to my office to plead for me to take him back, he mentioned Andre had broken two knuckles, and said he was in a fight with some guys. That just might be it." Then the light faded from her eyes. "Do you think that girl would help Charise after how Charise traumatized her?"

"Hell, I've been traumatized by Charise, but you see where I am. What do we have to lose by asking? She is an officer of the court. She would have a certain degree of obligation, right?"

I am so thankful to God for giving me the insight on what to do. One call to Arnold had Andre behind bars the next evening. For the next two weeks, Arnold brought Jarod to the hospital, hoping that would help Charise wake up. She's been in a coma for just about a month. And I, of all people, have been prayerfully vigilant over my baby sister the whole time. Who would have thought?

It's going to be really difficult letting Charise know that Jarod is the last child she will ever bear. When they did surgery, they had to remove her uterus. Hopefully she'll be able to get herself together to at least get some type of joint custody with Arnold or good visitation. Speaking of which, I don't know why she let that man get away. He's a really good one, and he adored her. She wouldn't be lying here all messed up behind that fool-ass Andre.

And poor Harmony; she's getting ready to give birth to triplets and no longer with her husband. Todd is an insensitive jerk, but what man isn't (in a woman's eyes)? Hopefully they can find a way to work through their issues for those babies' sakes.

Before all this Charise and Andre madness, Todd and Harmony were like a perfect match, unlike me and Lewis. With him, I kept trying to fit a square peg into a round hole. It just wasn't meant to be. I should have listened years ago when Charise first told me Lewis tried to hit on her. Then all my sisters warned me, but I wouldn't listen. I was too damned determined to make him Mr. Right. A lot like Kelly is doing now.

Eric was a better choice for me, but I messed that up. I couldn't deal with that nonsense when he told me he was going to be stripping professionally. All I could think about were the tons of women he'd be screwing. Instead, I chose jackass Lewis who still screwed tons of women. Déjà vu for me. Now, Eric is chasing my sister around the globe for an opportunity to be with her because he supposedly loves her so much. What a twist.

I guess I can't really point fingers at Charise for letting Arnold slip away from her. I did the same with Eric, and now Shawnee's doing it with Brad. For a few lustful moments with Eric, Shawnee's about to let

Brad slip away from her. She can convince herself that it's all because of Tatiana if she wants to, but it's really about Shawnee's lust for Eric. Harmony is about to let a good man slip away because of one—well, maybe two—insensitive moments concerning his own flesh and blood. Doesn't make it right, but I'd probably think like he did when it comes to my own children. I may have even hidden their crimes. I may have also gone off the deep end a time or two as well.

Now the one I'd wish would slither away is that sneaky-ass Sean. I know something ain't right with him. All of us know it but Kelly. I like that Kevin guy. I think if Elaine can get over her Miss Diva act, Kevin might just be the one for her. He's been calling the hospital to check up on Charise just as often as Elaine has been calling.

A nurse walked up to me in a private waiting area, interrupting my thoughts. "Ms. Wiggins?"

"Well that's my maiden name. I'm Mrs. Taylor, but that's fine to call me." I stood up, hoping she came bearing good news about Charise.

"Charise is awake and alert. It's like a miracle how alert she is. Come and see her," the nurse instructed, all excited. "The doctor is with her right now. I wanted to come and get you since you have been by her side so long."

"Give me a moment. I'll be right there."

I want to first say a prayer before going to face my sister after such a tumultuous relationship these past couple of years. I also need God to help me say the right words about what happened to her and her disfigured face. Finally, I'll have to get the family on the phone to let them know to head back to Houston. Elaine can tell Charise herself about her intentions to take her back to L.A. with her.

23
Kelly

"I now pronounce you man and wife. You may kiss your bride."

Sean didn't waste any time getting his tongue down my throat once the Officiate announced us husband and wife. I know my sisters are going to die when I let them know Sean and I found our way to Vegas and are now married. To hell with what they think anyway. They just don't understand what Sean and I have.

Sean wanted us to be together all the time, but I wasn't willing to do the 'play house' thing when I have my own home and business. That's when he suggested we come to Vegas to get married. I had never been before now, so although I hadn't yet made up my mind on the marriage, I did agree to at least come to Las Vegas with him for a mini vacation.

We stayed in a suite at the Palms. The place was beautiful. By day, Las Vegas offered scenic mountain views from every angle that leaves one in awe. By night, there are the bright lights and the glittering skyline of Las Vegas Boulevard. I could do without the heat, but Sean and I spent most of our days in our suite making love. It was the third day here that I impulsively told him I wanted to get married. And two days later, here we are, Mr. and Mrs. Sean Greene.

After returning to our suite later that evening, I decided to check my voicemails. I heard Sandy.

"Kelly, I was calling to let you know that Charise is finally awake. I wasn't sure if you got my first message. She awoke in good spirits, but that was short-lived when I had to tell her all that has happened to her. Needless to say, she's not too happy. Even worse, she feels I wished harm on her and she doesn't even want me near her anymore. I really need you guys to come back to Houston to help with her. I don't know what to do or how to help her. I am calling everybody because I don't know who will be the one that she'll be okay with. I think your relationship with her was pretty decent, so that's why I need you to come. Hopefully you understand what we are faced with here, so come as soon as you can. Love you lil Sis. See you soon."

Now what the hell am I supposed to do? I just got married! What am I supposed to say to make Charise feel better about what happened to her?

"What's wrong, babe?" Sean asked stepping in the room.

"I just received two voicemails from Sandy letting me know Charise is awake and now Sandy wants me to come help console Charise."

"How does she think you're supposed to console her? That's what doctors and psychiatrists are for. She's going to need a lot of professional help from what you told me. But tonight, Mrs. Greene, I need you. You are mine, all mine tonight, and I'm going to make love to you like never before," Sean said, running his fingers up and down the sides of my arms, causing the hairs to rise up on the back of my neck.

My husband is right. There isn't much I can do for Charise. She needs professional help that I can't give her. Hell, Harmony is a professional. She's there in Houston. Fuck it! I'll call her tomorrow, but tonight I am about to consummate my marriage. I wouldn't want this good man to slip away on a silly technicality such as 'consummation.'

A bit concerned, the next afternoon I checked my voicemail again, only to hear a shitty-gram from Shawnee.

"Kelly, where the fuck are you? Why haven't you called about Charise? I hope you're not stuck under that loser-ass nigga. You have a fucking sister—flesh and blood—who needs you here. I got the call in Europe and somehow I made it to Houston along with Elaine and Angelo only to find no one has heard from your ass. Answer the damn phone or call some-fucking-body. I hope that sneaky bastard isn't the reason you are turning your back on your own family, because if it is, you better remember that you'll need your family when he finishes dogging your dumb ass. Get your ass on a plane and get to Houston now, Kelly. I swear you will be cut the fuck off if I find you cut off your family in a time of need, for that bitch-nigga." Then the loud click followed with no goodbye.

I can't believe she'd act this way toward me. At least my man is *my* man. I'm not sharing some old white man with another bitch and too scared to speak up for myself. She thinks marrying him is going to seal her future. Yeah, right. She's just a judgmental bitch, always trying to tell someone how to live their lives while hers is all fucked up. And at least I'm not ashamed to be seen in public with my man. Fuck Shawnee.

"Baby, why are you letting them get to you like that?" Sean asked, wiping away my escaped tears. "You have every right to be happy, and I'm going to see to it you are. I'm not going to sit back and let them make my wife feel bad about a damn thing. I understand those are your sisters, but you have your own life. They need to remember that."

It was so romantic how Sean felt the need to protect me, even from my own sisters. I tried to smile through my tears. Sean took my face into his hands and began kissing me. It wasn't long after he had my bare ass propped up on the bathroom vanity, with my legs spread apart up in the air, as he stroked me slowly and deliberately. My hands were searching for something— anything—to grab onto to squeeze. Oh, he felt so wonderful inside of me. When I couldn't find anything to grab onto, I found my own tits to squeeze and fondle. Sean took that as his cue to tenderly nibble on them.

"I want you to have my baby," Sean whispered in between strokes.

All concentration on that magnificent orgasm I was about to have just went "ZIP." Orgasm went out the window. I am not ready to be anyone's mother. I decided to ignore his comment and pretend I didn't hear it. I figured I'd try to refocus on that lost orgasm.

A lost orgasm is just what it is, because he repeated, "Please have my baby. Our baby. You are my wife now. Let me plant my seed inside of you." All of this conversation between strokes.

Now why he gotta talk about some baby shit when I'm trying to get mine?

"You okay? Are you cumming? I need you to cum all over this big dick. Wet this dick, baby."

Now that's what I want to hear. Talk dirty to me. Don't be talking about damn babies. Yuck!

After a bit more dirty talk and changes in position, I finally got that nut I was trying to concentrate on. He let go shortly thereafter. That's what I love about Sean. He won't let go before I cum first.

But a baby? NOT!

24
Elaine

"I don't believe this shit! I just got a damn text message from Kelly saying Sean is her husband now and unless we accept him, she won't be coming around us without him."

"Elaine, can you blame her? You and Shawnee have been rough on her when it comes to that guy. I mean, to be quite honest, I think there's something suspect about him as well, but with my stupidity when it came to Lewis, I certainly knew I wasn't in the best position to say anything derogatory about someone else's relationship."

"Sandy, Elaine and I weren't being rough on her about the guy. I simply wanted her to keep her head on straight and deal with him the same way she would any other guy who entered her life," Shawnee said.

"That's Shawnee's take on the situation, but I knew something was wrong with him when he drugged Kelly to get her into bed."

"Yeah, you have a point there, Elaine. I'm kind of with you on that drugging thing. The Kelly I know would have never dropped those drawers before three months and a thorough background check. I am also bothered by the investment in his company. I mean, I know I didn't finish college like the rest of you, but that whole deal sounds shady as hell."

"Please don't get me started with that shit," Shawnee huffed, pushing her food away, which we'd ordered down in the hospital cafeteria. "Ya'll done spoiled my damn appetite. And the bitch didn't even have the decency to return my call from two days ago. Instead she's running off marrying the muthafucka! That bitch deserves everything she's about to get."

"Who deserves what?" Harmony asked, wobbling to the table to join us.

"Elaine just received a text message from Kelly announcing her marriage to the shifty guy. She said she's cutting us off if we don't accept her husband. As you see, Shawnee is now pissed since Kelly never tried to return her phone call. Hell, she never returned mine either, and I called first and twice."

"I think you all are going to cause me to go into an early labor. What the hell . . . Never mind. I don't even want to know. I have my own problems."

"So, Harmony, what are you going to do about your marriage? You have to find a way to work things out."

"Funny, I was just upstairs having the same conversation with your boyfriend Kevin. He too feels I need to find a way to work things out. You guys just don't understand that it's not that simple for me. I married the inconsiderate asshole that fathered the monster who tried to kill my sister."

"Don't forget he also fathered the children that you're wobbling around with."

We couldn't help but burst out into laughter. Watching Harmony wobble is comical. She better be glad she's 5'10, because she'd look worse carrying three babies if she were shorter.

"Fuck you, Sandy! You try carrying three fucking babies," Harmony yelled.

Sandy tried to stop her laughter. "I carried four. Remember?"

"You know what the fuck I mean. You didn't carry them all at once."

"That's why you need to be with your husband so he can massage and rub you and make you feel all better," Shawnee said.

"Well Shawnee, did it ever occur to you how the babies got inside my ass? From massaging and rubbing! Duh! Stop acting like you don't have a clue. Besides, I don't want Todd touching me. And don't think I forgot all of the other shit he said to me that day I got into my car accident."

"Oh, get over it! Half the shit was true." I laughed.

Shawnee jumped to Harmony's defense. "Speak for your damn self, Elaine. You didn't have to deal with his bitch-ass sister Tatiana."

Sandy twisted her lips. "Glad I can be lighthearted about this now, but Tatiana helped get you Eric back. It might have been underhanded as hell, but I know firsthand that was the best dick of your life."

"Eew, Sandy! You don't have to bring up that whole dick-sharing thing again. You know this pregnancy makes me get nauseous easily," Harmony said, holding her mouth as if she were about to vomit.

To tell the truth, that was probably the best dick of my life, but I don't dare say.

"Speaking of Tatiana, how are you dealing with that situation, Shawnee? Have you spoken to Brad about his affair with her?" I asked.

"Yeah, I spoke with him about it, and he still denied it. I wanted to tell him his fucking secretary, driver, and entire Houston office confirmed the shit, but I can't do that without causing them to get fired or in trouble. I also noticed each time I've been in Houston, he's been elsewhere. I guess he doesn't want to be here with me because he's afraid somebody will call his ass out right in front of me."

"He has come by the hospital a few times while he was here. I thought that was nice, but I did wonder why he would never come with you," Sandy said.

"I really don't understand how you would still agree to marry him despite his indiscretions. I know you're worried about Tatiana getting hold of him and booting you out of the company, but marriage is not something to play with. Do you think I like going through this shit with Todd, especially while carrying his children? I got married because of what marriage meant to me," Harmony said.

"And I guess you don't think marriage meant something to me when I married Robert? They are going to take theirs, and I'm going to take mine. Fuck the meaning of marriage. Lot of good it did me. And when I'm done with Brad, I'll be a wealthy-ass woman as a result. If pussy is their weakness, then I'll capitalize on that."

"Wow, that sounds like the story of my life. And I have my wealth just the same. But at the end of the day, that wealth means nothing if you're empty and bitter and don't have love," I shared with Shawnee.

"Preach, girl!" Sandy shouted with one hand in the air.

"Who says I don't have love? I do love Brad, and I know Brad loves me despite Tatiana. However, I love me more, and if I'm going to have to tolerate any infidelity from any man, I'm going to make sure Shawnee comes out on top. I could tolerate infidelity when I know—not think—I'll end up a billionaire as a result. Now if he was a broke ass . . . Oh, that's a whole other story. Next! He would have to get the boot immediately."

Sandy raised an eyebrow. "So I guess that part was meant for me?"

"Not particularly. It's just a broke-ass cheat ain't meant for me. So if Brad wants to get married, so be it. The sooner, the better. If he wants to sneak off and fuck Tatiana and/or others, then let him. And when we get married, just watch how I'll pull the plug on him getting this pussy.

The Queen

He won't be able to do a damn thing about it, other than what he's already doing."

Harmony laughed. "Who would have thought that old man Neely was an old freak? Damn! Is he taking Viagra or something? I know you are a freak, but if you're not enough for him, then he's something else."

We all laughed because Harmony made a good point. Shawnee was always highly energetic when it came to sex. She should have been too much for Brad if anything.

"Whatever works for you," Sandy said to Shawnee, shaking her head. "At least you have Eric as your back-up dick."

I wasn't too sure if Sandy was still being lighthearted about Eric and Shawnee together.

"Changing subjects, what's up with you and Kevin, Elaine? Do you think this will be someone you will settle down with?" Shawnee asked.

"I bet you do want to change the subject, Shawnee." Harmony giggled to herself. "I like Kevin. Even Angelo likes Kevin. You might want to watch that before Angelo takes him away from you." Then she laughed harder at her own joke.

"Ha, ha! I don't think so! I could see Kevin being a keeper. As you can already tell, he's always around when I need him. And after my big announcement about how I earned my money, he chose to hang by my side. He could have bounced from that point. The hard part is trying to commit myself to him knowing we can't sleep together until we're married, and then having to get rid of all my sponsors."

"Now that's some hard shit there! No dick at all! You went from 'dick musical chairs' to no dick. Whew! My hat's off to you."

"Sandy, I thought you're supposed to be all saved and sanctified now? You've been doing a whole bunch of cussing and talking about dicks?"

"Tell her, Shawnee!" Harmony said. "Elaine's been cursing just the same. Maybe we're being a bad influence."

"I haven't been doing a lot of cursing, Harmony. Besides, I'm still trying to change things in my life, but I'll curse a bitch out in a New York minute. I'll cut a bitch too," I said, making a cutting motion.

After we shared a good laugh, Sandy said, "I don't know why people think I'm supposed to be so perfect. I haven't been to anybody's church since I've been single-handedly keeping vigil here at the hospital. And furthermore, I have a bad taste in my mouth right now concerning church. It was a bitch from the church who's been creeping with my husband."

"Sandy, everyone's been creeping with your husband. Hopefully he's history for once and for all," Harmony reminded her.

"You damn right he's history. And to prove it, when Elaine takes Charise back to L.A. with her, the kids and I are going as well."

I choked on the water I had just sipped. I didn't see that one coming. Charise is one thing, but a house full of half-grown, teenaged kids, a baby, and Sandy all up in my business is a whole other can of worms.

Harmony laughed at my choking. "Obviously somebody forgot to give Elaine that memo. How are you just going to plan to take you and your four kids to live with Elaine? That's just flat-out inconsiderate."

I was so thankful to Harmony for stepping up and not have me be the heavy here.

"I have my own money. I'll find some place to live on my own. It's not like I haven't done it before. I usually don't have a problem finding a job when I want one. Maybe I could get a job over where Elaine and Angelo are."

"Sandy, you have a toddler. A baby, really. How are you going to an expensive-ass state like California, with all the job shortages and foreclosures, and think you could make out okay? I know Lewis has helped spend up your inheritance by now. From a business standpoint, Elaine can't afford to just give you a job when she's just been open a few months. Remember that Angelo is only there as part of a larger

The Queen

business deal, and if the other part of the business goes belly-up, there's a domino-effect," Shawnee also defended.

"Stop worrying about me. I'll be all right. I have never asked anyone for anything, and I won't start. I know I'm getting away from this whole Lewis fiasco, and I figured after this whole ordeal with Charise, that I need to bond better with my family. And for the record, Lewis was paying for everything while I banked my own money. You didn't think I put up with all of his shit AND let him spend me broke, did you? NOT! And you can believe that my other child support sufficiently covers my children's needs. I just have to get an order for the baby, and we're good to go."

"She told you, Shawnee." Harmony laughed. "Well, Sandy, I'm glad to hear that you somewhat got things in order. I just don't want things to get too financially hectic for Elaine, to the point that she feels she needs to revert to familiar territory."

"Hell, Elaine will revert if she can't get some dick soon. I'm not the only dick-happy bitch in the family."

"Go to hell, Shawnee!" I said in fun. "I can hold out as long as I need to. And Sandy, if you can find someplace reasonably priced, I will help you pay a portion of your rent for the first year only. That, or until you find a man to pay it for you. 'Cause you know I'm not paying for any place you're going to have some man in."

"Oh, thank you, Elaine." Sandy reached over and hugged me. "I don't plan on having any man around. I have a daughter to think about now, and I am saved."

Shawnee, Harmony, and I looked at Sandy then at each other before we broke out into a roaring laughter. One, because having her first daughter didn't stop Sandy from having a new boyfriend every time you blinked, and two, Sandy and "saved" almost don't belong in the same sentence. We took our laughter back upstairs to Charise's room, while Sandy cursed us the whole way.

25
Harmony

"Todd, we don't have anything to talk about. Get out of my office and leave me the hell alone." I ran for a safe distance behind my desk. I hate that I married such a gorgeous man who makes me weak in the knees on sight— most of the time.

"We have three precious babies on the way. We have a new marriage. We have plenty to talk about."

"Oh, so now my whorish babies belong to you?" I asked, taking my seat while shooting him with optical daggers. "Didn't you question their paternity? And as for our joke of a marriage, you fooled me good, but I don't have to stay your fool."

"Harmony, I can't believe you are going to hold that nonsense against me. I was confused and angry about what Andre, who is also my child, just threw my way. I admit I handled everything poorly, including my insensitivity to what he did to your sister. Now in my right mind, I don't feel Charise or anyone deserved what Andre did, even if they were the source of his infection. Harmony, this is hard on me. I don't expect you to sympathize, but I hope you understand what all is at stake here."

"Well, I guess I just don't understand. Thanks to both your fucked-up comments and your lunatic son, I've come to realize the importance

The Queen

of being closer to my own family. I tried to accept your family as my own, but when the going got tough, you made it perfectly clear that *your* family is *your* family, and my nutty, mixed-up family is *my* family. So on that note, I have decided to take my three illegitimate babies and move to L.A. nearer to my own damn family. You and your family can go to hell." I dismissively turned in my executive chair away from him.

"Fine, we'll move to L.A. near your family, but know that where you go, I will go with you."

My neck snapped from turning it so fast. "What did you say?" I asked, pretty certain I heard correctly the first time.

He inched closer to me as he looked directly into my eyes for some hint that he said the right thing to neutralize me. "I said, I will go wherever you go. Harmony, you are my wife and you are my family. For my wife, I am supposed to leave my family to cleave. I didn't do that before as I should have, but I will now. Don't get me wrong; I am happy about the babies, but my need to leave my family for our marriage has nothing to do with the babies. I love *you*, Harmony. I chose you for my wife. You chose me for your husband. We didn't come to that decision because of any babies. We came to that decision because of our love for one another. The babies just sealed our love. Not one seal, but three. I promised to love you for a lifetime. I was a kid when I made the promise the first time, and didn't quite appreciate the magnitude of that promise. Now I am a full-grown man, fully aware, and fully intending to uphold that promise.

"Harmony, I will leave the practice and everything I own, but I will be wherever you are. If it's L.A., then L.A. it is. I want to be with you when you give birth, the way I'm supposed to be. And don't think I don't see those swollen ankles you're hiding behind that desk. I should be able to rub your tired ankles every day. I see how you hold your back. I want to rub those kinks out for you every day. I want to serve your breakfast in bed each morning as I did before I so foolishly pushed you away. I want to love you, Harmony. Please let me do that. Let me spend each day of the rest of our lives making up to you for my stupid behavior. Let me be there to kiss away your sadness or sorrows. Let me be there to catch each tear before it can fall." Todd took his index finger to wipe the tear that had begun to fall. He then took my non-resistance as his cue to kiss me.

What the hell was I thinking leaving my husband? I'm about to lose the best thing that ever happened to me. The father of my children. My husband.

"You meant what you said?"

"Every word, Harmony. Tell me what I need to do to prove that I am one-hundred percent devoted and committed to you, our marriage, and our family."

"I really do plan on going to L.A. to be closer to my family. How are you just going to give everything up to follow me?"

"I said I would, and I will. You just leave that part up to me. How soon do you want to go? Your OB is here in Houston. Were you planning on waiting for the babies to get here? It's going to be hard for you to travel being a high risk pregnancy."

"I figured the sooner I go the better. It's not like I have the most competent obstetrician. The jackass couldn't even tell I was carrying triplets versus a single baby. This is my last week at work."

"Fine, we'll go to L.A. to find a home to get you situated, and I'll fly back and tie up everything here in Houston. Hopefully I'll have everything all settled and be back in L.A. for good before the babies arrive. At least I'll know you'll be in good hands with your family nearby."

"Todd! You are serious? You are really willing to give up your life for me?"

"Harmony, you are my life, and without you, I have no life. So if that means moving things around a bit, then so be it."

The Queen

Todd picked up my office phone and called his travel agent to book our flight to L.A. and our hotel for the coming weekend.

Damn! Now how am I supposed to stay angry with him? Maybe he'll return to Houston and change his mind about giving up everything for me.

"Do you think we can go online and look for some potential homes tonight when you get home from work?"

Wow, it just dawned on me that we no longer live in the same place. I don't want to go back to that house. Too many bad memories came from that one day.

"Only if you are willing to come to my apartment. I can't bring myself to go back to the house."

"I'm okay being anywhere as long as I'm with you."

As Todd sat on the edge of my desk with one foot touching the floor, I took notice of the instant erection between his legs. The sight caused vaginal contractions.

Damn, I'm not sure if I can have sex anymore in my condition. You can bet that I'm going to call my quack doctor to find out the minute Todd leaves my office.

"I have to get myself together and make a quick phone call before my next patient arrives. I'll see you tonight?" I said, standing up with the intentions of directing him to the door so I could call my doctor.

Instead, he took all of me into his arms and kissed me as if it were our wedding day. Suddenly I was in love with my husband all over again. Just like that. And when he left, I called and got my green light to make love to my husband. I only have a few more weeks before I have to abstain from sexual activity, so we're going to have to use this time wisely. And I get my swollen feet and back rubbed too? Hot damn!

26
Shawnee

Huffing and puffing. I promise this is my last time with Eric. I have a wedding to plan, and Eric is getting too attached. This is the very last time I'll let his long tongue tickle my cervix. This is also the last time I'll take his bat-sized dick up my ass. No more shall I play rodeo when he bucks me up and down as I straddle him. Never again shall his massive hands massage and caress every inch of my body.

"Are you sure you want this to be our last time together, Shawnee? You know I'm going to follow your lead." He wiped the beads of sweat from my face.

"I'm getting married, Eric." I stood from the bed. "I can't be doing this. It has to stop. I have no business here with you now."

"Apparently he can't love you the way I can, otherwise you wouldn't be here. To me, it doesn't sound like you're ready to be getting married. I mean, I understand: that's your bread and butter and all, so I don't want to knock you for getting yours. I just don't understand why we can't keep seeing each other. Like how we are now."

I momentarily halted my guilty pace. "Eric, you are the infamous Mandingo. You have women out the ying-yang. You don't need to keep trying to be with me."

The Queen

"That may be so, but you obviously need to see me. The past few times we've been together, you've called and arranged it. I'm just trying to keep you happy. Despite how you feel about me, I still love you, and at this point, will take any crumb that you throw my way. I won't lie, it's kind of fucked up that you only view me as a piece of meat, while I value you as a whole woman. It's clear to me that you'll never love me like I love you, 'cause you wouldn't be planning to marry some other dude when I was around from your first marriage. I wanted to marry you . . ."

Eric got off the bed and walked his luscious body to the picturesque window. It was obvious he was fighting tears. I wasn't sure what to do.

Do I go and try and console him? Do I just get dressed and leave him to his own misery? To hell with that! I want some more of his loving before I go—particularly if this is going to be our last time together.

I chose to walk up behind him and press my chest against his back and let my hands reach around to his front. I sensually kissed his back as I let one hand massage his nipples and the other hand stroke his manhood. It took a minute, but I felt growth in my hand and nipples hardening. I turned his body to face me and bent down to take his enlarged head into my mouth. He got with the program real quick. Both of his hands were massaging my head as he pushed his dick farther and farther toward the back of my throat.

He led me to the blanket he'd placed on the floor earlier, which was still wet from an earlier round. On the floor, he spread my legs apart and buried his face deep in my alcove. Then he repositioned my hips to bring my asshole to his mouth, while his fingers massaged my clit. My pussy was squirting up a storm. The sensational feeling had me going crazy. Then he turned me over onto my hands and knees. Again he orally stimulated my asshole while his hand played with the kitty kat. I knew this was his prelude to putting the dick in my ass. And without fail, he lubed up and was in my back door giving me a play-by-play commentary of each and every stroke.

"Damn, look how your ass is squirting juice all over my dick."

"Damn your wet pussy is pouring in my hand."

"Your ass muscles are working this dick, baby."

When he was done from that position, he carried me and laid me on the table.

"I gotta eat all this cum from your hot pussy."

Then his mouth was sopping up every drop of cum my pussy could manufacture. While he sucked the honey that he drizzled on my breast, he slipped on a fresh condom and took his massive erection and filled my wet cave. Then he angled my body giving him free access in and out of my pussy. Keeping his dick inside me, he raised me up completely as he moved me from one part of the room to another. He'd turn me from front, to back, to side, and upside down.

By the time he was done, my legs were completely rubber and were of no use. My throat was dehydrated. And like always after a romp in the hay with Mr. Mandingo, my ass was sore as hell. A good sore that makes my coochie contract every time I mentally replay the cause of my sore ass.

I'm sorry, Brad, but I can't let Eric go.

I'll have to find a way to have them both.

You want me to be happy? So I will be. With both men. I'm still going to get that Tatiana bitch out of the picture. Then I'll be really happy.

~ ~ ~ ~

"Sweetie, do you have a free moment to meet me for lunch? There's something important we need to discuss."

The Queen

"Sure, Brad. Anything for you," I answered after being summoned to his office.

I wonder what he needs to discuss outside of the office. Why didn't he mention anything last night when we were together? Maybe he found out about Eric and wants to confront me away from the office. Maybe he wants to break up with me. Is he finally ready to come clean about Tatiana? I hate when people do that shit. He knows I hate that waiting shit. They have you sitting around wondering what the hell is up. Now I have to wait at least 2-3 hours to learn what's on his mind.

Finally, *four hours later*, we went to lunch.

"I'm sorry to have you waiting and wondering for so long. I know how much you despise anticipation of the unknown. I had to check with you early enough before your schedule got too heavy and I would have had to wait to talk with you," he said after we were seated at the restaurant.

"Why didn't you talk to me last night when I got back in town?"

"Because you were looking so wonderful and I didn't want to ruin the moment."

"Ruin? Wow, that doesn't sound too good."

"No, Shawnee, it's not looking too good either." His expression was very somber.

My heart began pounding audibly. Whew! I think there was a sudden heat surge or the AC just broke down in the restaurant during this summer heat wave. My hard gulp had to let him know I was in panic mode.

But why am I panicking? My work is beyond outstanding. It has to be Eric. Does he know Eric was in Europe with me last week? Does he have spies watching me? Maybe he's been checking out my expense account and saw the suite I booked separately for Eric.

He took my sweaty, fidgety hands into his and then kissed them. "Sweetie, I'm not trying to leave you and I still want to marry you. I see you're already bothered. I will admit that I am the one who is afraid you will leave me once I tell you what I have to say."

Oh, so he is ready to come clean about fucking Tatiana! That bitch! No—what if it's others? He better not be fucking anyone else. So what, I've got my nerve. My panicked expression quickly changed to anger.

"Brad, so help me. You and that fucking Tatiana! Why?"

"Who? Tatiana? From the Houston office? The one I fired for you? Gosh, no!" Brad said, sticking to his lie. He had the nerve to laugh as if I'd said something so ridiculous. "How about I just tell you and stop this emotional rollercoaster you're on?"

"Yes, that would be good."

I don't know what's more unnerving: knowing he's fucking Tatiana or sitting here watching him lie so boldly about Tatiana. Now he wants to act like he barely knows her. I guess 'bare' is the operative word with his lying ass.

"Shawnee, I would like to move up our wedding date if you're still willing to marry me."

"Why wouldn't I want to still marry you?" I asked suspiciously.

Brad nervously chuckled. "For the longest, this old man thought he had eluded what seemed to be a family curse—the very curse that made me choose to never have any kids to bestow the curse upon. And now, well actually a few months ago, I've learned that I wasn't so lucky after all. I've gotten further in life than all the others, but didn't quite escape altogether."

"What are you talking about, Brad? What curse?"

A fucking sex addiction.

"Prostate cancer. Shawnee, I have prostate cancer. The doctors are not too hopeful because of my family history and age."

"That's bullshit!" I yelled. As the words sunk in, a tear fell. "Then find another doctor. Brad, find another doctor. You don't take the word of one and just give up like that. You said you loved me. How are you just going to accept that bullshit?"

Now my eyes were flooded and my voice was cracking. I've been so hard on him and now he tells me he's dying. I don't want him to die.

Brad tried wiping my tears away and moved his chair nearer to me to hold me in his arms. I slightly squirmed because we were out in public together and I'm sure people were watching us.

Taking note of my body's language, Brad said, "I hate telling you this in a public place, but every time we're together alone, the moment seems perfect with you, and I don't want to ruin that moment."

Brad's trying to comfort me when I should be trying to comfort him, and then I'm sitting here with my silly hang-ups worrying about what other people are thinking. He's been carrying this burden all this time by himself, while I've been carrying on with another man.

Maybe he really wasn't with Tatiana all those times, I tried to rationalize. So many times he seemed elusive about his whereabouts.

Oh, my Lord, I am so confused right now.

"Brad, have you consulted more than one doctor? What are your treatment options?"

"Yes, I have consulted several doctors both here in the states, as well as in Europe. Everything is too invasive or requires cutting here and cutting there. I have already opted to skip all of that and make the most of the days the good Lord gives me. I prefer a quality life rather than a quantity life with no more quality."

"What about me? Us? Haven't you thought about that?"

"Yes, Shawnee. There's not a day that goes by that I don't think about you and us. That's why I want to marry you sooner rather than later, and when something happens to me, you will become the heir to my estate without any challenges. Instead of me spending my days in hospitals with one surgery or treatment after the other, I want to spend those days pleasing you and getting you ready to take over the company."

"So you're asking me to marry you just to watch you die? Is this some punishment or something? How am I supposed to deal with that, Brad? I don't give a damn about being an heir."

I expected half if we divorced, but not all from him dying.

"Maybe I'm being selfish. There is no easy answer. I loved you and wanted to marry you long before I found out about this cancer. You also wanted to marry me before I learned about the cancer. But the bottom line is, the cancer is here and won't be leaving this earth without me. I want us to still be able to marry while I have quality time left. I want us to make some beautiful memories together. Even if you elect not to marry me at this point, you will still be my heir whether you like it or not. Shawnee, I just want to spend my last days happy with you as my wife. I don't want to spend my time fighting a losing battle."

CHA-CHING! And that trampy-ass Tatiana gets nothing! I would kill him if I found out he provided for her ass.

"I went through this death thing with both my mother and father. Mama fought for as long as she could. Daddy went kind of quick."

"And then they lost. That's my point exactly. I want to be happy, Shawnee, and nothing will make me happier than you marrying me and helping me fulfill the desires of my heart."

God, this is the toughest decision I have ever been faced with. He's right about fighting a losing battle. Yes, there are those few who have survived cancer battles. Daddy went quicker than Mama from some kind of liver failure, but in the end, they both lost their fight. How do I expect Brad to choose to suffer his remaining time rather than be happy?

"Fine, Brad, we'll do things how you would like, but don't expect me to be happy about this."

The Queen

And I hope those desires of his heart don't include me letting Tatiana come around at will or vice-versa.

"I don't know how or what to feel right now, but I'll go along with this."

"That's a start I can live with. I promise, you will be happy. I love you."

I tried to smile, but under the circumstances, a smile was too difficult. "So when did you have in mind to get married?"

"As soon as you can assemble your family together for a European cruise."

"Well, that is synonymous with never. There's too much going on with all of them, and you're talking about a week or two for the cruise. None of them can get away that long."

"Then tell me what you would prefer."

"I'm not pressed for my family to be there. If you want a European cruise, then you and I will do that. You say when."

The truth is, none of them are all that excited about my marrying Brad anymore since they know about Tatiana. They wouldn't take the time to come wish us well in what they believe to be a farce of a marriage. Well, Sandy is the eternal optimist when it comes to marriage, so she'd probably want to go, and Angelo would go just for the free trip. That is, if Elaine would let him. Probably not.

And two weeks later, just Brad and I were off to Europe to be married. This is not going to be easy. Now I feel like I have to sit around and watch my new husband die each day, little by little. Talking to his many doctors didn't help any. They were all doom and gloom. Although Brad is the picture of perfect health, they make it sound as though I should expect him to be gone within the next week or so. Assholes!

What's even more difficult is trying to be loving and compassionate to a dying man who is STILL fucking Tatiana every chance he can despite our marriage.

Apparently, Tatiana is still hell bent on getting me out of Brad's life. His marrying me wasn't enough to let her know that she wasn't going to have him. The bitch had the nerve to send me a date-stamped videotape, she took of her and Brad recently fucking. As disgusting as it was, I watched every bit of it. I was kind of jealous watching him fuck her better than he does me. The way he seemed to savor her tits in his mouth as if they were covered with his favorite flavor of something. In the video, his dick appeared almost longer as it was going in and out of her pussy. This bitch obviously used multiple cameras. At times, it seemed as though there may have been a camera crew on hand, because there were some really close up shots. Close enough to see that no condoms were used.

Did she convince him to do a porno movie with her before he dies? I sat and watched him bury his face in her pussy and her ass. I watched her sucking on his dick. And the big kick in the gut was watching the anal sex. Damn, we don't even have anal sex together.

The damn tape went on for about an hour and 45 minutes before he finally came. Never has he lasted that long with me. Apparently she had the thing edited.

No! The *coup de grâce* was listening to him tell her how much he loves her and she's the most important thing in the world to him. In the video, she told him that he needed to get rid of me so they could be together every day, and that I was only a gold-digger after his money.

His dumb ass responded, "I wish I would have married you instead. I just felt stuck between a rock and a hard place at the time, and she pressured me into getting married."

Is he fucking kidding? I pressured him?

The Queen

I pondered my next move since Tatiana is probably counting on my leaving Brad because of the video. Brad is "supposed to be" dying. If I walk now with this video, at the very least I'd take half of everything Brad owns, but since he'd probably be dead before the divorce is final, I'd still get just about everything. However, if I leave Tatiana an opening, she'll have her opportunity to get in and take everything before he dies. Not an option. If I stay with the motherfucker, I have to deal with this bullshit of him and Tatiana. But in the end, I'll have everything, and she'll have nothing. I need to check into that and make sure she's not getting anything. He could already be supporting her somehow without my knowing it, and planning to set her up in his death. I'd exhume his dead body just to re-kill his ass if I find he left anything to her in his will.

I really have to think about how I am going to handle this Brad and Tatiana affair now that I found out I am pregnant. I don't know if I should mention it to Brad or not. He may have been sterile for years, which is why he said he chose to never have kids. Then, with the prostate cancer, I didn't think he could get a person pregnant. I don't understand how this shit happened. I was taking birth control pills and I always kept a condom. Not that I wanted any baby, but I'd die if this turns out to be Eric's baby. Brad would probably boot me out of his life with nothing. Then again, I'd hate for this to be Brad's sickly baby. I wouldn't want a child conceived while he was sick with cancer. And if he could make babies still, is he trying to impregnate Tatiana as well? They obviously aren't using condoms. Then her and her bastard child would be trying to fight me in court for a piece of the inheritance. I'd kill the bitch first. And her baby.

Since I needed a leg to stand on when I told Brad about my pregnancy, I decided to confront him about the video.

"Come on, honey. Watch this video with me. We haven't had time to just sit and share a video together." I had my best game face on.

This motherfucker won't even see what's coming.

"I was hoping to make love to you tonight. It feels like an eternity since I last touched you," he answered.

"Well I'm sure this video will definitely set the mood," I responded with a smile.

He got so happy and started feeling me up. I jumped up from the sofa I was sitting to avoid his filthy clutches. "Not just yet."

"Okay, put it on. Do you think you can slip on something sexy before you start the movie?" he asked.

"How about I undo some buttons on my blouse, remove my bra, roll up my skirt to make it a mini, and remove my stockings? That way I can give you a nice little peepshow. I know how much you used to love that, Brad. Then maybe we could pretend I had to come into your office and you can't keep your eyes off my body while the television is on."

"Yeah. I'd like that," he responded in his perverted laugh that used to turn me on for some odd reason.

I did what I said I'd do, and then returned to the den with him. I decided to sit across from him as we used to do before consummating our relationship. I'd move in certain ways to expose just enough to turn him on, but not everything.

"Oh, Shawnee, I'm about to burst here. Come over here and let me touch that beautiful cunt of yours." He patted the seat next to him and was rubbing his dick, which was standing in the air out of his pants.

"Not before watching the video." I turned the video on and kept my eye on Brad. It took a minute for Brad to finally look at the television and see himself with Tatiana. He had been so busy stroking his own dick and watching my exposed pussy.

His dick instantly deflated when he saw the video.

"Yeah, your bitch felt the need to send this to me. She obviously wants me to know how you feel I pressured you into marrying me and that you really want to be with her." Brad looked like death at that very moment. "How could you, Brad? How could you look me in my face and lie to me each and every time I asked you about your involvement with her? And if you want to be with her so bad, why would you marry me? Why would you want to hurt me and complicate my life, knowing the fucked-up marriage I had just left?"

"Oh, Shawnee, I am so sorry. I obviously never wanted you to find out about this. I never wanted to hurt you. I love you, and that is strictly lust," he answered, nervous as hell.

"I heard you say to her that she is the most important thing in this world to you. I heard that come from your mouth, Brad. I sat and watched one hour and forty-five minutes of pure lustful fucking and sucking, Brad, with the ending saying I pressured you into marriage. Why did you fire the bitch if you were fucking her? Why were you fucking her, Brad? Why did you lie to me, Brad?" My voice was getting louder and my tone was going back to the ghetto from whence I came.

This motherfucker still had his eyes locked between my pussy and tits. Maybe he does have a sex addiction.

"How many other women are there, Brad? And don't you dare lie to me, because you know I'll find out. Then you won't have to worry about dying from cancer because I will kill you if you tell me one more fucking lie." Now I was standing over him as though I'd fuck him up any minute.

"Please sit and let's talk about this rationally. I'll tell the truth. Please," he said, taking my hand to get me to sit next to him. "Okay, the Tatiana thing. Yes, I was wrong for lying to you. I love you and didn't want to lose you so I lied about her. I had been intimate with Tatiana for some time, and when I had to fire her, she threatened to sue for sexual harassment. I offered her a very large payoff, but she decided she didn't want any money, but only to continue our relationship. I will admit I had feelings for her, but not what I felt for you. Something about her just turned me on and made it hard to resist her."

This was hard to listen to. I don't know why I even asked. "Who initiated your relationship? How did it start?"

"Does it make a difference?"

"I asked, you answer," I said through gritted teeth.

He was hesitant and looked down at his fumbling hands. "I guess I would have to say I did then. She had a lower position when I first saw her. I wanted to touch her. I found ways to get closer to her without raising eyebrows, and eventually I was able to get her in my office alone. I couldn't help myself. I just touched her breast. She was a bit put off, but when she didn't resist, I took it further and she let me. Maybe she was afraid of losing her job if she didn't cooperate. I don't know. That same evening I had her at my house and the rest is history. With you, you had this professional sexiness about you. You were intelligent and bold. You were about business and would do whatever to get the job done. That turned me on. I've had my eye on you long before there was any thought of Tatiana, but you were much more intimidating, much harder to read. You were very professional, but the way you wore your clothes made me salivate. You could wear a suit like no other. But you were also married. Tatiana wasn't married and she wasn't intimidating. I also wasn't worried about losing Tatiana professionally because she in no way compared to your level of intelligence. I did promote her to give myself easier access to closed-door meetings without arousing suspicions. You, I promoted based on your work. But I still wanted you sexually. When you came to New York and we were in my limo that first time, I didn't know what to do. I didn't want to compromise our professional relationship, but I wanted every bit of you. I wanted my cock inside of you so bad. I was scared of losing you then.

The Queen

"I also didn't know what to do because I was already involved with Tatiana. I didn't know how she'd react if she knew I was involved with you. After you and I went all the way, I spent less time in Houston to avoid Tatiana. She's a lot needier than you are. One time she showed up here in New York. I'm not sure where you were that day, but you didn't see her. I took her to a hotel, gave her what she wanted, and sent her back to Houston. She did it a few more times, which really made me start getting worried. Then she asked for me to transfer her to New York since I was spending so much time here. I told her it would be difficult. She threatened to make more frequent trips so she could find out if I was seeing someone else. I told her I would work something out.

"I really had been working on that overseas position for some time, and when I offered it to you, it just seemed like the perfect time. The crazy thing was, I was doing so much to accommodate Tatiana, but you were the one I actually loved. You are just so much more mature-minded and well rounded. With you, I could see a future. I couldn't see a future with Tatiana without a whole lot of headaches. The phone call to your ex-boyfriend confirmed how immature she is, and now this video. But still the physical attraction and chemistry was difficult to resist.

"Although I began as the aggressor, she became very aggressive. She eventually picked up on the fact that I was seeing you. She couldn't tell when you and I were in the office, but she realized I was always unavailable to her when you were in town. She'd frequent my office for intimate moments when you were away, but I never allowed her into my office when you were around. I also wouldn't see her outside of the office. When she confronted me, I told her the truth about you and me, as well as let her know that I loved you and wanted to marry you. She was in denial about it and behaved as if I never said anything. It kind of scared me as to what she would do. All she wanted was for me to keep being intimate with her. She didn't care about what I told her.

"I got greedy and wanted to have my cake and eat it too. I was able to have you both, and I loved it. I hesitated getting married when I learned of the cancer. The doctors told me the treatment would more than likely kill my sexual appetite, and I may not even survive treatment. I thought about just refusing the treatment and maintaining my blissful sexual life with you both. I planned on being completely faithful to you once we were married, before I learned of the cancer. After I found out, I wasn't sure about getting married only to have you watch me die away. I also only wanted to continue to be with both of you. Eventually I thought of who I would want in my corner in my final days and who I could trust to handle my company and everything I have built. That would be you.

"I had every intention on being faithful to you once we were married, but Tatiana can be very convincing. I am just weak when it comes to her. I'm sure that's not what you want to hear, but it's the truth, Shawnee. I swear I never wanted to hurt you. I don't know why she felt the need to send you that video. She said she wanted to have it for her memories when I pass on. I never thought she'd use it to try and hurt you. The stuff I said in the video was only to make her feel better when she'd watch after I was gone. That video is all she will have of me. You on the other hand, will have everything of me."

Is that supposed to make me feel better? I didn't hear him say he won't see her again. "So Brad, will you keep seeing her and lying to me? It doesn't sound like you plan on ending this affair."

Brad looked down. "I don't want to lie to you, Shawnee, but I don't want to lose you. I can't seem to help it. I don't want to keep seeing her."

"And that means I'm supposed to be all right with sharing my husband?" I was pissed that my voice cracked when I was trying to sound

firm. "If it's not enough that I'm supposed to accept you dying, but I'm supposed to accept sharing you—with a bitch I can't stand, no less?"

"But, Shawnee, I have already signed over my company to you while I'm still healthy and well. I have left every dime to you and a few charities. She's not getting anything. Please let me have this one thing before I die. I know it's asking a lot, but I can't tell you with honesty that I wouldn't want to be with her again. I get very turned on by both of you. I know I'm being selfish, but even now I want to fuck you. I love the way you give me a private peepshow. I love how your pussy feels on my cock and your plump breast feels in my mouth. I love burying my face in your ass and driving you crazy. But if you've watched that tape, then you would see there is a different type of chemistry between Tatiana and me. Maybe it's because she's younger, I don't know. I can't let go, Shawnee. That's the ugly truth. I can't let go."

I stood up and paced back and forth before sitting back down. "Brad, how do you expect me to be okay with letting you fuck me every other day you're not fucking her? I can't do it and I won't do it. If you want to fuck her until your dick falls off, then be my guest, but you will never touch this pussy ever again." I opened my legs to show him my pussy.

He looked and then his dick had the nerve to stand back up.

"Please, Shawnee, I need you. Okay, I promise, no more Tatiana. I won't be with her ever again," he said, putting his hand on my pussy and massaging it. "Please let me make this pussy feel good. Forget about me. Just let me make you feel good."

Now his fingers were inside my pussy, and he was making it feel good. And when I didn't resist, he pulled one of my tits from my blouse and sucked it. When he laid me back, he ate my pussy, and it felt so good, I didn't give a damn that I knew he was lying about not fucking Tatiana again. Damn, I wonder if this is the same lame shit Lewis would pull on Sandy every time she had to confront him about all the women he was fucking.

I am too much of a sex-a-holic to never let him fuck me again. I don't like the shit, but I'm going to have to tolerate Tatiana's dumb ass or make her disappear for good. If Brad's driver could fuck worth a damn, I could fuck him and resist Brad, but no such luck. When I tried him one more time and I got the same lame result.

After Brad finished making me 'feel good' and I looked up at the television showing Brad still fucking Tatiana on it, I said, "By the way, I'm pregnant. I'm due in March."

Brad's reaction was a combination of shock and anger. I figured one way or another, I was about to find out if he was capable of procreation. "But how? You can't be," he managed to say.

"I am."

"But when did you become pregnant? How long have you known this?"

"I found out two days ago. I considered an abortion, but thought against it with my age. I became pregnant before we got married."

"Shawnee, I can't have children. I couldn't before the cancer and especially not now since the cancer. You've been cheating on me this whole time? Tatiana was right about you cheating on me I told her you would never, and now you're carrying his baby. How could you do this, Shawnee? Do you know how much I love and respect you?"

Right at that moment, Brad's tongue was licking Tatiana's ass, still on the television. I pointed to it. "Yeah, I see for myself how much you love and respect me . . . with last week's date stamped on the film. And don't you ever tell me what Tatiana had to say about a damn thing."

I got up from the sofa and left Brad downstairs to finish watching his homemade porno tape alone.

And that was the last time Brad's dick ever made it inside of this pussy. A few weeks later, Brad's health started turning downward.

The Queen

Right before that turn, Brad got real blatant with his affair, but that downward turn ended their relationship. Not only was he bold enough to talk about Tatiana openly, but he had the nerve to confess about Daisy in his Chicago office and Cynthia in the Los Angeles office. Not even Tatiana knew about them.

Tatiana started calling our home like it was okay. Ironically, Brad told her I was carrying his child. That pissed her off.

She left a message on my cell phone saying, "You may have Brad fooled about that baby, but I know you are not carrying his baby, and as soon as I find proof, I'm going to expose your ass for once and for all. That baby is not going to make him love you any more because he's always going to be with me and there ain't a damn thing you can do about it. Whore!"

Brad's illness prevented him from being able to fly anymore. One day Tatiana had the nerve to come to New York while I was in town. Did she really think she was going to be with him while I was there? She came into the office wanting to meet with him in private. Brad's secretary called me quick-fast. I had been out of the building for a meeting. I was in his office just about as quick as Tatiana could finish unbuttoning her blouse. Unfortunately, not soon enough. I walked in on her trying to seduce him there in his office and him a willing candidate. She was standing in front of him braless with buttons to her blouse already undone and her boobs standing to attention. Her skirt was up, showing her waxed pussy, with one foot on the sofa he was sitting on. Brad's hand was on her upper thigh, with his thumb massaging her clit and wetness from her pussy around his mouth. Brad quickly pushed her away from him when he saw me, but hadn't tried stopping her before I opened that door.

"Brad wasn't getting any good pussy lately and I figured I'd deliver it to him," she said smugly while fastening her buttons back.

"Keep standing there and you'll be leaving in a body bag, bitch."

"I didn't come here for this shit. Brad, I'll see you later at the hotel."

I wanted to snatch her ass so bad, but had to remember I'm carrying a baby. "We'll see about that shit," was all I could say as she smugly left his office.

Brad claimed he had no knowledge she was in New York. He said she was upset because he wasn't calling or seeing her anymore, and said she came because she would refresh his memory but couldn't help himself when she exposed herself to him. He just wanted to feel her one last time.

I know Brad was mad as hell he missed out on the pussy she was offering that day, because two days later, he totally lost his ability to get an erection. He played one porno tape after the other, and still nothing. He begged to play in my pussy to see if that would help. I only let him watch me play in my own pussy. I did let him suck my tits. They were begging for some attention. Still, no erection. And with the demise of his erection, was the demise of his spirit. When his spirit went, his health got worse. He had no more drive or desire to work.

Eventually, I felt bad for him. Somehow I forgave him for everything. Maybe I didn't want to live with a guilty conscience. Although he could no longer perform, every once in a while he'd ask to touch my naked body or taste me. I didn't get much thrill out of it, but I'd let him, not sure if he was getting anything out of it.

The hardest part was when his mind started slipping. Every now and again, he'd call me Tatiana or Cynthia. When I'd correct him, he wouldn't have knowledge that he was doing it.

Then he got so happy about us having a baby together. I started wondering if he was lying about not being able to procreate. He went to his doctor and told him that he needs to start treatment to get rid of the cancer because he has his first child on the way and he needs to be

The Queen

around for him or her. The doctor said it was too late because the cancer had spread to his bone marrow, bowels, and brain.

I am truly devastated. Despite the Tatiana and my own infidelity issues, I love Brad. I don't want to lose him. The guilt is tearing me apart. I am going to be the best wife possible from here on out. That I promise.

27
Charise

"Okay, Charise. It's time to get dressed. You've imprisoned yourself in this room for over a month now. Enough is enough. God spared your life, now let's go live it."

"Leave me alone, Elaine. My life is over. I'm just waiting to die."

"Yeah, yeah, yeah. Sounds all good. Now get in that shower and get dressed. We're going shopping today. Beverly Hills. Remember when you were a kid, you always talked about getting older and rich and shopping in Beverly Hills? Well ya might not be rich yet, but you're going shopping."

"I can't, Elaine. I'm just an ugly old cripple now. Nothing in Beverly Hills can change that."

"Well, we'll have to go and find out if that's true or not. And as for being crippled, the only thing crippled right now is your mind and spirit, but even that's just temporary."

"Why are you doing all of this? Why are you being so nice to me? You hate me."

Elaine's face suddenly saddened. She came and kneeled before the chair I sit in each day, looking out the window. She took my hands in her hands.

"Look at me, Charise!"

I looked at her, but turned my eyes.

"I love you with every fiber of my being. I have never nor could I ever hate you. I've had my own personal demons I have been battling, which is how I came to realize I had turned my back on you and anyone else needing me. That same day you were hospitalized, I had just announced that I was going to Houston to bring you back here with me. I was finally ready to be the sister that you needed.

"I won't lie, I was afraid of the task I was taking on given your previous lifestyle. Charise, everything happens for a reason. That man intended to kill you because he was afflicted with a disease he thought you gave him. Not only did God spare your life from the beating, but he spared you of that virus that you so narrowly escaped. He could have been infected before he slept with you, or he could have picked it up from the girl he was with only moments after being with you. You don't take something like that for granted. That scar you have under your eye and over your eyebrow is a small thing. And before you say, so is the split on your lip. You are in the land of plastic surgery. I talked to someone who assured me those are easy repairs, but you have to get yourself together mentally and spiritually first. You have to work on the inward woman before dealing with the outward. I know firsthand."

"And we're going shopping why?" I pessimistically asked.

"Shopping is good for the soul. Besides, the person I just mentioned is also in Beverly Hills. You remember your favorite television show, *Nip/Tuck*? Well, we're going to our very own 'nip/tuck' doctor."

I couldn't help but giggle at Elaine's many attempts to sway me.

"I thought you'd like that. Come on. Get dressed and let's get going. I still want you to come and see our boutiques and spa, but we'll do that when you're feeling up to it. I also was hoping to surprise Harmony with a visit. You know she's feeling miserable these days from the pregnancy, and Todd is in Houston trying to wrap things up. I wasn't sure if you were ready to face Todd yet or not, so I figure we can go to the house while he's away. And maybe tomorrow we can go visit Sandy. She's been so worried about you."

"Really? How come she doesn't hate me after what I did to her?"

"Sandy hates what you did, but she could never hate you either. Sandy took a lot of the blame for not getting rid of Lewis when you first mentioned him making a pass at you. But whatever the case, he's gone now, and we have our family back together. Well, partly have our family together."

"Why do you say partly?"

"Kelly has allowed that idiot she snuck off to marry while you were in the hospital to isolate her from her family. She has the nerve to be living right here in L.A., but won't provide any info about where. She only sends an occasional text message to say she's okay and very happy. Now you know that's bullshit right there. Who could be happy not being able to get on the phone or visit your own family to brag about your happiness? She's fooling her damn self, but as always, we'll be here to clean up the mess he's making in her life," Elaine said with a disgusted look. "As for Shawnee, she's still living in New York. She married that old guy and now he's dying, so she's going to also need all the support from her family that she can get."

"He's dying?" I asked, genuinely hurt and shocked.

"Yep! He has prostate cancer and it's too advanced for treatment. Shawnee said it's killing her to watch him try to be so strong for her. He's leaving her everything when he goes. He already signed the company over to Shawnee. He wanted to get things done before dementia started setting in."

Tears fell from my eyes. I was sitting there, wallowing in my own self-pity and with each passing day, a man is slipping closer to his death, and my big sister has to just helplessly watch as she did with Mama and Daddy.

Damn!

"I know it all sounds hard to hear. This is why I need you to get up and let's start living. No one is guaranteed tomorrow." Elaine looked at me with pleading eyes as she gently coaxed me up from my seat.

That hot shower felt like the first one I had in I don't know how long. Elaine fixed my hair up to be presentable for going out in public and picked out my clothes. I was still afraid of going out in public. I felt like Whoopi Goldberg's character, Celie in *The Color Purple*.

Surprisingly, no one even paid me any attention as we walked the few feet from Elaine's car to the doctor's office. I thought for sure everyone would stop and look as if I were the most hideous looking creature they'd ever seen.

I was glad when the doctor said my scars would be easy fixes. I was shocked when he said twelve thousand and Elaine said it was no problem. Twelve thousand dollars doesn't sound like an easy fix, but then again, this is Beverly Hills. Elaine was about to set up my appointment for the procedure, but I had her hold off since I felt a little uncomfortable about her spending that kind of money on me.

As expected, Harmony was glad to see me out of my room in Elaine's mini-mansion. I opted to go see Harmony instead of shopping. I still wasn't all that comfortable out in public. I kept feeling like everyone would know what type of person I was just by looking at me and then say I deserved everything that happened to me.

It seemed like we had good timing. Harmony was feeling down because she was no longer so certain Todd was going to follow through on his promise to be with her in L.A. She said he seems like he's making one excuse after the other of why it's taking him so long to return from Houston. She's already scheduled for her C-section, and Todd says he'll have everything done long before then. We'll see.

To be quite honest, I'm not really looking forward to having to face Todd. I remember overhearing Elaine and Harmony talking at the hospital about how Todd blamed everything I did on Harmony and she almost lost her babies in a car accident. He also blamed me for his son being infected. I don't want Harmony to have to struggle with three babies by herself, but since Todd has shown his ugly side, I have a feeling my big sister is going to be alone one way or another.

After visiting Harmony, we decided to pay Sandy a surprise visit. Boy, did it feel good to finally make peace with my sister. The crazy part is I don't know why I was the one who had beef with her. She had every right to beat me to a pulp, but I had no right to be angry toward her.

Then, on top of everything, Lewis had been screwing a few women from the church in addition to both of us. If anything, I felt shame. I felt even worse about making her leave my hospital room and it was her who'd stayed with me the whole time I was there. She quickly whipped up a good dinner for us to eat and it made me remember all the great times we had before Lewis slithered into our lives.

My greatest surprise came when Arnold brought Jarod to see me a week later. That did my heart wonders. I looked at my son for the first time and was overcome with even more shame for how I just tossed him away like he was last week's lunch. I even felt guilty about how I had treated Arnold. I had a good man in my corner, and I pushed him out the door so I could be my own worst enemy. And now, I'll never be able to bear children again and have to settle for whatever crumbs Arnold sees fit to give me with regards to my own child. I won't complain, though, because one, he didn't have to give me anything, and two, my foolish lifestyle almost robbed my son of his mother forever.

When I was a bit more comfortable in public with my slightly disfigured face, Angelo and his crew gave me the makeover of a lifetime. That makeover made me decide to go forward with the cosmetic surgery procedures. I was kidding myself into thinking I could go the rest of my life trying to wear the badges of my shame. Harmony said I was

The Queen

feeling that way because I was trying to punish myself for all that happened. She was right. I did want to punish myself, but now I think I'm ready to start healing from the inside as well as the outside.

Ultimately, the surgery left me looking better than ever, and with the help of my baby brother, his crew, and Elaine, I think I'm ready to start living again. Smarter this time around.

I finally entered through the church doors with the rest of my family, thanks to Kevin. Elaine's boyfriend has been instrumental in my recovery. I remember when I first saw him in the hospital and wondered why he was there since he didn't work there. He didn't know me, but still he was always there. I later learned that he was always calling when he wasn't in town, to check on my status.

He was the one who found the psychologist who came to Elaine's house each day trying to help me deal with all of my traumas, including the loss of my parents. I will admit that although I give her a hard way to go, I actually like her. She also attends the church we're now all attending. Needless to say, she and Harmony clicked on a friendship level. She kind of reminds me of our mother.

Kevin asked me what I aspired to do professionally with my life. I told him I always had this secret dream of owning a magazine. I wasn't sure what type yet. He offered to be my very first financial backer when I decide. Is this guy an angel or what? It seems as though he brightens everyone's life that he comes into contact with. He's Angelo's new best friend now. He doesn't care about Angelo being gay or anything. Most straight guys wouldn't get caught in the same room as a gay guy. Even Arnold is hesitant about being near Angelo, as if he's going to somehow contract Angelo's gayness.

It broke my heart when Elaine told me she was a prostitute and that's how her wealth began, but then she rolled that into her shoe boutiques. I'm glad she has let that life go. She said that caused her to realize she and I weren't that different in our lifestyles. The only difference was that she was afforded a more lavish life that ultimately left an emptiness in her life just the same. It was incredible that Kevin accepted her with all her baggage and has been not only a rock in Elaine's life, but our whole family's life. I hope she doesn't blow it with him like I did with Arnold.

After careful consideration, I've decided to pursue my magazine goals. I chose to create a fashion magazine for people of color. I found that all the magazines catered to Caucasian people, and I wanted a magazine that I could relate to. Elaine and Angelo loved my concept and offered their business expertise to help me get it to fruition. Elaine has so many celebrity contacts, it's not even funny. She said with all of her contacts, my magazine articles are only a phone call away. Angelo also has tons of contacts in the fashion industry. And true to his word, Kevin came with the financial backing. Elaine also provided some financial backing.

It would have been great to have Kelly on board to help plan the kickoff party, but she's been MIA with Sean. Her text messages to Elaine, which once read, "I'm okay and I'm happy!" now simply read, "I'm okay." I guess she's not happy anymore. She's been leaving that part off. I wish she'd at least take my calls. I never said anything bad against Sean. I'm not sure why she's cut me off as well. Guilt, perhaps. Hopefully she'll find her way back into the fold soon.

28

Harmony

"Just a minute!" I had to yell to the lunatic ringing my doorbell like someone was killing them.

It can't be Todd, 'cause he has the key and he said he'll be back later this week. I only have two more weeks left before the babies arrive and still Todd hasn't moved to L.A. It's been more like mercy or guilt visits lately. I knew I shouldn't have taken his ass back. His lying ass is too umbilically attached to his mama. All that 'leaving the family for his wife' bullshit!! I don't know the last time I've had breakfast in bed from his ass. He really doesn't see any reason to come around now that he can't get any pussy. That's when his trips started slacking. I guess if he can't have my tit to suck on, he has to go suck on his mama tit.

"Wait a fucking minute! I'm coming to the damn door!" Why must people be so impatient? They know I'm carrying triplets. This ain't no easy shit for me.

I swung the door open, ready to kick someone's ass for working the hell out of the doorbell. Okay, so I can't kick anyone's ass anymore. I found a sobbing Kelly looking like she ran away from home.

"Kelly? What are you doing here? What happened to you?"

"Please, Harmony, let me come in. I don't know where else to go."

"You look a mess. Get in here before one of my neighbors see you. How'd you get my address?" I insensitively inquired as I stepped back to let her in my house.

"I contacted your old office in Houston and got the info."

"Hmm! That easy, huh?" That pissed me off. Over the phone, Kelly could have been anybody. "So who are you running away from? That nigga started beating your ass already?"

That comment made her break down uncontrollably. I wasn't moved. Not when I have my own shit going on.

"He put a gun to my head and said if I tried leaving him, he'd hunt me down and blow my brains out," she said when she composed herself enough to speak.

"So just bring your mess to my house and let him kill us both, huh? What kind of shit have you gotten yourself mixed up in and now want to drag me into?"

"I didn't know. This just happened last night."

"Bullshit, Kelly! You did know! We all knew something was wrong with his shady ass, but you cut all of us off and gave us your ass to kiss. Now you're here saying 'fix my stupidity,' knowing the motherfucker is hot on *your* trail."

"I didn't know where else to go."

"How about the police? If a nigga puts a gun to your head, you go to the fucking police." I know I wasn't cutting her any slack, but it's been months, and she doesn't deserve any slack. "So how did he end up putting a gun to you head last night?"

"I confronted him when he got home about the woman who came to my door earlier stating she is his wife and wants me to leave her husband alone."

I had to wobble my way to a chair for that one. I didn't think that was the sneaky secret he had. I figured he was into drugs or something like that.

Kelly continued. "And when she saw the ring on my finger, she said it was her original wedding ring that went missing, but Sean had recently purchased a newer and bigger ring for her. She said they have two sons, and have a home in Salt Lake City. When I told her I was Sean's wife, she said he does that all the time to women. Then she told me that I must have had a lot of money and low self-esteem. She said that's who he usually targets, and then comes home to her when he's done with his victims. She went on to say that she felt the need to come burst my bubble because he's been with me longer than the others. She couldn't sit around while her husband fell in love with another woman.

"After telling her to go to hell and closing the door, I went online to check my accounts and credit cards only to find my cards maxed out and my accounts almost empty. I should have called the police at that time, but I wanted to confront him first. First he tried kissing all over me saying that was some jealous ex-girlfriend messing with my head. When I asked about the money, he claimed I told him it was okay, and all the purchases for women and children were to help one of his artists who was having financial difficulty while her record deal was pending. The jewelry purchases were for his clients to have the right image.

"Harmony, I never told him that any of it was okay because I didn't know. When I fussed about him putting me $300,000 in debt in addition to cleaning out my savings account, he blew me off as if I was bothering him. Thankfully he wasn't able to access my business accounts. I got up in his face about the money and he pulled a gun from his desk drawer and put it to my head. He told me to stop bothering him with that nonsense, then reminded me that we are married and in this together. He said these are small investments into our bigger and brighter future. Then he tried to kiss and touch me. When I refused his advances, he just took what he wanted. Afterward, he warned that I better not ever try leaving him, and then professed how much he loves me. He said this is real love and he doesn't plan on letting go."

I sat and stared at Kelly for a brief moment before answering her rambling. "Well, I guess you better make your way on home before he comes looking for you, 'cause this sister can't and won't help you."

"What? How could you say such a thing, Harmony? What happened to you? Didn't you hear what I just told you that he has done to me?"

"No, Kelly, you did it to yourself. Now you want to be the poor victim. First off, since when have you stopped monitoring your bank accounts? The Kelly I know checks her shit DAILY, so I'm inclined to believe you have given him open access and permission. Second, how did he gain access to all of your accounts and credit cards? Because with your nose wide open, you authorized him onto all accounts. Otherwise, you would have called the police immediately regarding your FDIC insured accounts. You didn't have any qualms about the spending until the woman showed up saying she was his wife and he was playing your ass, which we all figured long ago. But now realistically, what woman is going to foolishly show up volunteering 'we're scamming you so now you need to go away' without worrying about going to jail right along with his scamming ass? And if you really wanted to know who you were getting yourself all involved with, you should have checked him out. And on a final note before I put your ass out of my home, there were no amount of words he could have said that would make you cut off your own family. That was your choice. He didn't hold you hostage 24-7. He has a 'big multimillion dollar company,' remember? Now go home to the husband that you chose, and sleep in the bed that you made." I worked my way out of my seat and to open the door for Kelly's departure.

"Harmony, please. I can't go back there. He's going to kill me."

"Then go to the police if you're that worried. From what you've told me, he's committed at least five felonies. There's no reason he wouldn't be locked up tonight. Have him locked up and then I'll take you seriously, but not a minute before."

And she left the same way she came—sobbing. She'd look back every now and again with pleading eyes, as if waiting for me to call her back. I didn't. I just closed my door to put her out of her own misery of thinking there was any hope.

When she was gone, I called the others to fill them in. They were split on how I handled her. All agreed that she voluntarily gave him all access to her accounts and only went ballistic when the other girl showed up.

As Elaine pointed out, she couldn't have gotten $300,000 of debt in one month without the banks notifying her personally, and if it was accumulative, then she would have reviewed the charges or purchases on her statements and had her account flagged then.

Kevin took it upon himself to have Sean investigated based on the info Angelo and his crew was able to gather. It turns out that Kelly's marriage is legally binding because Sean was never married before. However, he does have two sons, 9 and 11 years old, (which he pays child support through the courts for), living in Salt Lake City with the nutcase that showed up at their door. It would have been an easy find if Kelly would have done her homework. There were also multiple visitation orders with Sean as the petitioner, that his baby's mama wasn't complying with. He even filed for full custody this past February, with the case still pending.

The record company is all legit, not worth any damn forty million, but it is struggling financially. The only real estate he ever had his name attached to is the condo he and Kelly just purchased together two months ago. I don't know about a fleet of cars, but he does have a Chevy Tahoe and a Mercedes, and neither of them is brand new. That's it.

He has a couple of domestic violence cases on his criminal record. Both with his kids' mother. He also has an aggravated assault from some club fight six years ago, which he was only given probation. He had two financial judgments, which were just paid since his marriage. Probably with Kelly's money. His background wasn't as bad as I expected it to be, but Kelly should have checked these things out and made an educated decision rather than a sexual decision. Additionally, Kelly never got around to filing those charges against him for the gun to her head or him cleaning out her bank accounts. No surprise there.

True to his word, Todd showed up with all of his possessions packed in a truck two days before my scheduled C-section. I guess he found his balls after all and cut that damn umbilical cord. He got to cut the babies' umbilical cords, though. There are two girls, Alana and Alisha, along with one boy, Alonzo. Thankfully, each of them is healthy. The girls were over four pounds, while Alonzo was five pounds, two ounces. Todd is equally happy with each of them. He hasn't picked a favorite yet. I figured he'd gravitate toward our son given he doesn't have Andre around anymore.

Andre wanted to fight his criminal case concerning Charise because in his warped-ass mind, he's still convinced that Charise infected him somehow, and Charise's beating was justified, but not even his cousin Terrance is infected. Todd spent the past month helping Andre accept his fate and convinced him to take a plea deal of 20 years. Whether he'll survive those 20 years is anyone's guess, but Charise is satisfied with the deal. She sort of feels badly for him because he is HIV positive, but then she feels he can't spread his infection to anyone else.

Harmony's Epilogue

Charise has been really getting herself together in every way. Mr. Nose-Wide-Open Arnold once again gave up everything and moved to L.A. to be with Charise. At least his job transferred this time. He proposed to her on Christmas Eve, and she actually accepted. It's sad how it takes a tragedy to grow people up. I think a lot also has to do with the support she's been getting from Elaine and Sandy.

Speaking of Sandy, she stayed true to her vow of being done with Lewis. She finally filed for divorce. When he received his divorce papers at his girlfriend's (Sandy's former friend) house, suddenly he was interested in trying to put his family back together. Sandy wasn't having it this time. Yea!! Also, Sandy started back to school to complete her bachelor's degree online. Since Sandy loves to write, Charise has brought Sandy on board with her magazine. Their relationship has been getting back to the way it was before Lewis surfaced in their lives.

Kevin proposed to Elaine on Christmas day. He was playfully disturbed that Arnold got to make his proposal before he got to make his. In one sense, Elaine wants to plan a big celebrity filled wedding. On the other hand, she's ready to run to the courthouse to get married because Kevin will not touch her until they are actually husband and wife.

For the first time in years, we had a big family Christmas gathering. Todd's parents and brothers came with their families. Thankfully, none of Todd's sisters came.

After I filled in the blanks, Todd didn't feel it was a good idea for Tatiana to be around my family. Todd was remorseful for putting Tatiana in Shawnee's life. He said he never knew the guy his sister was dating was the same man that Shawnee was involved with. Tatiana kept her personal life secret from her family. Since Tatiana couldn't be invited for Christmas, his other sisters thought they were doing us a disservice by not attending. They tried to keep Todd's mother from coming, but she had no intention of missing the babies' first Christmas. She's actually a truly wonderful woman when you can get her away from her controlling daughters. I know I talk a lot of shit about her, but I love the woman to death.

Surprise, surprise. Kelly showed up with her *HUSBAND*. Apparently after Elaine provided her with the details of Kevin's investigation, she wasn't bothered enough to kick his lying, sneaky ass to the curb. She's also been trying to help Sean obtain custody of his sons from the nutty mama who knocked on Kelly's door claiming to be his wife. Kelly can't stand kids, so she's probably only helping him to get back at the mother. Apparently a gun to the head was enough to make her stand by her man. Those kids were probably why he was in such a rush to get married to whoever was dumb enough to marry him on a whim.

Watching the two of them on Christmas day, trying to play the happiest couple in the world was nauseating to say the least. Everything was "Sean this" or "Sean that." "Oh Sean is so smart."

"Oh Sean is so funny."

"Sean is the greatest."

Then he acted like he couldn't keep his hands off of Kelly. Sandy eventually had to check him on what she and everyone else felt was inappropriate behavior around her children.

The Queen

Actually, there were many kids other than Sandy's. Arnold had his nieces and nephew along with Jarod. Kevin's nephews came, and two of Todd's younger nieces were there. Not to mention my trio. Sean expressed his hopes to have his kids by the beginning of the year. He also kept talking about him and Kelly having their own little one together soon. From someone who knows Kelly very well, that subject obviously didn't sit well with Kelly. Annoyingly, Kelly has been gravitating more to helping build Sean's business.

As she puts it, "I'm just doing my wifely duties."

Someone needs to write a book called *Being a Wife for Dummies*. Page one should read: "NEVER GIVE UP YOUR OWN IDENTITY FOR ANOTHER." The end.

Angelo brought over a few of his friends. Most of them were from the spa and boutique. He even brought this one girl. We were all wondering what was up with that until she mentioned some gay club she hangs out at and that all the beautiful and professional women are there. Although I have for the most part accepted Angelo's sexuality, I cringe about the day he will walk through the door to introduce us to a man as his partner. Not quite ready for that. I guess it's like no parent wants to ever think about their children having sex with anyone. That's the same feeling I get when it comes to my baby brother.

Last, but not least, Shawnee, Shawnee, Shawnee. Sadly, Brad's health was not well at all, so he wasn't able to travel. He wanted Shawnee to attend, but her pregnancy has been causing her difficulty. The *coup de grâce* is the baby belongs to Eric, not Brad. Her amniocentesis provided that bit of info.

Shawnee had been taking birth control pills, but for some reason or another, her body began rejecting them. The doctor speculated that it was probably due to her frequent international travels. Shawnee didn't want to tell Brad about the paternity confirmation. She said he was in so much pain, that it's horrible to sit and watch.

She didn't tell Eric about their love child. She didn't want Eric to create any grief for Brad, particularly since Brad made financial provisions for the baby.

Sandy wasn't too happy to learn about the baby's paternity, but then decided any baby that made it through both a condom and birth control pills was destined to be here. She was glad the child was at least conceived prior to the marriage. Somehow, that made it all better for her.

On January 14th, Brad's cancer battle ended. Shawnee was so devastated, as if it were some big surprise. Damn if Tatiana didn't show up for the funeral telling anyone who'd listen that she was Brad's true love.

Sandy and Elaine had about all they could stand of her, and tripped her down the steps outside of Brad's home into the mud from some melted snow. She tried to press charges, but the police said it was an accident. All the witnesses backed up my sisters, although it was clear that they blatantly bumped her off the side, while one put a leg in front of her when she was facing the steps. She sprained an ankle, scraped her knees, fractured her elbow, chipped a tooth, and had an ugly lump on her forehead.

After the funeral, we were able to convince Shawnee to move to California with the rest of her family. We should have known that telling Eric about the baby was going to bring him as well. It was an adjustment to say the least. Eric is now part of the family forever. He loves him some Shawnee. Shawnee said she doesn't feel the same about him. That's understandable as she's still grieving the loss of Brad. Time will tell what will come of the pair, plus baby girl Shayla.

Elaine and Kevin decided to tie their knot on my anniversary day: February 14th. They took a nice little cruise without any family, but decided to have a June wedding so everyone could be there. I think the

#

Valentine's Day wedding was more so for Elaine's hormones. She wasn't going to get any dick until she said "I Do."

Charise and Arnold elected for an April wedding in Vegas. At least they had a real wedding with family and friends, and didn't sneak off like Kelly and Sean—the Sean who's still trying to impregnate Kelly. Kelly is playing instant mom to Sean's sons, so a baby is not on her list of priorities at this time. Unbeknownst to Sean, Kelly is popping a birth control pill daily. She was taking depo shots, but when Sean wanted a baby, she stopped the shots to make her periods come regularly, but taking the pills to prevent the actual pregnancy. I guess she's not a complete fool. Why she can't just be honest, I don't know.

Kelly is still somewhat distant from the family because no one wants to hear her do nothing but complain about how bad those boys are. When we do get together, Sean chooses not to take part, and calls Kelly every five minutes 'til she leaves from us. She thinks that behavior is him "missing her" so much.

I really got pissed when she told us how he can't get enough of her sexually, that he just touches her in front of the kids. Since she doesn't feel comfortable with how far he goes in front of them, she'll take him in the bedroom. I'm half tempted to call child welfare my damn self. Obviously, Sean doesn't give a shit about them. He can't if he's trying to have sex right in front of them. Kelly said the boys used to see him with their mother all the time. It was no big deal to them. After all, according to Sean, "they need to learn about sex at some point." Whew! That's some shit Kelly has gotten herself into.

So I guess that's about it for the Wiggins' family adventures. Well, I didn't mention the part about Charise inviting both Mama and Daddy's families to her wedding. It was pretty much a repeat of my wedding with the addition of Aunt Willie Mae snatching off Aunt Harriett's wig, and the brawl that got them all locked up overnight in Vegas.

What happened in Vegas, got to stay in Vegas; at least for a night.

Other than that, there's nothing else to tell right now. So, again...

The End??

(For Now...)

Caught Up Between Sisters

(Book Three)

Enter the story of the men in the Wiggins sisters' lives. Each man shares tales of their lives now that they are part of the Wiggins clan. With such a complex set of women, life can't be easy for them.

Dr. Todd Palmer no longer finds his wife physically appealing now that she's had the children. What's a man to do when residing in a land of beautiful young women? That fragile home is at risk of being completely shattered when the opportunity surfaces to make a fantasy a reality.

Eric Bradshaw a.k.a. Mandingo worships the ground his daughter's mother walks on. The problem is that the feeling is not mutual. That becomes apparent when she starts dating someone new. Now the owner of an upscale restaurant financed by her, how does he cope when the woman he wants no longer wants him, while women shamelessly throw themselves at him every day? Those are small fish to fry compared to the big shark on its way.

Arnold Hamilton always tried to do what he thought was right, and marrying the mother of his son seemed like the right thing to do at the time. But his heart says otherwise since his wife previously left an opening for another woman to lay claim to his heart. Who wins the battle? Does he do the "right thing," or follow his heart? Sometimes it's not what's on the outside, but what's on the inside that should be paid attention to.

Sean Greene knows the music industry like he knows the back of his hand, but he had no clue about the family he married into. What's worse is when you're despised by the family, and they'll stop at nothing to get you.

The time for confessions of past demons has come and gone, but "Forgiving Kevin Dobbs" held onto a few of his own secrets, afraid he'd lose the woman he had come to love. It won't be long before those demons rear their ugly heads. But if he thought those demons were bad, he'll experience a whole other type of demon married into the Wiggins family.

NOTE FROM THE QUEEN:
Caught Up Between Sisters will be released at the same time with The Evolution Between Sisters. Unfortunately, it is impossible to give you the story-line without providing clues to Caught Up Between Sisters. Caught Up Between Sisters is the tale told from the men in the Wiggins sisters' lives. The Evolution Between Sisters is the story told from the sisters, in response to story told by the men. I didn't want to leave you with a lengthy cliff-hanger, so this way you will have your answers almost immediately.

The Queen

Thank you for reading *Between Sisters and Between More Sisters*. If you enjoyed these two novels from The Queen, be sure to lookout for:

Caught Up Between Sisters
The Evolution Between Sisters
Never Again Between Sisters
Sisters Daughter
Revenge Between Sisters - The finale
(all part of the Between Sisters series)

A Scorned Woman
Queendom Shorts (anthology)

Also, log onto our website at www.queendomdreams.com and take part in the *Between Sisters* discussion or see what The Queen is talking about on "Ask The Queen".

To find out what other books Queendom Dreams will be releasing and other authors with Queendom Dreams Publishing, please visit www.queendomdreamspublishing.com.

About The Queen

The Queen has been writing for many years, ranging in short stories, poetry, plays, professional, and other writings. She is a native of (Queensbridge) *Long Island City, New York*. ***Between Sisters*** is her debut novel of the series. She is also the author of ***Tapioca Pudding Next Door***. Her education includes Business and International Business. When she's not writing, she loves to travel to sunny climates with clear and turquoise waters or near the mountains for inspiration.

www.ingramcontent.com/pod-product-compliance
Lightning Source LLC
LaVergne TN
LVHW091632070526
838199LV00044B/1032